Master of the Bluffs

B.J. Irons

spectrum books

Spectrum Books

Artwork: Adobe Stock – © ysbrandcosijn, luliia.

Cover designed by Spectrum Books.

Paperback ISBN: 978-1-915905-08-6

This book is a work of fiction. Names, characters, places and events are fictitious.

First edition, Spectrum Books, 2023

Discover more LGBTQ+ books at www.spectrum-books.com

Contents

"Unfortunately, every season roughly 30% of the clothes produced by major, high-end designers are never sold. So, to make room for newer, shinier and 'in-season' items, that unsold stock has to go somewhere and usually it's burned or buried in landfill. These designers would rather their products be destroyed than sold at cheaper values. After all, they need to maintain their value and reputations."

Chapter 1

Jackson

Every writer and journalist has their *tick*, or rather that *thing* that needs to be happening around them constantly in order to drive their concentration. For some, it's a specific song that gets played on a loop to keep their creative juices flowing. For others, it could be nature sounds like the soothing noise a gentle gust of wind makes against the bristling of leaves on a tree or the crashing of the ocean waves against a sandy shore. Let's not forget the ever-annoying constant clicking of a pen cap: *in, out, in, out, in, out, in, out* (we all have that one colleague that comes to mind when we think about that damn clicking noise).

But for me, it's an odd one. And right now, I'm finding myself focused on my laptop in my office performing that *tick*, I'm so used to—tapping the metal end of a pencil against a desk. I'm not sure if it's the metronome I'm craving or the higher pitch that it elicits, that the wood of the pencil or rubber eraser can't produce. Perhaps it's the resilience and forceful yet easing bounce that ricochets from the desk when I beat the pencil against it. But ever since I can remember, it's just something I've grown accustomed to. An unbreakable habit that makes me feel comfortable, that honestly makes me a better writer.

It's not like I even use pencils. Hell, all the ones I have in my drawer are all unsharpened. But I keep them on hand still, knowing that during a frustrating time or a moment when I have that uninvited *writer's block*, I'll need that tapping to calm my nerves, to get me back on track with my work.

And right now, I was vigorously tapping my pencil on my desk at a greater rate than I normally would. It was 8:30pm on a Tuesday night. Half of the office lights were already shut off. The custodial staff was nearly done with their evening vacuuming and trash removal. Soon, I would be the only one left in the building, alone in my cubicle with the brightly lit computer screen staring straight at me. My soul companion for the remainder of the night.

I traced my hand through my wavy brown hair, stressed as fuck over this draft I was writing. But it wasn't just any draft. This was the *mother* of all initial drafts. As a columnist for Chatterbox News, a magazine company that gives you the most up-to-date and latest developing news in the entertainment industry on celebrities and gossip, I've been covering small meat and potatoes stories on lifestyles of the rich and famous for my entire career here at the company. But none of my stories were groundbreaking. Not a single one was worthy enough to put me on the map. Not only did I have dreams, aspirations of becoming the next Carrie Bradshaw, but I wanted all the perks that came with it. The money, the wealth, the fame, the Instagram followers, the fashion designer endorsements, among the countless other benefits.

Yet, I had a feeling in my bones that the story I was now covering would be my big break. The one that would launch my rocket to the moon, and thereby take my career to that next level I've been wishing for. And what was said story that would be catapulting my life? It was *Dean Cargill*.

So, what's the scoop on Dean Cargill? What's so great about him? Some people may be asking. Well, Dean is a modern socialite in the gay community. A sexy, twenty-seven-year-old hunk who just experienced his third divorce nearly a month ago. All three of his husbands being well-established, rich men, much older than Dean. A famous actor, a politician, and a movie producer, each who have been very quiet and hush-hush when it came to the press begging them for stories about their relationships to Dean Cargill after their divorces. But it was quite the astonishment when all three of these men remained firm in their *no comment* stances, even all these years later.

Yes, Dean Cargill was no A-list celebrity that has been covered by countless news and media outlets, but what was most unique about him was that no one was able to get a story on him at all to begin with. That is until *me*.

Just a couple weeks ago, I covered the divorce of movie producer Roger Friedman and Dean Cargill, like many other celebrity columnists. The story was straight-froward, unbiased, and without direct quotes or comments from both parties. I assumed it to be an average story of mine. One of the many I've written for Chatterbox over the years. So, when I learned that it did gain some attention, I was stunned, to say the least. Never in my wildest dreams did I ever realize that it would lead me to garner an actual interview with *the* Dean Cargill, himself.

Famous and more highly established journalists have been banging down the door to get an exclusive interview with Dean Cargill. Yet here I was, new and unheard of, Jackson Cartwright, able to get in on the action that none of them could. *Action Jackson* is what I should really call myself now after this. It has a nice ring to it.

Journalist Action Jackson Nails Interview with the Elusive Dean Cargill. I can already see the headlines now. Who knows, maybe other expert journalists will want to do a cover story on me after this is all said and done. If I play my cards right, I could come out of this as a world-famous columnist. Major media corporations and outlets would be begging me to come work for them. Hell, I could even smell a potential book deal after this.

I closed my eyes as I sat at my desk, envisioning my future, picturing that Carrie Bradshaw lifestyle that I've always wanted. The glitz, the glamor, the designer clothing, the high-rise New York City apartment gaining invitations to the most exclusive dining events and parties with expensive wine and champagne. As I opened my eyes, I began actively typing the strokes on my keyboard, trying to finish this initial draft for my boss before the morning deadline.

I will be the next Carrie Bradshaw!

I will be famous!

I will be an amazing and well-respected journalist!

I kept repeating these words over and over again in my head as I continued to write. I knew in my gut that I would get there soon, on the ride to this opportunistic lifestyle that I wanted to play in. And Dean Cargill would be my one-way ticket to getting there.

Chapter 2

Jackson

One Week Ago...

"Happy Birthday, Jamie!" the entire group of us at the table chanted, raising a motley crew of various glasses and drinks—red wines, white wines, rosés, martinis, margaritas, you name it, in the air to toast the man of the hour. Our friend Jamie had now hit the big three-zero. We were a tight-knit group, the twelve of us, each a gay couple who did everything and anything together.

My fiancé, Darren, sat to my right as we all imbibed, laughed, and told crazy stories, celebrating Jamie's milestone. I could feel Darren's hand squeeze my thigh from underneath the table. There was a menacing glint in his eye as he stared at me out of his periphery. I knew that look far too well. That glimmer was a tell that my boyfriend was horny as hell and looking for some action tonight.

He and I had our very own language. A language that didn't require words. We could easily pick up on each other's thoughts just from our cues and subtle facial expressions. All I had to do was move my hand to rest just above his knee and give it a light rub to let him know that *yes, we'll get to it later. Don't you worry.*

For now, a soft peck on his cheek would just have to suffice, which I willingly gave him, before we diverted our attention back to the others who were deep in conversation at the dinner table.

Darren was only two years older than me. His thirtieth birthday was actually just around the corner, too. Of course, I was already planning a huge surprise party for him, but on top of that, I was already in the midst or researching different hotels and places to stay at for a two-week getaway in Italy. The plan was for solely him and me to travel up and down the Amalfi Coast. We'd begin in Florence and then venture out to the rolling green hills of Tuscany. We'd stay at a villa and drink chianti and toscanas. Nothing but the freshest sangiovese grapes. That would be our only inland stay.

Then we'd head south and strictly travel along the coast, starting in Naples, then hitting up Positano and Sorrento, before we would cross the sea and stay in Capri. I could picture it now. Gorgeous cerulean seascapes at every turn, mornings at local cafés, brunches with aperol spritzes, and then the authentic Italian dinners with the finest wines. We'd stuff our faces with everything that ended in a vowel (which is pretty much any Italian dish possible). Every hotel we would stay at would have windows that overlooked the breathtaking crystal Amalfi waters. The scent of lavendar and sandalwood ocean breeze would permanently linger in the atmosphere during our entire vacation. I closed my eyes briefly, imagining all of it. *Just a few months away*, I kept reminding myself. Almost there.

But a light tap on my leg brought me back down to this birthday dinner we were at. "Don't you agree, Jackson?" my husband asked me.

I had a bewildered look on my face, unsure of the question that had been posed for me to respond to. All I could do was nod, hoping that was the correct thing to do. "Yeah. I completely agree," I uttered. The smile on Darren's face was the reaction I got, which reassured me that my reply was pleasing enough to the group, much to my relief. I'm not sure what the hell I even agreed to, but whatever.

Darren must have sensed my distractedness, which is why he guided me back to the dinner party, not wanting anyone to think I was being rude. That was the thing with Darren. He always knew the right thing to do. He kept me in line and was my constant voice of reason. Whether it was an issue I was having at work, a minor argument with a friend, or dealing with family drama, Darren was right there to talk me off a ledge. That's just who he was, and he had always been that way since I met him at the tail end of when I was in college. One month after I graduated, we officially started dating. Three years later, he proposed. And now, it had been three years since our engagement. The agreed upon arrangement was for us to tie the knot after Darren turned thirty.

It was just the right amount of time to finally pay off our student loans, become financially comfortable, move into a beach house together we've both been dreaming of, and potentially start our own family, thereafter. Darren was the one who had the luxury of really moving anywhere. He worked as a graphic designer for a national marketing company. So, as long as he had a laptop and internet access, he was golden. As for me, I could technically work from home, since my job really only required a computer too. But I had a less laissez-faire type of company I worked for. The Editor-in-Chief of Chatterbox News was a stickler for wanting us all to still come into the office, even post-pandemic. He managed to meet us halfway with offering all employees to work from home two days a week, and we all figured that's as much as he would be willing to budge.

Suddenly, I could feel my phone continuously vibrate in my pocket, meaning that someone was calling me. Since Darren was right next to me and it was nearly nine o'clock at night, it could only be one of two things—a family member with an emergency or something work-related. A tight deadline, perhaps?

I reached and retrieved my cell phone and stared at the brightly lit screen. It was actually an unknown number, which seemed even more of a mystery to me. It would be rude of me to take it here at Jamie's birthday dinner, but what if it was indeed an emergency that couldn't wait? What if someone was badly injured or in the hospital? I couldn't risk it.

Abruptly, I stood up and patted Darren on the shoulder. "Excuse me, I need to take this call," I informed him and our group before stepping away from the table. I barely was able to notice the worried look on Darren's face as I moved away.

"Hello?" I said, holding my cell phone to my ear as I quickly paced through the restaurant to go outside, where it was more quiet, so that I could hear whoever was on the other end of the line. But this was L.A. we were talking about. There was no place outside that was *quiet*. I should have thought sooner about that. The hustle and bustle of the streets was definitely active right now. I was probably better off inside, to be honest.

"Is this Jackson Cartwright?" a deep manly voice asked me.

"Yes. This is he. Who am I speaking to?" I returned with.

"Jackson, this is Edgar Baxter, Executive Editor of Chatterbox News."

Edgar Baxter!? The Editor-in-Chief? Well, speak of the devil that I was just thinking of a bit ago...

Needless to say, I was stunned to be receiving a call at this late of an hour from him. Hell, I was shocked to be receiving a call at all from him, to begin with.

"Hi... I mean, good evening, Mr. Baxter..." I anxiously replied, hoping my nerves that were running amok were undetectable to him.

But there was a long, awkward pause after I greeted him. Was I supposed to be the one to then ask him how he was doing or the reason behind his call, or should I wait and let him get to it? God, I wish there was a manual for shit like this.

Luckily, he did make the next move. "Jackson, I'm sorry for giving you such an impromptu call at this late of an hour, but it seems a matter of urgency has fallen into my lap that requires your attention."

"*My* attention?" I repeated back to him in complete disbelief.

"Yes. Would you happen to be available right now? I think it's best if we discuss the situation in person."

Now!? At 9:00pm on a weeknight? What the hell could this possibly be about!? Did I screw up? Oh shit! This couldn't be good. What could I have possibly fucked up on? The worst of thoughts continued to permeate through my mind.

"Ummm. Yes. I am finishing up at a dinner with a few friends, but should be able to meet you at..." I then paused, assuming that there was a desired location Edgar Baxter wanted to have this untimely meeting with me at.

"Petrossian. Ever hear of it? It's a French restaurant just..."

But before Edgar could finish his statement, I boldly interceded, not wanting him to waste his breath on giving me directions when I already knew of the place. "Yes. I'm aware of Petrossian. It's roughly only twenty minutes from where I am now," I informed him.

I couldn't help but laugh at my response on the inside, being reminded of a line from one of my favorite movies that I've watched over and over again. *Everywhere in L.A. takes twenty minutes, Cher!* Although, technically, that wasn't true in reality. Many places in L.A. could take over an hour to get from here to there. It just so happened that I was roughly twenty minutes away from Petrossian, though.

"Great! What a coincidence. So then, will I be seeing you in twenty minutes then?" He threw the ball over in my court.

There was only one acceptable answer I could give to my boss' boss' boss. "Yes. I'll book an Uber right now and head on over."

"Looking forward to seeing you soon, Jackson," Edgar's strong, confident voice echoed.

"Yes, you too," I managed to get in before the call ended.

Locking my phone, I returned it to my front pants pocket, just staring ahead at the traffic going by on the street in front of me.

I was rendered speechless, motionless. What did I do? How could I have possibly captured the attention of the Editor-in-Chief of Chatterbox News? After several seconds of standing still, confused as ever, I finally allowed my mind to drift back to the party and everyone else who was inside. I'm sure Darren was getting worried about me being outside for longer than expected.

Going back inside, I returned to sitting in my seat. Everyone was still talking amongst themselves, but it was Jamie who glanced over at me. "Is everything okay, Jackson? You look like a truck just hit you dead on."

I didn't even bother to fix the horrified expression on my face, which is what I probably should have done if I didn't want anyone to be concerned about me.

"Yeah. What's going on, babe?" Darren tilted his head to get a better look at me.

"That was the Editor-in-Chief that just called me..." I said out loud, with a sort of numbness in my voice. "He wants me to meet him at Petrossian in twenty minutes."

"In twenty minutes!?" Darren repeated with incredulity. "Why so suddenly?"

"He says it's urgent," I replied. "And didn't give a reason as to why."

"You don't think..." Darren then paused, scared to even finish that statement. But based on his panicked tone, I knew the very exact word he spared. *Fired*.

"What if it's a promotion?" Jamie piped up once again. "You have to go, Jackson, if you want to know what it is. You don't have much of a choice."

"But I feel terrible. I don't want to ruin your birthday dinner," I stated, but with defeat, knowing he was absolutely right.

"You're not ruining anything," Jamie assuaged. "Besides, we're probably going to wrap up here in the next hour or so. Go ahead. I promise I won't hold it against you."

"Thank you," I softly stated back to him, before turning to look at Darren to get a sense of what his reaction was.

He simply shrugged. "I mean, go if you have to, babe, but I think it's pretty shitty of him to practically summon you this late at night out of the blue. Hopefully, it doesn't become a habit."

I kissed my boyfriend on the cheek before rising out of my chair. "I don't think it will. But you're right. If this becomes a pattern, I won't hesitate to put my foot down."

"I figured as much. I should know better than to think anyone could just walk all over you," he stated.

"Exactly," I simply said, before hovering my gaze over the entire table. I said my goodbyes to everyone with haste and then bolted out of the restaurant. My phone was already out of my pocket, opening up the Uber app.

The ride would be the longest twenty minutes of my entire life. I would sit in the backseat twiddling my thumbs, rocking my right leg up and down, having my elbow prop my face up as I glared out the window at the passing lights that were lit up by the tall buildings and cars beside me. If only I had a pencil on me right now to tap against a hard surface, to calm my nerves.

How would one describe Petrossian? Well, there are a total of five locations of their restaurants and boutiques around the world—New York, Las Vegas, Brussels, Paris, and of course, Los Angeles. The luxury French restaurant sells six different types of caviar. Their most simple of salads costs close to thirty dollars. But the Kumamoto oysters served with caviar powder, that's a whopping one-hundred and twenty dollars. And believe me, you would need three of those meals to even feel remotely satisfied and close to having a full stomach.

It's not an overly large place. Very elongated, with two rows of seating. The place can fit up to roughly twenty people. It was adorned with black leather seats and a long stretched out sofa with fine white table cloths. But here's the real kicker. To my knowledge, Petrossian is only open during lunch hours. Only those who have great connections can get an exclusive and private reservation on rare occasions, which means Edgar Baxter had some really damn good connections.

As I entered the restaurant, I didn't even have to scan around to spot him among a crowd. He was the only one seated at a table for two towards the far end of the restaurant. So, it was obvious who he was. The walk on the gray-slated tiles across the floor was a long one to get to him. What was a twenty-foot distance felt like a mile trek. As I inched closer, I felt as though my fate was sealed. A terrible omen would befall me.

But as I approached, the Executive Editor rose from his chair, holding his hand out to me, with a wily grin on his face. I graciously accepted his hand firmly in mine and shook it. Not exactly what I was expecting.

"Ah. Jackson Cartwright! It's a pleasure to finally meet you," he announced.

I continued to hold my grip on his hand, trying to be the macho professional I'm sure he was used to dealing with. Old-school firm handshakes among men. The more pressure applied, the better the first impression, I was taught. "The pleasure is truly all mine, Mr. Baxter."

We then released from one another. "Please, call me Edgar. There's no need for formalities."

Yeah, right, I thought. If that were the case, then why were we at one of the fanciest French restaurants in all of West Hollywood?

Edgar Baxter was a polished gentleman. The kind that comes from a "remarkable pedigree" as I picture other well-established individuals refer to their lineages as. Smooth, white hair swayed back, with a very tan complexion, likely from his weekends spent on yachts and reclining on a lounge chair by the pool, basking in the warm Malibu sun that overlooks his grandiose estate. The man was in his mid-sixties, tall and skinny. Honestly, he was the spitting image of *Dateline NBC*'s Keith Morrison. At least, in my eyes, he was.

"Very well, Edgar..." I replied, hopefully appeasing him.

"Yes. Please have a seat," he offered, holding his arm out to usher me across the table from him, to which I obliged.

Edgar Baxter was dapper in his silver suit jacket and matching dress pants. He wore a white buttoned-down shirt beneath, along with charcoal designer shoes. He just reeked rich, expensive.

As for me, I had on skin-hugging, dark denim jeans and a tight black buttoned-down shirt, also known as the gay version of *business casual*. I felt very under dressed compared to the big boss man across from me, but hey, it could have been a lot worse. I tried not to let it bother me so much. After all, there was a lot more looming here between us that I should be worried about than my current dress attire.

Edgar's attention then shifted to the menu he had in his hands, perusing it intently. A waiter approached us the second he saw Edgar browsing through it. "And can I offer you both anything to eat or drink?"

"I actually just came straight here from a friend's birthday dinner. So, I'm alright," I commented. Truthfully, I could have gone for something else to eat, but based on these prices I would have to pay, *no thank you, mam!*

"Nonsense, Jackson. You have to have something," my Editor-in-Chief recommended.

Clearly, he wasn't taking *no* for an answer. So, I would just be polite and at least meet him halfway on this. "Maybe a drink wouldn't hurt."

"Ah! There we go. Would you prefer red wine, white, champagne?"

I shrugged. "Anything really is fine with me."

"Well, let's go with a bottle of the Louis Roederer Cristal then," Edgar responded to the waiter. "And bring us out a charcuterie and assortment of caviar, if you wouldn't mind," he added.

All I needed to hear was the word *Cristal* to know that this bottle he ordered was at least two-hundred dollars minimum. I just prayed Edgar Baxter wouldn't expect me to pay for half of it. No. That would be a faux pas on him, right? He surely would use his own Amex Black or even the company credit card, if he even had one.

"Very well, sir." The waiter retrieved the menu and lightly bowed to us. "I will be right out with that momentarily."

Edgar then leaned back in his chair, arms crossed over his chest, seeming relaxed as he stared at me once the waiter left us in peace. "So, I'm sure you're wondering why I requested us to meet in person so suddenly."

To put it bluntly, *fuck yes, I was wondering.* But that most certainly was not the answer I was going to give him. "Yes. I am curious to know."

"Well, I guess we will get right to it then," he suggested.

Right to it? Could I at least have two glasses of Cristal in me to numb the bruise I was likely about to be inflicted with?

"I've heard from my subordinates that you have quite the work ethic, Mr. Cartwright. Chatterbox News is lucky to have someone like you as a journalist," Edgar began to explain, before the waiter returned with our champagne flutes.

Well, so far, so good. If the head boss was going to fire me, he wouldn't make an introductory statement like that, would he?

"And it's likely the reason that one of your news stories has captured the special attention of a certain someone," he added.

I couldn't imagine which news story he was referring to. To be honest, even I wouldn't consider some of my celebrity gossip columns as groundbreaking and worthy of a journalism or literary award by any means.

"Which news story are you referring to, sir?" I curiously asked.

"The one you wrote recently, covering the divorce of Roger Friedman and his much younger ex-husband, Dean Cargill," Edgar revealed.

Roger Friedman and Dean Cargill? But that article was so... *plain*. I pretty much cut right to the facts, leaving an unbiased and objective viewpoint on their divorce when I initially wrote it. Hell, I couldn't even get any direct quotes from either one of them. No one could, for that matter. Their lives were beyond private, even more so than Natalie Portman's, who wouldn't even let her PR managers into the details surrounding her life.

But I was in complete disbelief now. Who would even have paid that close attention to the story? Was there something terrible I wrote in there or offensive that I failed to realize? Perhaps Roger Friedman filed a complaint, or worse, even a lawsuit against Chatterbox News. Against *me*.

"I don't quite understand..." I admitted aloud to him.

Edgar must have sensed the grim cloud I had lingering over me. "Oh! It's nothing terrible, Jackson, if that's what you're thinking. Did you think I brought you out here so suddenly to share bad news with you?"

I shrugged. "I honestly couldn't tell you."

"Well, it's nothing like that, rest assured," he stated, now alleviating all possible worry I carried on my shoulders coming into this meeting.

"Then, what is it?" I boldly asked, wishing we would stop beating around the bush here.

"It's Dean Cargill. His agent reached out to us. Apparently, he wants to do an exclusive interview with Chatterbox News, and not just on his marriage to Roger Friedman, but the two preceding ones as well. His entire life," Edgar informed me.

"Wow! Are you serious?"

"Dead serious," he quickly replied back. "And he requested specific terms regarding the interview."

"And what exactly are those *terms*?"

"He wants to do a one-on-one interview. And you are the only person he wants to do it with. Otherwise, he is out." Edgar was now studying me carefully, like an interrogator, trying to gauge my reaction to the bombshell he just dropped on my lap.

This couldn't be real, could it? Dean Fucking Cargill actually knew who I was? I was actually *somebody* in the world of a celebrity. It was pretty crazy to even comprehend right now. I couldn't wrap my brain around it. What did this mean for me? What did this mean for my career?

There was a lot to consider here, but I knew one thing going forward, and that was that I would be a fool not to take this opportunity and run with it. "I'll do it!"

"Perfect! I was hoping you'd say that," Edgar revealed. "But I'm sure you're still wondering why I called you out here at the eleventh hour to tell you all of this instead of waiting until the work day tomorrow?"

I nodded. This was true. I was still digesting the idea of getting the chance to have a solo interview with Dean Cargill that I failed to wonder why the Editor-in-Chief couldn't wait until tomorrow to tell me this. There was something I had to have been missing here.

"Yes. I was wondering why this couldn't have waited until tomorrow, but I am thrilled that you told me about it right away," I tried to explain, not wanting to seem rude.

"Well, you see, Dean Cargill has a very strict timeline. He has made it quite clear that he is only available at his new residency in Malibu for one week, beginning next week. He'll then be vacationing in the Mediterranean for a few months. Needless to say, time is of the essence, Jackson, if we want to make this meeting happen."

This still wasn't adding up to me. If I had nearly a week left before I would be meeting Dean to interview him, then what was the reason behind all of this sudden urgency? Why all of this commotion *right now*, this very second?

"So, when do I head out to Malibu? Will the company be putting me in a nearby hotel?" I asked.

Edgar nodded, affirming my thoughts. "Oh, of course. Except Mr. Cargill proposed that he be the one to cover all expenses for you, and *then some*, for when you see him next week. And believe me, you're not going to want to turn down all that he has most generously offered for your comfortability... and beyond that."

Seriously!? Is this even real!? I was on cloud nine. This was definitely a once in a lifetime opportunity. I couldn't believe it. This was the leap in my career that I had been hoping for. That I had been *dying* for, to happen.

Yet, Edgar still didn't give me full detail in his enigmatic explanation.

"But if Dean Cargill is paying for everything, why would the company need to put me up in a hotel?" I inquired.

"Like I mentioned, Mr. Cargill is flipping the bill only while you will be interviewing him, which is next week. But in the meantime, you'll need to head to Malibu well before then. You have quite the amount of research to gather, to *unearth*, ahead of time. Although Mr. Cargill thinks you will only be in Malibu to interview him at his residency in Paradise Cove Bluffs, there is another angle you will take in all of this."

"Another angle?" I repeated back to him, in a confused tone.

"Yes. I want you to speak with all of his neighbors in Paradise Cove Bluffs. At least those that are currently there and not out of town. You need to get intel on Dean well before you actually interview him. Based on some of our preliminary findings, it seems that everyone is skeptical about him. And I don't mean just about him being many years younger than all of his former rich and wealthy husbands. What I mean is, they are all suspicious over his finances and his ability to even be able to afford to buy a home in Paradise Cove Bluffs. I'll be honest, based on his financial history and what we've uncovered at Chatterbox, we're inclined to think the very same thing. There is still a mystery that lies there, with how Dean Cargill accumulated all of his money. It couldn't have been just from his former husbands, based on the court's financial records. There had to have been some way he gained so much money so quickly. A lucrative undertaking, perhaps? Or maybe something is happening under the table. Who knows? But it's your job to find out."

So, there it was. I knew this interview couldn't be all lollipops and rainbows. I was going into this undercover, technically. I would be needing to deceive Dean Cargill, with this ulterior motive that was now presented before me. But it was something I was used to. Such is journalism, after all. Just get to the heart of the matter and to the underlying truth of the story, by any means necessary. It really was a cut-throat business.

"Yes. I understand the assignment, sir. Loud and clear," I confirmed to him. "And when exactly will I need to leave?"

"Well, if you're planning to interview Dean next week, I think you'll need all the time you have between now and then to track down his neighbors and meet with them. I'll have a car out front of the office at noon tomorrow, ready to take you to Malibu. How does that sound?"

You're telling me I have nearly twelve hours to drop my entire life, pack up and head to Malibu for what could be a two-week assignment? I thought to myself. And he has the nerve to ask me, *how does that sound?* But I couldn't reveal these opinions aloud to him. So, I answered with the only appropriate reply that I could give. The only response that was warranted under these circumstances with all that I had riding on my career with this interview with Dean Cargill.

"It sounds great. I'm looking forward to it."

Chapter 3

Jackson

Three Days Ago...

"So? How is it? Any luck with getting a hold of his neighbors?" Darren asked me over the phone.

My hands were tied as I held my cell phone to my ear to chat with my fiancé and the other to brush my hair, studying my face in the hotel vanity mirror in my bathroom. I had now been in Malibu for the past three days and still I could not manage to get hold of a single one of the neighbors in Paradise Cove Bluffs.

One neighbor was busy performing plastic surgeries all week and was completely booked, while another was shooting a film in Brazil. It seemed that everyone was out of the city and was not expected to return to Paradise Cove for at least a whole week, which didn't bode well for me. However, I did get a return call from a Mrs. Van der Sarm, who was a direct neighbor of Dean Cargill. She was willing to take me up on my proposition to meet her, but under one condition. The widow that married into the Van der Sarm, Dutch billionaire family, that owned some of the greatest cruise ships in the world, stated that she had no desire for me to conduct the interview at her home. Instead, she requested we meet nearby at The Sunset Restaurant, which was just down the road from my hotel, overlooking Zuma Beach.

Of course, I accepted her invitation and so I was now getting ready to head out to meet her once I finished my phone conversation with

Darren. "Just one, which is where I'm heading off to shortly. Meeting her at a nearby restaurant," I informed him.

"And let me guess, you've done nothing but work the past two other days?" he asked me.

My future husband knew me all too well.

"Yes. I've been busy drafting up questions and planning the flow of the conversations, rehearsing when to pivot and digress on certain topics. You know I've painted and organized an algorithm in my head of how this is going to go down."

He began to laugh on the other line. That cute, dorky laugh of his made me melt on the inside. And to think it would be a whole two weeks of me not being able to hear that chuckle, or rather cackle, of his that I dearly missed.

"I can't say I'm surprised," Darren stated. "But hey, maybe if you get some downtime, I'll come up and pay you a visit. I could just work from the hotel or something. As long as they have free Wi-Fi, then I'm all set."

"I would love nothing more than that, babe," I let him know.

"But in the meantime, please, please, please try not to be cooped up in your hotel room the entire time. Get out a little. You're like, what, a walking distance from Zuma Beach? It's Malibu! Enjoy the sun."

Darren was right. I've always been one to try and not take advantage of my work trips where I was out of town conducting my investigative journalism on celebrities. I did my best not to turn it into some pleasure cruise. I've always maintained a professional work ethic both in and out of my office, no matter where in the world I was. But this, without a doubt, was my top assignment in my entire career, yet I did have a whole three days before I would even see Dean. Maybe I should lounge on the beach and possibly grab a cocktail at a close by beach bar. Why not do that after my interview with Mrs. Van der Sarm? Once she would leave The Sunset Restaurant, I could just venture out right onto Zuma Beach and enjoy the rest of the afternoon. That sounded like a decent plan. Let's go with it.

"I think you're right. I'll try to get out there this afternoon. But listen, I gotta run, babe. I wouldn't want to be late. Just based on our phone conversation from earlier, I can tell Nora Van der Sarm is someone that's not meant to be kept waiting," I informed him.

"Yeah. No worries. Just FaceTime me later tonight, before you go to bed. And I better hear that you managed to get to the beach, or at least somewhere that's not the hotel today," he jokingly threatened me.

"I promise, I'll find the time to do that." And I meant it.

"Alright. Love you, babe."

"Love you too. Take care." I hung up the phone and then returned to gazing at myself in the mirror. Now, I knew Mrs. Van der Sarm was a billionairess, and I should probably dress to the nines for her. But we were going to be dining at The Sunset Restaurant, adjacent to the beach. The temperature was in the high eighties today, but felt like it was in the nineties. I wouldn't want to wear pants and wind up creating a puddle of sweat on my chair, so white khaki shorts seemed to be most appropriate given the circumstances, with a dark blue short-sleeve buttoned down shirt. I continued to brush my hair until it was gelled to perfection. Being pleased with the final results, I slid into my sandals, put on my tan Ray-Bans aviators, grabbed my swimming trunks, which I planned to change into in a nearby restroom along the beach afterwards, and left the hotel, shutting the door behind me.

My nerves were starting to now get the best of me when I began to realize that this was it. This would be my first official interview related to the Dean Cargill case, and I had the highest of expectations for this project. Failure was not an option for me.

As I arrived at the restaurant, I was sort of taken aback by the variety of clientele that were in here. Yes, there were some people that seemed slightly hoity-toity, but for the most part it looked like people here were thinking along the same lines as I was, which was ready to hit the beach after a nice cocktail and meal.

It gave me much more of a relief to see that I was surrounded by my kind of people and not some rich aristocratic millionaires. However, it left me to wonder why a woman such as Nora Van der Sarm would choose to dine and be interviewed here of all places in Malibu. Was I casting judgment on her too soon? But who wouldn't? She was a billionairess after all, and that title alone came with stereotypes that anyone would automatically presume.

I made my way over to the hostess at the front counter, who greeted me right away. "Welcome to The Sunset Restaurant. Do you have a reservation or…?" she trailed off.

"I think so. Is there one under Nora? Nora Van der Sarm?" I asked.

The second I mentioned her name, I could sense the hostess' demeanor change. She expressed a stern look on her face, before her eyes darted up and down, scanning my body, likely wondering who I was. Evidently, she must have known who Nora Van der Sarm was and let her mind wander to trying to guess my relationship to her. An affluent family member? A celebrity, perhaps, or someone with superb connections? No matter what the case, the situation left me slightly giddy on the inside, enjoying the entire experience. Someone actually assumed I was someone big, someone famous. It was a feeling I'd always wanted to have, and now I was finally able to live it. It only left me wondering what else this Dean Cargill assignment had in store for me. And hopefully, it would entail more encounters such as this.

"Yes. She's upstairs. I'll take you to her," the waitress instructed.

"Great. Thank you."

I followed behind as she took me upstairs to an area of the restaurant that was more secluded. There were fewer dining tables here, but it seemed much more private. An elongated bay window with a few tables meant for two hovered over the beach. I could see the close-up details of the salty waves crashing into the shore, but with a gentle ease as the tide line continued to rise, as it typically did into the afternoon.

At one of the tables directly in front of the bay window sat a woman with semi-thin gray hair. She had on thick white designer sunglasses, which I knew to be expensive based on the large forward and backward "C's" that were on the rims. She wore an off-shoulder, lacey, ivory tulum dress that cut off just inches above her knees. On her feet, the woman sported trendy taupe wedges. Gucci? Valentino? I couldn't quite tell, but I'd definitely be sure to make note of it once I was close enough to inspect them further.

"Mrs. Van der Sarm, your guest has arrived," the hostess told her as we approached.

"Ah! You must be Mr. Cartwright." She didn't bother to rise from her chair, but her pearly white veneers were displayed with the smile she had on her face in greeting me.

"Yes. But please, you can call me Jackson," I replied, not really wanting anyone to ever refer to me as Mr. Cartwright. I still felt too youthful to be called a mister. I was not quite at the age or even at that prestigious of a level to be comfortable with it, just yet.

"Very well, Jackson. It's very nice to meet you. Please, have a seat." And so, I did as she said.

Meanwhile, the hostess bowed to the two of us. "Your waitress will be here momentarily," she stated, before ambling off downstairs back to the front counter.

"Thank you, Mrs. Van der Sarm. I appreciate you being able to respond to my requests and take the time out of, what I'm sure is, your busy schedule to have this sit-down with me," I politely said.

"Well, if we insist on foregoing the formalities and are referring to one another on a first name basis, then you can call me Nora, as well."

I wasn't too sure whether or not to take this remark as her being friendly or perhaps sort of shady, based on her delivery. I decided that I would try to tread much more lightly from here on out.

But before I could even reply back to her, our waitress made quick timing in already arriving at our table. "Hi, I'm Ashley and I'll be your server for today. Are there any drinks I can get you two to start off with?"

Nora spoke up first. "I'll have the usual, and a glass of water, if you don't mind."

"Of course," Ashley responded, before she gazed over to me. "And for you, sir?"

I barely had any time to sit down, let alone scan the cocktail options. I instantly grabbed the drink menu and began scrutinizing it. The variety of beverages were daunting and overwhelming, to say the least. Roughly three full columns of various wines by the glass and bottle. A small section to the far right displayed the beers and cocktails. And a cocktail is ultimately what I was in the mood for, based on this relaxing cool beach scene that was just outside the window next to us.

"You know, I always judge a person by their drink choice," Nora coyly blurted out.

Oh geez. I mean, no pressure, right?

"And I'll have your…" I paused, stalling for a moment before finally making a selection. "Let's go with *The Westward*." It sounded refreshing based on its description. Pearl cucumber vodka with freshly squeezed lime and watermelon juice, and an added cucumber wheel to garnish it.

"Sounds good. And I will also bring you a water with that as well. I'll be back momentarily." And with that, Ashley took off, leaving us to ourselves.

"Interesting choice," Nora announced.

"Oh? And what is the *usual* that you typically have here?" I inquired.

"The same, ironically." She smirked at me.

"Really?"

"Yes, really. Let me guess, did you picture me as a dirty martini kind of woman? Gin, not vodka?" Her brow arched at me.

I couldn't help but chuckle at her insinuation that was definitely on point. "I mean, only partially," I kidded back with her.

"Well, at least you're honest. I'll give you that," she commented. "So, you are a journalist covering a story on my most recent neighbor, Dean Cargill?"

I guess we were jumping right into it then.

"Yes. I am actually interviewing him next week for my story. But before then, I wanted to get the opinions of those surrounding him, including his neighbors in Paradise Cove Bluffs."

"I see..." Nora then removed her white Chanels, revealing a set of bright, yet calming, cyan-colored eyes. "Well, once you've heard from one of us, then you've practically heard from all of us."

I didn't want to lose any capturable moments from here on out, so I abruptly reached for my small recorder in my pocket and placed it on the table between us. "Do you mind?" I asked.

She shook her head, allowing me to hit the record button.

"And what do you mean by *once you've heard from one of us, then you've practically heard from all of us?*" I repeated back to her, to make

29

sure that line was captured in the recording.

"I mean that all of us that live in Paradise Cove Bluffs share the same sentiments about Dean Cargill."

"And that is...?"

"That he doesn't quite fit in," she blurted out. "He's so young, and quite the party boy, based on some of the raves I've seen from my home."

"How would you describe these raves?" I followed up with.

"They can vary. There have been nights where I've seen nearly fifty men in speedo's frolicking on the beach that his pier leads to, just behind our homes. On other nights, I've seen more modest dinner parties. But it's nearly all men in attendance at all of these gatherings."

Well, that was a given. Duh. I didn't want to disrupt the ebb and flow of the conversation, though, so I just nodded.

But before one of us could utter another word, our waitress returned with our drinks. We clinked our glasses together before taking sips. The refreshing taste from the cucumber and watermelon with vodka on top of the gorgeous oceanic scene before us left an invigorating wave of feelings overcome me. I couldn't help but lightly moan in pleasure after I took my sip.

"It's really good! I can see why it's your regular," I shared with her.

Nora grinned. "Yes. It's definitely my go-to here when I'm not in the mood for wine."

As I placed the glass back down on the table, I averted my attention back to the interview. "Now where were we? Oh yes! The parties and the opinions of all the neighbors. Tell me, what were these conversations like between you and everyone else? Clearly, everyone has the same viewpoints with their disdain for Dean Cargill, no?"

"To put it bluntly, yes. We have a group chat going on about him," she stated.

Ugh! If only I could get access to this! If I had that communication log, I wouldn't have to do anymore interviews after this, besides with Dean. However, I knew it was out of the question to request for her to add me to their chain. I was already pushing my boundaries, but luckily, Nora Van der Sarm was much more open to giving me details than I had expected. I assumed I would have to use a vice grip and pry the information out of her, but surprisingly, she was an extremely willing customer.

"If you don't mind, can you tell me about some of the conversations that have been going on in this Paradise Cove Bluffs group chat?"

"Well, just things all of us managed to scavenge about Mr. Cargill. Obviously, the three divorces he's had in the span of six years was a hot topic, along with his age. But then, I guess all of us decided to go down this rabbit hole. Don't you find it odd that Dean Cargill can afford to live in a twenty-million dollar home?"

I shrugged. "I don't see why not. His former husbands were fairly well-off, right? An actor, a politician, and a movie producer."

"Yes. But we've all looked up his husbands' net-worths. Three million, eight-million, and ten-million. And I won't mention which neighbor, but one of us had a P.I. further look into things. The alimony and divorce settlements were not that extreme to somehow allow him to outright buy and afford a twenty-million dollar estate in Paradise Cove along with sustaining the sort of lifestyle he lives."

"So, what you're saying is, you think he has some other business endeavors or private person that is bolstering him?"

"I suppose so. How else would you explain his financial situation? Look, we did not mean for this to turn into a witch hunt or anything of the sort, but the more we dove into everything, the more questions arose. We've kept things private among our little Paradise Cove clan, because we don't want the media to use our names and risk us potentially facing a defamation lawsuit. But I will say, I have always been a good judge of character. And I'm telling you, something is just not settling well with me about Dean Cargill. There is more to that young man than meets the eye. He's not just the gold digger that the media has painted him as. There's something more there. Something far worse, I fear. *We all* fear."

I didn't expect the histrionics there, but the more dramatic flares, the better for my article.

"Thank you, Mrs. Van der... I mean, Nora." How quickly I forgot our nomenclature rules. "And yes. Per our agreement over the phone, I promise to not use your name in my story. But would you be willing to elaborate more on..."

Before I could even finish my sentence, she was holding her phone up to her ear. "Sorry Jackson. I have to take this." She then abruptly rose from her chair. "Oh, Abigail! It's so good to hear from you! Yes... Oh really?... For how long?.... Just two days!? Well, you must stay with me. I'll make you feel right at home!... Of course, it's not an inconvenience at all! I will see you soon, my love." Nora hung up on the call, glancing over at me. "I do apologize, Jackson, but my daughter is visiting L.A. out of the blue, unbeknownst to me, for just a short while and I rarely have the opportunity to see her and the grandchildren but on holidays. I'm sorry to cut our meeting short, but I really must be going." She quickly proceeded to head down the stairs and out of The Sunset Restaurant.

I couldn't help but flail back in my chair, annoyed that I barely put a dent in the information I could have potentially gotten about what the Paradise Cove Bluffs neighbors uncovered about Dean Cargill and their further negative opinions on him. I highly doubted I would be able to get any other meetings on the books with any of the other neighbors besides Nora. And I only had three more days remaining until I would meet Dean. This was not what I imagined my week would be like leading up to my interview with him. Things were not going according to plan, but I wasn't a quitter. I would have to use the info Nora provided me and make the most out of it in my story, in *my angle*, as Edgar Baxter so well put it.

The sudden buzzing of my own phone inside my pocket, then distracted me. I pulled it out to see that I had a recent email notification. My eyes bulged when I saw that it was from Gregory Kindoff, one of the lead divorce lawyers of Roger Friedman.

Gregory Kindoff

<GKindoff@gkpartners.org>

To: Jackson Cartwright <jcartwright@chatterboxnews.com>

Subject: RE: Interview Request — on Dean Cargill

Good Afternoon Mr. Cartwright,

I am definitely intrigued by you somehow gaining an interview with Mr. Dean Cargill and developing a story on Roger Friedman and him. I am happy to provide information for your story. My availability is a bit chaotic, but I can manage to arrange my schedule today to meet you in my office at 4:30pm, if that works? Otherwise, I'm afraid I will have to wait a few weeks to rebook you as I will be attending the needs of one of my other clients in New York. Please, let me know if you will be available during this time at your earliest convenience. Thank you.

-Gregory Kindoff

I was already in Malibu and Gregory Kindoff's office was back in inland Los Angeles, over two hours away at this time of the day, assuming there was traffic. But did I really have a choice in the matter?

No. So, I immediately replied, letting him know I would be there by 4:30pm.

I guess I would be recanting the promise I made to Darren. There was no way I was going to make it out to the beach today.

The clock struck 4:30pm on the dot as I bolted out of the car and made my way into Gregory Kindoff's office, hoping that he hadn't already left. I approached his receptionist who had a bun in her hair with librarian glasses on. "I have a 4:30pm appointment with Mr. Kindoff... is he in?" I asked, gasping in between words, attempting to catch my breath.

"Yes. Mr. Cartwright, I presume?"

I nodded.

"He's been expecting you. Please, head straight back. He's in the main doors at the end of the hall," she instructed.

I passed by her and trekked down the long, narrow hall. I knocked on the mahogany door that was slightly ajar. "Mr. Kindoff?" I asked.

"Yes. Ah! Mr. Cartwright! Welcome! I'm glad you could make it on such short notice."

"I am too..." I stated as a matter-of-fact. But I would not let him know of the rush and stress I had undergone just to get here on time, all the way from Malibu.

"So, I must say, I am quite at a loss for words here, Mr. Cartwright. You truly managed to get an interview with Dean Cargill?"

"I did. I will be interviewing him three days from now," I let him know.

"And how on God's green Earth did you manage to pull that off!?"

He sounded intensely exasperated.

I couldn't help but shrug. "I'm honestly not sure, but I do intend to find out. All I know is that I did a story on his and Roger Friedman's divorce recently. He or someone from his team must have read the article and liked what they saw, because they reached out to my Editor-in-Chief and requested I conduct an interview with him."

"Wow! It must have been quite some story that you wrote on them."

No. It wasn't at all. I didn't think much would come of it when it was published. It was one of my most average pieces of work, honestly. At least, I thought it was.

"Evidently..." I responded.

"But it seems your interview with Mr. Cargill isn't enough, is it? Otherwise, you wouldn't have requested to have this meeting with me, would you?"

Gregory Kindoff was a shark. It was in his blood. When you're one of L.A.'s top divorce attorneys, of course a shark would be your likely *Patronus*.

"I just want to make sure I am taking all viewpoints and opinions into account before I develop this story. Just doing my due diligence."

"Well, let me just say that your *due diligence* is rather unethical, Mr. Cartwright. Seeking out Mr. Cargill's enemy attorney doesn't exactly sound virtuous."

"No. But with your knowledge and records, I think you can give me the evidence I'm looking for, for this story," I replied back, hoping to gain his attention all the more.

"And the evidence to which you are referring to is...?"

"Financial records," I revealed. "I've also had the opportunity to interview some of Dean Cargill's neighbors in Paradise Cove Bluffs. It seems they are under the assumption that Mr. Cargill's public finances aren't adding up to him being able to afford his twenty-million dollar estate in The Bluffs. Other sources at my company have uncovered the same details."

"I see... And you somehow think I am going to risk my career and my ethical integrity to allow you to see his financial records?"

I couldn't help but nod. "Look, I'm just following the trail of crumbs here. Any information you can provide on Dean Cargill and his financial records upon his divorce to Roger Friedman would be great. I swear, I will not implicate you in any sort of way," I said, to try and alleviate any worry he may have had.

"Hmph!" Gregory grunted, before he spun around in his black leather chair, opening one of his desk drawers. He browsed through a few of his files before finding a manila folder. He pulled it out and tossed it across his desk at me. "Here. You can look through these, but only under my watchful eye. You cannot pull your phone out nor take any pictures. Am I understood?"

Jackpot! This was exactly what I needed!

"Understood," I replied.

I spent nearly thirty minutes searching through the records, while Gregory sat at his desk, studying me very closely.

"But this doesn't make any sense..." I said aloud after reading through almost all of the files he had provided. "You're telling me that Dean Cargill had a larger annual income than Roger Friedman!?" I asked in disbelief.

"Yup! There you have it!" Gregory Kindoff exclaimed.

"How is that possible? Dean married into money. He has no former career, no pedestal to have made the income that is shown here. How could he have possibly earned this much money without..."

But Gregory held his hand up in protest. "That subject is beyond me now, Mr. Cartwright. When I suggested the very same sentiments to my client, Mr. Friedman, to try to get alimony from Mr. Cargill, he outright refused it and did not want me to further investigate the financial background of Dean Cargill. The whole thing left me in a tizzy."

"So, what then?" I was beyond confused at this point. "That's it? We now know Dean Cargill's insane annual income and we just sit on it and not try to figure out where he is getting all of this money from?"

Gregory Kindoff shook his head. "There is no *we*, Mr. Cartwright. My obligations to Mr. Friedman and investigating Mr. Cargill are long gone. Further finding out about what's going on with Dean Cargill is now *your* job." He pointed his index finger directly at me as he spoke. "And I really hope you nail the cocky little fucker!"

Chapter 4

Jackson

Current Day...

I stood just in front of Dean's lavish beach house on my phone with Darren. I had called him once I made it all the way down the driveway. If I needed anyone to give me a decent pep talk to help alleviate my worry, it was him. Darren gave me faith, motivation, and confidence. The moment I heard his voice, I was already feeling a bit better.

"You got this, babe. Just treat this like any other interview," my fiancé advised with great enthusiasm.

But my inner saboteur was whispering to me. *This isn't like any other interview, though. It could make you or it could fucking break you,* it kept telling me.

"I know, I know." I let out a deep and heavy sigh to Darren. "I just... I don't know. What if I blow it? I don't know how to handle this situation, though. Part of me wants to be on good terms with Dean. After all, he was the one that specifically reached out to request me to be the person to interview him. So, technically, I should be in his corner, right? But then, what about everyone else? The Editor-in-Chief, the Paradise Cover Bluffs neighbors, even the lawyers. Everyone but Dean expects me to go after him. I'm kind of stuck between a rock and a hard place, here."

"You just have to go with your intuition, Jackson. Look, there's a damn good reason Dean picked you out of every journalist across the country. You're smart, you're talented, and most importantly, you're loyal. Whether Dean is shady, a gold digger, or whatever, shouldn't matter. *He's* the one giving *you* this once in a lifetime opportunity to excel your career. You should at least give him the benefit of the doubt and hear him out. Anything anyone else has to say about him is just hearsay," Darren advised.

I scratched the back of my head. "I guess you're right... damn you!" I exclaimed jokingly.

"I know. It's why you love me. Now get your ass into that twenty-million dollar house and do what you were meant to do," he wittily commented.

"Fine. I'll call you right afterward. Love you."

"Love you too."

I ended the call and shifted my attention back to Dean Cargill's new Paradise Cove Bluffs property. The sun was blazing, blurring my vision. So, I used my hand as a visor over my eyes to get the full scope of the place from the outside. The home was two stories, and pure white. Its architecture was extremely modern, with obscure, diagonal angles going in every which direction. Although the trims and framework of the house were ivory, those extravagant features were overshadowed by the massive amounts of windows along the house, which drew the naked eye.

Soon, the front grand entrance doors opened, and a young, cute guy that looked to barely be in his twenties emerged from it, wearing light blue faded jeans and a ripped white t-shirt. His sun-bleached brunette hair was swayed back as he sported a pair of silver Giorgio Armani sunglasses.

"Ah! You must be Jackson Cartwright," the boy announced.

"Yes. That would be me," I confirmed.

He stepped forward into the driveway. "Welcome to Mr. Cargill's residency. I'm Luke, one of his personal assistants."

Wow! I didn't realize personal assistants could come in this attractive of a form. I guess I was remiss in not realizing that they do come in all shapes and sizes.

"Nice to meet you, Luke." I politely greeted him back with. "It's a gorgeous piece of property," I commented, raising my arms out wide.

"Yes. This is Paradise Cove Bluffs, after all." He sounded non-committal, seeming unimpressed. "But I'm sure you didn't come here just to marvel at the place. Mr. Cargill is waiting. I'll take you to him."

Luke turned his back and headed back into the home, to which I promptly followed close behind him.

As we entered the main foyer, Luke snapped his finger towards the floor. "Shoes off, please."

So, I removed my shoes and socks too, just to be on the safe side. Wouldn't want to risk the chance of leaving any trail, even a small fracture of a piece of fuzz on the floor to set a bad first impression of myself. If Dean was that strict about the tidiness of his home, I figured it was best to accommodate that as much as humanly possible.

As we stepped further into the belly of the beast, I was awestruck. This was not how I envisioned the place being at all. I thought it would look more like a bachelor's pad. Lots of black leather and dark gray furniture. Clean geometric lines and black granite countertops in the kitchen. But this was not the vibe this house invoked. Everything was milky, cream-colored, and bright, from the rays of the sun striking every surface of the home through the glass windows, covering nearly every inch of the walls. Natural light was not scarce one bit in this house.

The open concept definitely made the place seem even more spacious than the five-thousand square feet that it already had. The ceiling was made of shiplap and it was angled, with added white beams to provide even more character. The kitchen was pure white, with Calcutta marble countertops and an island surrounded by six stools. The backsplash possessed a subtle sheen, and had the full spectrum of watery blue hues. It looked like a sea glass mosaic, probably hand-crafted by a professional artist. The floors were made of a luxury vinyl plank but stained to look like a light wood. This property screamed elegant beach house, to say the least.

As we ambled past the kitchen and the main living space, I realized we were heading toward the patio. The entire back wall had floor-to-ceiling glass sliders that were fully open, leading to a deck that wrapped around the home. Once we stepped outside, I could see where the true value of the place came from. It was this astounding outdoor vantage point. The views were breathtaking of all of Paradise Cove. I was at the center of the "C" of the coast, able to see the beach with the soft marine waves brushing up against the shoreline. Nearly all the Paradise Cove homes on the water were visible from where I stood. But this was only the beginning.

Luke walked us around the outdoor fireplace and luxurious, patio furniture sets. We went down a set of stairs to another vastly open lower terrace. But there was a small structure that we were heading towards as we descended. It looked to be a smaller home, no more than twenty hundred square feet, but still a considerable size.

"He's waiting in the casita," Dean's personal assistant disclosed.

A casita? So, not only did Dean Cargill have the huge, gorgeous beach property that was behind us, he even had an additional home here that stepped right out onto the golden sands of Paradise Cove. We moved around the side of the casita and towards the end of it that led directly out to a wooden pier that veered off and disappeared into the sands. Just like the main house, this casita's back wall had glass sliders that opened up directly to the outside. As I stepped inside with

Luke, I could see taupe love seats and accent chairs. Behind them was a small kitchen and to the left was a mahogany bar counter with a back wall full of mirrors and stocked shelves full of top-shelf liquor brands. Various assortments of glassware, cannisters, and decanters were also prevalent in this bar area. Now, here was the sort of bachelor pad I had pictured, although it still had a slightly nautical feel to it with the different natural watercolor hues, mainly navy blue, and lighter beige and taupe coastal colors accentuated throughout.

And there, behind the bar counter, was a man with his back to me. His dark brown hair was gelled and sleek, combed to perfection. A light, celeste blue blazer covered his slim, yet toned frame. A buttery-shaded collar barely peeked out along his neck, letting me know he also had on a flaxen-yellow buttoned-down shirt underneath.

He must have sensed our presence, because the man quickly spun around, holding two Baccarat crystal glass tumblers in his hands, half-filled with ice. I glanced up to notice his flawless smooth, yet oily, skin on his face. His jawline was just as perfect as the gossip media columns had displayed. No Photoshop necessary. Dark designer aviator sunglasses hid those baby blue eyes that the GQ Magazine covers he modeled for, highlighted so well. His rosy lips were plush and looked permanently puckered, but maybe that was because a lit cigarette was dangling from them.

"Ah! The infamous Jackson Cartwright. Welcome!" he enthusiastically stated, after taking one final puff from his cigarette before disposing of it on the crystal ashtray at the counter.

I found his facetious introduction to be quite ironic, because in the eyes of the media, or rather the world for that matter, Dean Cargill was really the *infamous* one.

"Thank you. It's a pleasure to be here. Your home is spectacular," I shared with him.

"Yeah. It better be for the amount I paid for it!" he declared. His eyes then darted up to his personal assistant. "I think we're all good here, Luke."

"Very well. Just let me know if you need anything else." And with that, Luke took off, returning to the main house.

"Please, Jackson, have a seat, or perhaps you want to sit outside on the beach? It's a pretty damn gorgeous day out. Well, that tends to be a majority of the time here in Malibu, but still..."

I nodded. "Sure. Let's talk out on the beach," I agreed.

"In the meantime, do you want a drink?" He held out the glass tumbler full of ice.

"That would be great. I'll just have whatever it is you're having," I said, making it as simple as possible for him, not wanting to heavily impose.

"Coming right up." Dean reached for a decanter full of dark brown liquor and poured it into our glasses. He grabbed both tumblers and came out from behind the bar counter.

"Let's head on out then," he instructed.

I followed Dean as he led us out to the beach. There was a white round wooden table with four matching white chairs that were teal-cushioned surrounding it. Dean sat in one of them, while I chose to sit in the one that was directly across from him. He passed my drink across the table to me.

"Dare I ask what's in this drink?" I smirked in his direction after taking a sip from it. It was biting, but very smooth as the liquid trickled down my throat.

"Just Hennessy Paradis Rare Cognac," he replied, so matter-of-factly.

I would make a mental note of this and be sure to check the price of it when I returned to my hotel. I had a hunch it was in the thousands of dollars just for a bottle, if not more. After all, this was Dean Cargill's tastes we were talking about. And that didn't come cheap.

We just sat still, admiring the majestic waters of Paradise Cove and its vastness. The silence that existed between the two of us was a bit awkward at first. It felt like a game of chess. Both Dean and I were being strategic, but it was just a matter of which of us was willing to make the first move as pawn.

"I guess we should just get right down to it," he finally broke the ice with, surprisingly.

I shrugged as I took another sip of the cognac. "I mean, I'm okay with whatever you're comfortable with," I said, to appease him.

"Well, I'm pretty comfortable right now," Dean confessed, with a coy smile written on his face.

"So, I guess I'll get started with the questioning, then?" I suggested, still trying to get a feel of where Dean's head space was and if he seemed willing to want to start the conversation right away.

"Yeah. Let's get down to it, Jackson. Do your worst!"

Chapter 5

Jackson

Current Day...

"Yeah. Let's get down to it, Jackson. Do your worst!"

I was shocked that Dean was so enthusiastic about this. Trepidation, reluctance, beating around the bush. All of these reactions were what I was half-expecting Dean to display, but he was showing no signs of hesitance whatsoever.

"Well, I like to ease into my interviews," I stated, willing to share with him my methodologies. "Make everyone feel comfortable and treat the entire situation as more of a candid conversation. It makes the discussion all the more authentic, on all counts."

Jackson took a sip from his cognac after burning out another cigarette he had lit. His designer sunglasses remained on, concealing his eyes. As he scanned the beach before us, his hair slightly blew with the gentle sea breeze. Even I was caught off-guard for a second, just by this picturesque scene of him. He was definitely in his element here in Malibu, in his dapper suit on the beach. Dean was sexy as hell, and dare I say even intimidating, as a result.

"Well, I want to be authentic as humanly possible, so I will follow your lead," he willingly said.

We were already off to a good start. Dean's openness and his wanting to get his real story across was making this easier for me. I don't know why I was so timid about this whole thing earlier. It was proving to be a cake-walk.

"Great!" I then pulled out my tape-recording device and set it on the wood table between him and me.

Dean scanned it closely, just staring at it as I laid it before us. His demeanor slightly changed the moment I hit the record button. I could get the sense that it made him a bit distressed.

"Do you mind if we use alternative tactics to conduct this interview?" he suggested.

"Oh? What do you mean?" I asked, curiously.

"This interview being recorded... it just doesn't *feel* right to me. Would you be able to go old school and just do it in on pen and paper? Jot things down that way?"

Well, this was an unusual request. I didn't see the difference between using a tape recorder and putting words down on paper. Having to write everything out on a pad would definitely be an arduous process, and I didn't want to miss anything in the interview because of me being so consumed and focused on getting my notes down. There would be a disconnect there.

Yet, I knew my goal during this interview was to also make Dean Cargill calm and relaxed while we spoke. So, I would offer to meet him halfway. "Would it be okay if I typed out my notes on a laptop?"

He nodded. "That sounds perfect."

Except the issue was I didn't have my laptop on me. It was back at the hotel. Me leaving here and returning to get it would be extremely unprofessional. I was in quite the conundrum. What the hell was I supposed to do? I had to be upfront with Dean about it.

"Unfortunately, my laptop is sitting on the desk in my hotel room," I confessed.

"Oh. Well, no worries. I'll have Luke bring down a spare device for you. You can just email your notes to yourself. Will that work?"

My face began to turn red from sheer embarrassment. This was not how things were supposed to go. Not the best jumping off point. I hoped Dean wouldn't consider me an amateur or unprofessional from here on out, because that was not the case by any means.

"Yes. That would work for me."

Dean then pulled out his cell phone and began typing into it, likely texting his personal assistant. "Luke is on his way down now."

And he was quick. Within two minutes, Luke arrived at our seated location on the beach and placed the silver laptop on the table in front of me. Opening it, he powered it on and pulled open a blank document for me.

"It's all set to go for you. Internet and all. Can I get you both any-thing else?" Luke asked, with his eyes darting back and forth between Dean and me.

"I think I'm all squared away now. Thank you," I replied.

"We're all good. I appreciate it, Luke." Dean said, before Luke headed back in the direction of the main house.

I placed the laptop on my thighs and began to firmly type out my proposed questions to him.

"Now, where were we?" Dean checked.

"Just getting started," I told him. "Okay. So, Mr. Cargill..."

"Dean... please," he interjected.

"Apologies, *Dean*," I corrected myself. "Tell me, why did you choose to move here, to Paradise Cove Bluffs of all locations? There must be something special about this place that drew you into it."

"Of course. Just look around us," he briskly declared. "We're in Malibu and in one of the most exclusive communities in all of L.A., well, all of California, really. The weather is perfect. The privacy is to die for and this property is one of a kind. The second my agent sent it to me, I knew I had to have it. I had a few of my assistants check the place out for me in person, just to make sure it was up to par with my standards, but otherwise, yes, I actually bought this place sight unseen, technically."

I did my best to keep up my typing pace with what he was telling me. "Yes. It is pretty spectacular. I suppose they don't call it *Paradise* Cove Bluffs, just for any reason," I responded, trying to add some fluff in between so that I could catch up on my notes before I would proceed to my next round of questioning. "And you bought this place for... what? Twenty-million dollars?"

Dean remained silent for a moment. His attention from the beach diverted to now looking in my direction. His brow arched just over his shades. I wish I could see those crystal blue eyes of his behind his sunglasses. I could at least get a read on what he was feeling and thinking.

"Yes. But what does that have to do with anything?" he asked, sounding accusatory.

I did my best to brush this off and change the topic altogether. "Sorry. Just small talk around you living here," I tried to explain, hoping he would buy the excuse. Maybe I should have waited to discuss my financial inquiries with him far later in the interview. "Anyway, let's change gears here. I'd love to know more about your family. Any information you're willing to share about them?"

He grunted at the mention of them. "Pshhh. I barely even talk to them anymore. We'll give the occasional birthday and holiday text message exchanges, but that's the extent of it."

"Oh? Is there a reason you don't see them as often? Was there some sort of falling out?"

Dean took another generous sip from his drink before nodding. "Yes. When I came out of the closet during my freshman year of college, my parents practically disowned me. Both raised me to be Roman

Catholic. I went through the whole church phase of going to C.C.D., receiving Communion and then going through Reconciliation and then Confirmation. My family is very religious, so them having a gay son was a sin in their eyes. We got into some heated discussions back then. Comments were made that I will never forget. And because of this grudge I can never let go of, there will always be a permanent strain in our relationship."

This was a lot. But I was pleased he was being so forthcoming with providing me this information about his personal life. "What about other family members? Siblings? Cousins?"

He shook his head. "I have an older sister, but she is so far up my parents' asses that she can barely think for herself and create her own opinions. So, I didn't even bother with her growing up. As for cousins... they're all the same too. Just like my parents and sister," Dean scoffed.

The bitterness was growing and growing the more we discussed his family. I didn't want to lose Dean altogether. I had gotten enough initial information about his family life. It was time to switch to a different subject, something that would evoke more pleasant feelings, hopefully.

"I know we're jumping around here a bit, but I'm trying to get the full scope of *who Dean Cargill really is*, before I get into the more specific questions I'm mainly here for," I informed him, hoping he would appreciate my full transparency. "Let's talk about your education. You went to a public school in Pennsylvania and then you went to major in Fashion Merchandising at the Miami International University of Art & Design. That seems like a pretty big leap to go from a rural Pennsylvania town to Downtown Miami. What was your reasoning for wanting to get into fashion merchandising and to up and go to Miami?"

Dean's face lit up like a child's face on Christmas morning. Clearly, this was a series of questions that he liked and he had fond memories of, at least based on my assumptions.

"I had always been into fashion my entire life, since I can remember. I loved watching Project Runway, America's Next Top Model, Sex and the City, Real Housewives... anything that covered high-end fashion and people living these extravagant lifestyles, that I hoped to live one day. Clearly, I was right in having these aspirations, no? Look where it landed me today," he spoke confidently but also cheekily at the same time.

"My hometown wasn't cutting it for me," Dean further added. "I needed a bigger scene. A bigger place that I could put my stamp on. I wanted to have fun, go to clubs, bars, just like I saw on T.V. I wanted to be included at fancy dinners with expensive champagnes, and drinking extra dirty martinis. I knew I was meant for that kind of life and by sitting in Pennsylvania, there was no way I could get a shot at trying to acquire it."

"That makes sense. I too had similar thoughts as you, growing up. It's ironic you mention Sex and the City," I revealed, wanting to share something that we both had in common. "I admired Carrie Bradshaw and wanted to be her when I grew up. It's why I got into journalism and working with Chatterbox News."

He smirked at me. "Yes. A common experience shared among many gay teenagers who are intrigued with that big city life."

"So, college must have been pretty expensive for you. Did you do anything else while you went to Miami for Fashion Merchandising?" I asked.

"Yes. I actually had a strong work ethic I instilled in myself. While going to college full-time, I also worked. Started out working in fashion retail at Michael Kors, actually. It was a good stepping stone for me to dip my feet into the world of fashion merchandising. I thought it was important for me to be able to put all of the knowledge I was learning in my classes to concrete experiences. So, getting a job in the fashion retail space was key to making that happen. Plus, it helped to pay the bills at the time."

Even this small amount of background information I gained from Dean Cargill would do wonders in a story. I was already jumping for joy on the inside from these simple facts and quotes alone. But I needed to keep going. It was time to push my luck a little to see just how far I could go and get the answers I needed to out of him.

"Speaking of money and finances, I know gossip columns and the media have had many questions and speculations about your finances. Some are asking how you are able to afford the lifestyle you live, stating that the money you received from your divorce settlements is nowhere near enough to cover your current expenses. Would you want to say anything to set the record straight with this?"

"No!" he blurted out in anger. "I have nothing to say about that. I'm shocked you would even ask me that, Jackson. That is not the reason you are here, to delve into where I got my money. I brought you here to tell my story—to share my life story with the world, without painting me in a negative light, like everyone else already is. Yet, you sit here and sound just like them, trying to be nosy as hell in figuring out my financial status!" he further accused, as he rose from his seat.

I needed to diffuse this situation. I needed to calm him down, fast. "Dean, I swear I didn't mean to get you this upset. All I wanted was to be able to..."

"I'm not upset!" he shouted in a rage.

Dean firmly planted his hands on his hips and let out a deep, exhausting sigh. "Look, I think this was a mistake in having you come out here..."

No! I felt like screaming. *Don't fucking do this to me.* I worked so damn hard to get here, to this moment. But there was no way I could reveal this to him. It would give him even more of a reason to shun me altogether.

"I'm sorry. Here, have a seat. I'll make sure to stay away from that subject," I tried to reason in order to placate him.

But Dean wasn't having any of it. "I think we're done, Jackson. I'll have Luke escort you off my property. I wish you nothing but the best," he nonchalantly stated, before walking up the pier and back towards his main home.

What the hell!? What in the *actual* hell!? This couldn't be happening. I was living a complete and utter fucking nightmare. I had ruined the entire interview with Dean Cargill. I had agitated him to the point where he now wanted nothing to do with me. For now, I quickly pulled up my email to send my notes to myself before Luke would confiscate the laptop from me. I needed to go back with at least *something*.

What would Edgar Baxter say about this? I could potentially lose my job at Chatterbox News for royally fucking this up. There had to be a way out of this. I had to try to make Dean reconsider his decision to cast me out completely.

Clearly, talking about finances was a sensitive subject to him. I would have to steer clear of it. But first, I needed to figure out how to get back into his good graces. There had to be a way.

Chapter 6

Dean

Nine Years Ago...

It had been a whole two weeks since I had moved into an apartment in Miami with two other roommates, not far from my college campus. It was much more cost effective for me to pay monthly rental on an apartment than to have to take out student loans in order to live in the over-priced residence halls on-campus.

I wasn't your typical eighteen-year-old gay boy. When it came to money, I was rarely frivolous with spending it on dumb shit like video games, expensive hair care and skin products, etc. I resorted to the cheapest items I could find that still managed to get the jobs done I needed them to. After all, the cost of food and a place to live pretty much ate my entire checking account at the end of every month.

My parents practically disowned me when I told them I had applied to Miami International University of Art & Design to major in fashion merchandising and was accepted. They were vexed to say the least, wondering why their only son would want to live in a *sinful party city*, as they so well put it, when I could just as easily go to school in Pennsylvania. Hell, they would have even been satisfied if I decided to go to a trade school over fashion merchandising.

I was forced into an ultimatum. Stay in Pennsylvania and attend college there, under the comfort of my parents' home or go to Miami. If the latter, my parents would not be putting a dime out towards my expenses. Their hands would be wiped clean of helping support my student loans, and during the summers and holiday times when I would be expected to return home from campus, they would refuse for me to stay in their house.

The arguments we had were so intense that I didn't even bother to speak to them for the entire three months leading up to my departure. I knew money would be tight when I went to college, so I picked up two summer jobs and worked over sixty hours a week, just to be able to save as much as possible before I would venture off to college. I worked at the local hardware and home improvement retail store, while also working closing shifts at the American Eagle clothing boutique at the closest mall, taking inventory, folding shirts, and then restocking the shelves and cleaning the entire store at night, so that the place was flawless the following morning to be re-opened for tomorrow's customers.

Maybe that's where my dedication and work ethic stemmed from. It wasn't from anyone in particular I inherited or learned it from. I was forced to have to work hard. It was a survival mode I was involuntarily put in. I could not live in Pennsylvania anymore. I needed to get out and no matter how many hours I had to work, I would be sure to do it in order to make a living in Miami happen. Failure to get the hell out of this bumfuck place wasn't an option for me.

Luckily, my work at the clothing store was something I could add to my newly improved and updated resumé, as well as now being a fashion merchandising major at Miami International University of Art & Design. So, in order to keep up with my upcoming expenses, I put my feelers out well in advance and applied for many jobs near my new apartment and the college. Much to my relief, a manager from the Michael Kors store at the Dadeland Mall in Miami gave me a call, saying she was interested in potentially hiring me. She conducted a virtual interview with me and then gave me a call two days later to let me know I was being offered a sales associate position. I accepted the job instantly, and now I was relieved to know that my stay in Miami would be permanent. And from then on out, I knew I was going to be okay.

And now, my first day on the job would be tomorrow from 3:00pm to 10:00pm on a Saturday. However, tonight, I wanted to celebrate. In my two weeks here, I had already become acquainted with a few other gay college guys. Who knew that all it would take would be for me to take my shirt off and lounge on a towel on the warm, golden sands of South Beach in order for a group of cute boys my age to flock over to get to know me?

We exchanged phone numbers after that day and stalked one another on social media. In just twenty-four hours, I was already being invited out to Twist, a popular gay club in South Beach Miami, with them. The only issue was that I was only eighteen-years-old and did not have a fake I.D. I could use. However, one of the guys claimed to know a bouncer and bartender friend there who could get me in and serve me drinks, respectively, despite my age.

So, I stared at myself in my small bathroom mirror, styling my hair with a comb, ready to make my official debut in the Miami gay night life. I had on tight dark blue dress pants, a pair of glossy black boots with a silver buckle on the sides of them, and a cream buttoned-down short-sleeve shirt. Now, I just needed to find a driver and hit the club.

Even I didn't anticipate that I would somehow be one of the ones at the venue that seemed far more overly dressed than most of the other occupants. I met the three guys from the beach yesterday, Hector, Luis, and Ramone, at the front entrance. Just as he promised, Hector escorted us up to the bouncer. The thick, bald man simply nodded at each of us as we entered the club. Once I stepped foot inside, any worries I held onto about getting in trouble for being underage here immediately vanished. This was my first time in a gay club and for how big Twist was, I was completely overwhelmed. The four of us passed through one of the bar spaces with a ton of music videos playing all around. Then, once we trekked to a new area of the club, I felt like I was in a completely different bar altogether. Twist was a complex that had a total of seven different bars, each area with its own unique *twist*.

Hector led us to a spot that made you feel like you were in an aquarium. The strobe lights that scattered throughout were all in a variety of shades of blue. The headlights over and under the bar were also teal. We sat on four stools side by side. I couldn't help but smirk once I saw that the panel underneath the bar had a zebra print decal on it. This place was definitely eclectic, but I loved it.

The crowd around us was pretty lively, too. It was definitely a packed night, although I wasn't sure what was defined as being *packed* since this was my first time here, but there was wall to wall people at every turn. Some were out on the main floors dancing the night away, raising their drinks in the air, while others, like us, were at the bar, trying to get the attention of the bartenders for a cocktail.

Hector waited until he caught the eye of a specific blonde bartender, which led me to believe this was the guy that he knew wouldn't card me. "What do you all want to drink?" Hector asked us. Luis and Ramone spoke up first, which gave me time to think for a minute before he repeated to ask me for my order. "And you, Dean?"

"I'll take a glass of pinot grigio." Honestly, I hadn't had much experience with alcohol, besides wine. There were a few parties I had with friends back in high school, and we managed to sneak a bottle of wine or two from our parents. Out of all the wines I've had, I distinctly remember liking a bottle of pinot grigio. Also, my first day on the job at Michael Kors was tomorrow. I didn't want to chance drinking liquor tonight, and I absolutely hated the taste of beer. So, wine sounded like the best option, even if it was a little unusual to be drinking a glass of wine at a popping gay club.

"Coming right up," the bartender said, as he made our drinks and handed them to each of us.

"Here's to Dean!" Hector announced. "Welcome to Miami! You're never going to want to go anywhere else. This, I promise!"

Everyone proceeded to raise their glasses in the air. I followed in suit and clinked mine with theirs before taking a sip of the mildly acidic wine.

"So, who wants to dance?" Luis suggested to our group.

"Count me in," Ramone announced.

"Yeah! Let's do it!" I enthusiastically declared.

We rose from our seats and strutted our way out to the dance floor just as a remix to Lorde's new song *Royals*, began to play. The four of us held our drinks high up and swayed to the music.

> *And we'll never be royals (royals).*
> *It don't run in our blood.*
> *That kind of lux just ain't for us.*
> *We crave a different kind of buzz.*
> *Let me be your ruler (ruler).*
> *You can call me queen bee.*
> *And baby I'll rule, I'll rule, I'll rule, I'll rule.*
> *Let me live that fantasy.*

We danced and danced for what seemed like hours and got a few refills in between. This was *everything*. This was the life I had dreamed of. I've waited so long to be able to leave my small town and go to a big city and dance the night away just like all of those scenes I've seen on television. And now, I was finally living it! A gay boy going to a nightclub for the very first time in his entire life. It would be an experience I knew I would never forget for as long as I lived.

After a while, I finally checked my phone to see that it was already 11:30pm. Earlier, I set my own personal curfew, promising myself that I would make sure I was home and in bed by midnight. Now, I was cutting it a little too close to that time.

I leaned over and whispered to Hector, Luis, and Ramone. "I think I'm going to hit the road."

"Really?" Ramone commented. "Come on, Dean. Just stay a little longer. You don't even have to be at your new job until 3:00pm tomorrow. You have nothing to worry about."

He really was doing his best to peer-pressure me, but I've worked too hard in my life to make any mistakes now. "Sorry. But once I get my schedule, we can hang out again next weekend at some point. I swear!"

"Fine..." Ramone rolled his eyes before leaning in to give me a hug.

"Take it easy!" Luis said.

I gave them each a hug and a peck on the cheek before I made my way through the labyrinth that was Twist until I got outside.

The brisk night air hit me in the face the second I stepped out. It was a nice welcome compared to the steamy atmosphere from the inside of the nightclub. Moving to the side, I leaned against the brick wall and proceeded to open up this new app called Uber to find a driver to come pick me up to take me home. But before I could click on the app to book the driver, I heard a man's voice speak up.

"Looking for a ride?"

I glanced up from my phone to see that he was directly in front of me. My eyes widened at his features. He wore a burgundy blazer with a white undershirt. He was in dress pants and expensive designer shoes. Ferragamo, I presumed, based on the symbol of the buckles. He had dark, jet black hair, but with slight traces of an ashy gray scattered throughout. His eyes were molten brown. Instantly, I swooned. There was something about this man that was beyond attractive. Was it his older, suave looks, or the fact that he was so well put together? Clearly, he had some sort of success in his life based on his attire.

"I was actually just booking an Uber home," I disclosed to him.

"Well, I don't mind taking you there," he stated. "That is, if you don't mind us making a quick pitstop. A few of my friends are meeting up at my place for bourbon and cigars. Always love new company. Would you be able to hang with that sort of crowd?"

I felt like I was being judged and also challenged at the same time. Yet, my parents' advice was ringing in my head. *Don't go home with strangers*. However, there was something different about this man. I could tell he was gay, and I wasn't getting serial killer vibes from him either. Perhaps it was just young, gay, teenage hormones kicking into overdrive, but I was beyond intrigued to see where this man lived and the types of friends he had where they all drank brown liquor and smoked cigars. The whole concept just reeked of wealth, and it sounded like a crowd I wanted to be a part of.

Maybe Ramone was right, earlier. Maybe I should stay out a bit longer. After all, I didn't have to be at Michael Kors until 3:00pm tomorrow. Even if I got back to my apartment at like 2:00am, that would get me at least a good ten hours of sleep before I would have to get up, shower, change, and head into work. I could make that happen. I had already convinced myself in just a span of seconds.

"I think I'll be able to manage," I spoke confidently.

"Perfect! I'm always looking to make a new friend here and there. I'm Frank, by the way."

"Dean..." I replied back.

"Well, my friend Mike is grabbing his car now. He's my D.D. for the night and will take us back, if that's okay with you."

I nodded.

"Awesome," he simply responded with.

And so, Frank and I became engrossed in idle chit-chat for a few minutes. I informed him of my recent move to Miami and the reason behind it, while he told me that he was a criminal defense lawyer and that we were going to what sounded like a pretty upscale penthouse in Downtown Miami. Soon, a black SUV pulled up beside us, to which Frank opened the back door for me.

In this moment, I knew I was making a major decision. It may not have seemed like it at the time, but it was one that would change me as a person from here on out. Should I be responsible and take the safe route, heading home on my own, or should I leap headfirst into an SUV with rich, older strangers, who I could form bonds with, make connections with, and experience the sort of lifestyle I've only dreamed of?

"I'm not much of a bourbon drinker, but do you have any wine at your place?" I asked Frank, as if that would be my determining factor.

He couldn't help but snicker at my naivety. "Of course, I do! Now get that twink ass of yours in the car!" he demanded of me, jokingly.

I was a little caught off-guard by him referring to me as having a *twink ass*, but at the same time, I couldn't help but enjoy the attention. So, I hopped in the SUV and off we drove to Frank's penthouse.

I could easily be identified as the black sheep of the group. All of these men at Frank's place were well into their forties, some arguably in their fifties, I presumed. But I did my best to remain a wallflower, trying to listen in on everyone's conversations and keep up with them. Many of these handsome and astute men were lawyers, like Frank, while some held other impressive and prestigious titles and careers.

Frank was not kidding when he described his penthouse to me earlier. It was unlike any place I had been to in my entire life. Places like this did not exist back in my hometown. The walls were nothing but glass, overlooking the brightly lit up city that was Miami. The furniture, the kitchen, the company, the glassware, the décor, the bottles of liquor and wine. It just screamed wealth. I couldn't help but picture myself living in it. What I would give to be able to have this sort of life and not have to worry about money and living from paycheck to paycheck. This was what I wanted. This was what I *needed*.

"So, what can I get you to drink, Dean? You mentioned you wanted wine. Do you like reds? Whites?" Frank asked.

"Do you have pinot grigio?" I felt like a parrot on repeat with this same drink request all night. Really, it was the only wine I had heard of, and I hoped people couldn't see through my bluff in that I was an inexperienced drinker.

"Yes. And coming right up," Frank said, as he moved aside and proceeded to move behind his kitchen island. He bent over to retrieve a bottle from his wine chiller and used an electric corkscrew to pop the cork, before pouring me a glass.

"Thank you," I replied as he passed me the glass.

"Come. I want to introduce you to some of my friends," he suggested.

All I could do was nod as he wrapped his hand around my waist and led me around to everyone at his small get-together. As the drinks continued to flow and the men stepped out onto the veranda to smoke their cigars, I realized it was already hitting 2:00am. As most of Frank's friends finished their cigars, they bid farewell to him and everyone else before departing. Soon, it was just Frank and me, with two others in his apartment. I was ready to leave, but I first wanted to get some alone time with him to truly thank him for inviting me over this evening.

Eventually, his two friends did head out, leaving the two of us to ourselves. "I really do appreciate you inviting me here tonight. I've only been in Miami for two weeks. So, I'm really trying to make some new friends and get acquainted with the city."

"Well, I'm glad I could bring you over. My friends absolutely adored you. And I don't mean that just because of how young and fucking cute you are. They were impressed with how smart and motivated you seemed. You're not like most other guys your age, you know," he shared.

These compliments made my insides melt. To be noticed and to be treated as though I was someone impressive was beyond elating to me. Tonight could not have gone any better.

"Well, you're not like most men I know," I admitted to Frank. "I've only known guys my age. And I'll be honest, I'm not attracted to any of them. I'm not sure what it was, but when I saw you tonight, something just clicked. I think you're beyond attractive and *just my type*."

Frank held a wicked smirk on his face as I admitted this to him. He placed his drink down on the counter and held his arm out, gripping me by the back of the neck. "You can always stay here tonight, if you want?"

The moment he said this, all I could think about was his sexy body against mine. His masculinity taking me over. Being able to be in bed with this hot, successful man was beyond exhilarating. I could feel my blood already warming up at the thought of being fucked by him.

All of my priorities were taking a backseat right now. My first day on the job tomorrow, my college and career, my morals. They were all now distant images covered by a wave of fog, while Frank was the one directly in my line of vision, right in front of the lights. The only thing visible to me right now.

"Yeah. I think I'd like that a lot," I intimately whispered to him.

Frank then pulled my head into him, so that my soft lips could grace his. We made out slowly at first, but the intensity quickly picked up and before you knew it, we were throwing our clothes to the floor of the hallway on our way into his bedroom.

He lifted me in the air to passionately kiss me more, before he softly laid me down on the bed on my back. The dichotomy of feeling the silky satin sheets against my back with the firmness of his cock and body pressed into the front of my torso sent chills down my back.

"God, you're fucking spectacular, Dean!" he said in between his breaths of kissing. "I'd give you the fucking world!" I had a hunch the alcohol or the sexual urges were doing the talking for him now as we had sex, but I could not help but simper from his remark, because it did sound really nice. A man being able to give you the world... what an amazing fucking world that would be.

I woke up with Frank to the sound of his alarm just hours later at 7:00am. He told me he had to be in the office before 9:00am. I was actually relieved to hear this. It made me have to get up early to get back to my own place, so I could sleep for a few more hours before having to get ready to go to work. While Frank was in the shower, washing off, I decided to make us a pot of coffee in his kitchen, grabbing the coffee grounds, filter, and sugar from his massive pantry.

Just minutes later, he emerged from his bedroom in nothing but long black dress socks, dark red boxers and a white undershirt. He looked so damn fine right now, but I knew better than to lean in to kiss him and seem desperate.

He began sniffing the air before his eyes darted over to the pot behind me. "You made coffee?"

I nodded. "Figured you could use some before you head into the office."

Frank smiled, displaying those ivory teeth of his. "You know, keep it up and you might make me want to bring you back around more often," he stated with a flirtatious wink.

"We'll just have to see about that," I commented wittily back at him, before he quickly stepped close to me to wrap me up in his arms.

"Actually, why don't you come back over after work and stay the night?" Frank suggested, while nibbling on my neck.

"Really? I don't get off until 10:00pm," I reminded him.

"So what? I'll still be awake. I'll have a nice dinner catered for us over a bottle of wine. What do you say?"

I was now in a dilemma here. Part of me knew that the best thing would be for me to keep my space a bit from this guy that I literally just met last night. But then the other half of me reveled in the thought of getting to see him here again and be treated with all the fine things that he had to offer. Another awful thought then permeated my mind. What if I rejected his offer? Would he be turned off and decide to no longer bother with me altogether, moving on the next twink at his disposal?

I couldn't let that happen. Now that I had access to this successful and wildly attractive man, I was unable to take a chance in leaving him behind. So, I succumbed to him against my better judgment.

"I'd like that a lot, actually," I responded to him.

"Good, because now that I've had a taste of Dean Cargill, I don't think I could go a whole day without getting more of you." Frank craned his neck to passionately kiss me on the lips, allowing me to taste his minty fresh breath from having just brushed his teeth in the bathroom. I leaned into him more, closing my eyes, getting lost in the moment.

I had to separate myself from him, being reminded of the time. "I should really get going, though. I wouldn't want to make you late."

"No. You're right. Just text me later and let me know how you're doing. Looking forward to seeing you later tonight."

I simply smiled and nodded, before walking around Frank and back into his bedroom to retrieve my clothes from last night, putting them back on in haste. I made it out of the room and towards the main foyer as he called back out to me. "See you later, babe."

And just like that, I instantly swooned at being referred to as his *babe*. At the same time, I now knew how into me he really was. Who knew that I had the ability to captivate a man in just the span of hours, overnight?

"Bye, babe," I returned with, before heading out the door to head back to my apartment. I held a permanent smile on my face the entire ride back to my place and until I crawled back in bed. I would sleep so peacefully for the next several hours until I started my first official shift with Michael Kors.

It was 2:45pm, and I stood right in front of the store to my new job. My hair was gelled and swept back, flawlessly. I had on a lavender buttoned-down shirt and slim, light gray dress pants that hugged the curves of my leg muscles well.

I needed to look like I was wealthy and refined enough to be working here. Also, being a sales associate, I knew I would have to resort to my charm and suave looks in order to make the sales I was expected to make.

Plus, I recalled the message in the email my manager sent me when I accepted the position in regard to the dress code protocols. *Michael Kors employees are expected to reflect the Michael Kors image at all times during working hours, in manner and appearance. Employees are expected to be well groomed and dressed in accordance with the Personal Appearance Guidelines. The Company's philosophy is that our employee's style represents both Michael's vision as well as the chic, sophisticated, jet set, luxury DNA of our brand. Employees will be wardrobed in the season's current looks.*

Truth be told, I was nervous as hell about stepping foot in the place. No matter how confident and prepared I thought I was, those first day jitters would somehow always manage to triumph in the end.

"Well, here goes nothing," I mumbled to myself as I entered Michael Kors. As I moved in, I realized just how small the place really was. I wasn't sure what I was expecting, but I pictured it being much bigger. So much bigger. But I appreciated the cleanliness of the place. Everything was shiny, bright, and tidy. The white tiled floors were glistening so much that I truly believed they were probably safe to directly eat off of. They were that spotless.

Purses with the MK symbol in all shapes and sizes lined the floor to ceiling shelves on the walls. A glass enclosed jewelry case was at the center. I hovered over it, admiring the thousands of dollars' worth of watches and other accessories inside it.

"Dean?" I heard a woman's sultry voice call from behind.

I spun around and instantly recognized Jennifer, the store manager, from seeing her face during my Skype online interview. "Yes. That's me. And you must be Jennifer. It's great to finally meet you in person!" I zealously shared with her, wanting to make the best possible impression.

"You too! It's so nice to finally have you here with us!" she replied, which made my cheeks change to a softer, scarlet hue. "So? Are you ready to begin your first official day on the job?"

"Ready as ever!" I eagerly chimed in.

It turned out that the job was pretty basic. I just needed to greet customers and ask if they were looking for anything in particular. A majority of them would always reply *just browsing* or *no, I'm just looking around*. It was a quick pattern I picked up on, that those people who made such responses were likely going to walk back out of the store empty-handed. It was those who came in on a mission, searching for a particular bag or piece of jewelry that would be the ones likely to make a purchase.

It turned out that I was a complete natural at talking to strangers, putting on the *old Dean charm*, as what some of my friends back home would refer to my social skills as. I really could hold a conversation with everyone and anyone.

My manager, Jennifer, was getting off at 5:00pm, but told me I would be closing the store tonight with one of the assistant managers, named Brendan. When I first met him, he was tall, lanky, but had well-kept hair that waved effortlessly. He wore Michael Kors prescribed glasses, of course. When Jennifer soon left, Brendan picked up the role of having to train me.

Right away, I could tell he was gay, just like me. Once he realized I was too, he immediately became more playful, making snide comments here and there about certain customers who were rude or just plain annoying and bothersome. But overall, I really did enjoy his company.

When the store finally closed, I let out a deep and heavy sigh. I had made it through my first day on the job and it wasn't bad at all. I even managed to get a number of sales in. Even more so, I was looking forward to having dinner at Frank's place in just a few hours which would likely end in an evening filled with steamy, hot passionate sex, again.

But before then, I would have to *close shop*. Brendan locked the front of the store up, so no one else could get in, before he went behind the registers to count the earnings for the day. As for me, I just moved around and straightened up a bit, but I didn't need to do much since the place was pretty much in order all day long.

However, once Brendan finished up, we still weren't ready to leave the store just yet. Some of the purses and bags on the shelves needed to be sent to the back room now that they were no longer *in season*. We stocked the newly open spaces with a fresh shipment of new purses and bags that had just arrived yesterday while bringing the older ones to the stockroom.

"So, what happens with these?" I curiously asked. "Do we mark them down for clearance and put them back up on the shelves at a later date?"

Brendan chuckled at my ignorance. "No. Not at all. They're done."

"*They're done?*" I repeated back to him, a little confused. "What do you mean?"

"I mean, they get shipped back to the warehouse," he informed me.

This was pretty surprising to me. I had always assumed they were just reticketed at a lower cost, but then I recalled other cheaper retail stores that also sold out-of-date Michael Kors products. It then clicked that perhaps they were sent to these other places to be resold at a discounted price.

"And then they get sent back out to other retail stores to try and sell them?" I inquired.

"Sometimes," he revealed. "But most of the time, I'd say around three-quarters of them wind up getting burned."

"*Burned!?*" I echoed back to him in disbelief. "But why waste the money in doing that, and not attempt to sell them at an alternative location?" It seemed that there was a lot to fashion merchandising that I would have to learn about in my college courses I'd be starting in the near future.

"Think about it, Dean. If every major, upscale designer brand clothing store decided to sell all of their unsold merchandise at lower costs, then the brand would depreciate its value. Everyone would be able to access a Michael Kors bag and it would no longer be the luxury brand that it's now known for. Does that make sense?"

To an extent, it did. But then I attempted to do the math in my head. Based on the amount of bags we just re-boxed to send back to the warehouse, it was nearly $20,000 worth of products. That meant that in just tonight alone, if Brendan's estimates were accurate, that $15,000 was going right down the drain, or rather on the stovetop to be burned.

I couldn't wrap my head around it. All that money gone to waste when it could easily be sold elsewhere. Hell, even I wouldn't mind taking the bags off of their hands to try and resell them myself, if I wanted those sorts of high margins and profits, which, let's face it, I did based on my current paycheck to paycheck living situation.

What Luxury Brands Do To The Leftovers
By The Lux Group

We are so consumed with owning the latest and greatest designer bags and products that we fail to see the age-old tradition of those companies destroying their unsold merchandise.

Did you know that the fashion industry is one of the world's greatest land polluters? It's about time we talk about it.

Things You May Not Have Known About Luxury Brands.

Have you ever seen a sale on luxury products? Never! Doing so would dilute the heritage of their brand. In order to protect their brand identity, they feel that they are forced to destroy their items.

Over the years, brands like Michael Kors have been accused of destroying their products.

Their justification in doing so: to maintain the scarcity of their goods and the exclusivity of their brands. They don't want to sell their goods at a lower price as it may harm their luxury image.

Chapter 7

Jackson

Current Day...

Fuck it! Fuck it all to hell!!!

After my failed interview with Dean, I returned back to my hotel with my tail tucked between my legs. But I couldn't just return to my room and slam my face into the pillow, soaking it with my tears. I made it to the bar to grab both a shot of tequila and then a martini to return to the room. *Alcohol.* It would be the only friend that was here at my side to console me during this crazy fucking turn of events that I did not see coming.

Once I got to my room, I slammed my door behind me and took another sip of my drink. Flopping down on the end of the bed, I lowered my head into my hands before tugging at my hair like a deranged maniac.

How could I have slipped up this badly?

Why did I even think it wise to press Dean on his finances so early?

Did I really think he would just flat out answer me without any sort of reluctance?

What the fuck was I even thinking!?

These thoughts continued to swarm through my mind. I was distressed and felt like a complete and utter failure. A loser.

If there was anyone who could talk me off of this ledge, it was Darren. I sat back in the bed, staring up at the ceiling as I pulled my phone out of my pocket, dialing his number.

"Hey babe. Everything okay? How'd the interview go?" he asked right away.

"Bombed it…" I admitted, without beating around any sort of bush.

"Bombed it? No. It couldn't have gone that bad."

"Oh, but it did," I said with sass. "In less than ten minutes, I was already kicked out of his house."

"You can't be serious. What the hell did you say to piss him off?"

"It all happened so fast," I replied, swaying my hand through my hair in deep frustration. "We were talking about his background and family history one minute, and then I dove into the topic of his finances and simply asked for him to set the record straight against those who have made defamatory claims about how he really makes his money the next. It set him off."

"But why? It's not like you said anything that he hasn't already heard of. Plus, you were actually the one willing to let him tell his side of the story, to absolve him from all those claims people were making against him," Darren explained.

"I know. I thought I handled that portion well, but evidently not. It seems Dean is triggered easily. And that's another bizarre thing. The minute I asked the question he was extremely volatile and full of rage. Then, almost instantly, he completely calmed down and kindly had me escorted off of his property, *wishing me nothing but the best*."

"Wow! I'm sorry all that happened to you, honey," Darren sympathized. "But I wouldn't just give up because of this. Dean didn't completely shut the door on you. Maybe he was just having a rough day. Being interviewed in person is a new thing for him. Remember, he lives a very private life and avoids paparazzi and journalists like the plague. Perhaps he just doesn't know how to navigate through some of the tougher questions that are bound to be thrown his way."

"Are you for real, Darren?" I asked in disbelief. How could my fiancé think that all was not lost? "Of course the door was completely shut. And it wasn't just slammed in my face, but it was locked and dead-bolted to boot."

I could hear the sighing breath of Darren from the other end of the line. He likely thought I was being overly-dramatic right now, but who wouldn't be? How does one react to the pedestal that is leading up to their dream and career goals, just crumbling before them?

"I get that you're bent out of shape right now, but just wait a little while. Once you've gotten your composure back, I think you should reach back out to him or his agent. Be friendly. Explain that there was a miscommunication and that you apologize and would be willing to re-do the interview from scratch and under Dean's terms."

"You really think that would work?"

"Why wouldn't it?" Darren stated with confidence. "Just promise that you'll avoid any topics that could be triggering to him. I think he'd actually come around to that, honestly."

Darren was somebody who often saw everything through rose-colored glasses. He believed everyone in the world was logical and un-complicated. That solutions to any problem were easy to come up with and would go off without a hitch. This was exactly what he assumed now with this Dean situation, that all of it would just blow over and I would be given a second chance.

But I was too sensible to think that things would be okay. There's no way Dean would come around and recant his decision to back out of the interview. Celebrities and wealthy people like him rarely went back on their initial word and decisions.

"I have to assume the worst, Darren. If I don't, then I won't be prepared to figure out how to work around it."

"And what is the worst possible thing that you think could happen, babe?" he asked.

"That I lose my job. That Chatterbox News fires me altogether," I revealed to him. "I wouldn't be surprised if somehow one of Dean Cargill's PR people already contacted Edgar Baxter to inform him that everything has been canceled. Who knows? They could already be working up an email telling me my employment will be terminated. Do you think they will at least offer me a severance package?" I knew I was beginning to sound hysterical, but I couldn't help it.

"Calm down. You're not going to get fired," Darren said in an attempt to alleviate all of my worries. "Let's look at everything from an outside lens here," he further recommended. "This interview would have never even happened from the get-go if it wasn't for you, Jackson. Dean or someone he knows clearly liked the story you covered on his and Roger Friedman's divorce. It was why they specifically were the ones to reach out to Chatterbox to get hold of you. Not the other way around. So, without you, Chatterbox News would have never even had an interview with Dean Cargill lined up to begin with. Everyone would just break even, cut their losses, and move on."

"But will Edgar Baxter view it that way? I honestly think it still reflects badly on me in the end," I pessimistically stated.

"Well, there's only one way to find out. Make the call. See if you can get through to Dean. That's the first step you need to take. We can only speculate on what's going to happen in the near future until you at least give it a shot."

"Fine!" I gave in, sighing with vexation. "You know, you can be a real stubborn, hard-ass sometimes?"

I could hear Darren laughing in the background. "And you think you're not? Puh-lease!"

We both snickered together. "I wish you were here," I broke the moment of relief with, appreciating him guiding me through my turbulent emotions. It made me miss him all the more. His smile, his touch, just his presence, period.

"Well, you will see me soon, eventually. Whether you come home early because everything happens to fall through, which I suspect it won't, or if you do wind up staying longer with interviewing Dean, I'll make the trip down to Malibu as promised."

"Perfect! I really need to see you soon, but let's hope it's under the latter circumstances."

"Oh yeah? *How bad* do you need to see me soon?" Darren's voice deepened almost into a sexual grunt, and I could instantly sense that his devil horns were growing through his scalp.

"Honestly, pretty fucking bad," I admitted.

"Ha! Well, how about this? Let me buy a sexy pair of underwear or even an outfit I want you to wear for when I come down. You'll wear it and do whatever I say… since you want me so *fucking bad*."

God, I could practically feel Darren's erection popping through the phone right now, poking me right on the cheek. "I love it when you're demanding!" I teased. "But it better be sexy."

"Oh! It will be!" My fiancé chuckled once more. "Anyway, eyes back on the prize. Focus on getting that interview back with Dean. Let me know how it pans out. Love you, babe."

"Love you too. See you soon."

With that, we ended the call.

I returned to drinking my martini just staring at the home screen of my phone, aimlessly. After a few minutes of debating, I decided to ultimately listen to Darren in the end. I made the call to Dean's agent, hoping to reach him. I would profusely apologize and try to make things right again. After all, this was my career and all my Carrie Bradshaw hopes and dreams on the line here. I would do well to continue to remember that.

Chapter 8

Dean

Eight Years Ago...

I stood leaning against the kitchen island in our penthouse, going over the menu with the private chef once more. "So, we'll have both a classic bruschetta and wild mushroom bruschetta to start off with. Can we throw a few more appetizers out there since it will be an hour before we all actually sit down for the next course? I want that out the second the first guest arrives at 7:00pm. We'll let everyone mingle and then once everyone is seated by 8:00pm we can have the antipasto salad served followed by the rosa di parma pork tenderloin as the main course. We'll only have two people who are vegetarians, but others might want a taste of the pepper ricotta primavera as well, so let's make a little extra of that. Then, we'll end the dinner with the fruit crostata. I believe I hit everything. Was there anything I left out that we discussed earlier?"

The Italian chef shook his head. "I think that covers about all that I brought with me. I'll also have carbonara arancini served as an appetizer along with the bruschetta."

I raised my brow to him with a confused look on my face, unsure of what the hell a carbonara arancini was.

The chef smiled. "It's an Italian rice ball filled with onion, garlic cloves, arborio rice, white wine, chicken stock, peas, parmigiano-reggiano cheese, eggs, salt and pepper."

"That sounds great. Just remember to leave some of those rice balls without the chicken stock for those few that are vegetarians."

"On it, boss!" he whimsically stated, before he turned around to gather the ingredients from the refrigerator.

It was already 6:00pm, and I needed to get ready myself before the guests arrived but I couldn't just yet since I needed to be available to let people in the building who rang our front buzzer. Frank was still in the office but would hopefully be home in a...

But no sooner than I thought that, the front door opened and in strolled Frank in his forest green Dolce & Gabbana suit. I retrieved his laptop bag from his hands, knowing he would likely lazily toss it on the floor beside the office door. The maid had already left for the day, so I did not want to leave any trail of a mess before the guests arrived.

"Welcome home, babe." I greeted him with a peck on the lips.

"Thanks, Gillbear," he returned with. Gillbear being the pet-name he came up with for me several months ago. It was a play off of my last name, Cargill. "Has the chef arrived yet?"

"Yes. He's in the kitchen getting preparations underway. I've already discussed the timing and plan with him already. So, he's good to go. The server and bartender will be here within the next half an hour. I still need to hop in the shower, which means you need to keep an eye on your phone to buzz the server and bartender into the building."

"Perfect." Franked leaned in to place another kiss on my cheek. "Thank you for handling all of this. Yeah. Go ahead and get in the shower. I'm going to freshen up a bit too and change, but I'll have my phone close to me."

"Great. Thank you." I sauntered off to our office, placing his laptop bag in the bottom cabinet of the credenza, before trailing off into our master bathroom to hop in the shower. As I closed my eyes and let the water strike me in the face, I instantly relaxed, submerging myself into its blistering warmth. It would be both a calm and sophisticated evening tonight. I began reflecting, which is where I got most of my thinking done, in the comfort of a hot shower.

I couldn't believe how quickly my life had changed in just one year alone since moving to Miami. Frank and I have now been together for nearly a full year. Just six months ago, I officially ended the lease on my apartment and moved in with him, here, in his penthouse. It wasn't too difficult for me to contort and adapt to Frank's lifestyle and fit in with his friends. It came easily to me. Call it my Gemini nature coming out.

Frank proved to be beyond generous since we've been together, buying me a new wardrobe full of expensive and designer brand clothing, a luxury convertible, and refusing my offer to pay him monthly to live here at his place. The man loved to treat me well. He never wanted me to spend a dime on anything. There came a point where he offered to cover all of my student loans, but I rejected the idea altogether, which he appreciated about me, that I wasn't some swindler strictly after his money. I wanted to make contributions to our relationship too. However, Frank was in much more of a better circumstance to be able to do all that. But I knew my time would come, where I could completely reciprocate for all that he had done for me, financially.

One thing I couldn't give up on was my job, though. I now worked at Coach, selling handbags and other accessories. I lasted at Michael Kors for about eight months before I made the switch to work at Coach. I just needed a new scene and a change of pace. Plus, the pay was slightly higher, not that that fully mattered to me at this point.

Frank practically begged me to give up my job, saying he could easily support me. He thought I was working way too hard with going to college full-time while also working in retail part-time. But I just couldn't let myself give it up. I wasn't sure if it was my work-ethic or independence in wanting to keep this job for me, but I couldn't relinquish my side income. Plus, this extra money I made in working with Coach allowed me to afford to buy Frank some lavish gifts on special occasions, even though my presents were technically modest compared to the things he spent on me.

But there was one gift he was stunned by that I got him just a month ago. On his birthday, we had a candlelight dinner together. I pulled out a perfectly square box from underneath the fine white tablecloth.

"Dean, you shouldn't have..." he commented once he saw the box on the table.

"But I couldn't resist. Here. Open it," I suggested.

Frank pulled open the box, revealing a sparkling watch. It was a diamond men's Rolex with a dark mother-of-pearl dial. The diamond bezel consisted of four carats.

"Try it on," I further added, seeing that Frank's eyes were bulged in shock and that he was rendered speechless.

"Dean! This is really extravagant. But how could you afford this?"

I did find his question to be completely insulting, but I could understand why he thought this. How could I have afforded a ten-thousand dollar watch working only a part-time job in retail? Well, I was just frugal with my earnings from Coach. I put my earned money into my own savings account and tried not to touch one bit of it.

"You know I work hard. I've been saving up. Happy birthday, babe," I simply uttered.

Frank leaned across the table to give me a kiss before placing the watch around his wrist, adjusting it. Once it was on, he held it close to the candlelight at the center of the dinner table, allowing the light to brightly reflect off of the diamonds.

"God, you are unbelievable. I am so lucky to have you in my life," Frank stated.

"Ditto," I replied back to him.

I had been standing under the scorching water in the shower, for about ten minutes now, daydreaming and reminiscing over those amazing nights the two of us had together, that I had completely forgotten that I should be in a rush to get ready for the upcoming dinner party.

I hurriedly washed my hair and rinsed my body before stepping out of the shower. As I dried myself off and wrapped a soft, white towel around my waist, I made my way back into our master bedroom to see Frank at our vanity, studying himself in the mirror as he straightened out his tie.

"Dapper as always," I remarked.

His piercing green eyes sprung up to stare at me through the mirror, spotting me naked, as I dropped my towel on the chaise in the room. "Sexy as always," he returned.

We both snickered as I stepped into the walk-in closet to retrieve my clothes for the evening, tossing them on our king-sized bed, ready to change into them.

"Both the server and bartender are already here," he informed me.

"Perfect. I think we are all set, then?" I asked, double-checking.

"Seems that way." Frank came over to passionately kiss me. His hands wrapped to the back of my head, pulling me into him. I closed my eyes, feeling the tug of his fingers through my damp hair.

I was the one to break our embrace, knowing that going any further would wind up causing us to spend an additional fifteen minutes in this bedroom having sex, when we were already getting short on time with having to go back out for the dinner party.

"You probably should head out there and make sure the server and bartender are on the same page and then be ready to greet our guests at the door," I recommended. "I won't be long. Just give me about ten or fifteen minutes to finish getting ready and I'll join you."

Frank let out a sexual groan, likely irritated that I had teased him and he would have to wait until the end of the night before he could get his hands on me once again. "Fine. If I must..."

He stepped out of the room, allowing me to get ready on my own. This dinner party would be no different from the rest that we've hosted on a weekly basis. The only variation was the dinner theme. Tonight was Italian, of course, and we were sure to always shuffle the theme around, trying not to repeat any from the past.

Frank's friends, which were now also my friends, were all scholarly and impressive in their own rights. Most of them were lawyers like Frank. Many of our dinners resorted to conversations pertaining to law, politics, and human rights. They discussed in depth context to their current cases, which I listened to intently, chiming in every now and again to share my unbiased and objective viewpoints. Every time I did speak up, I could feel Frank's hand squeeze my thigh from underneath the table, offering me a warm smile from beside me.

Overtime, I learned that Frank's friends were enraptured with me, and were quite impressed, making furtive comments to him along the lines of:

He is so wise for someone his age.

Where did you manage to find him? They don't make them like they do him.

You found yourself a great catch, Frank. Try not to lose him.

I've never met someone so young and so put together.

Bring Dean around more often, Frank. He's such a breath of fresh air.

Yes. In just one year, I had come a long way from being the college freshman who moved from bumfuck Pennsylvania to Miami and could barely afford his rent. Now, I was living rent-free with my super sexy, successful lawyer boyfriend in his lavish penthouse. I was becoming someone important, someone who could stand on their own two legs and no longer have to be obsessed with thoughts of money being on my mind.

Well, that was only partially true, actually. Money still was on my mind. But now, I thought about how I could make more of it and work towards an even greater lifestyle. When you have the work-ethic and motivation I have, with a newfound confidence and finances no longer being a looming concern, then there were no limits. Not even the sky. I was ready to go beyond that.

The day after that dinner party, I had a few morning fashion merchandising classes I had to attend. Afterwards, I barely had just enough time to get to the gym and back home to freshen up before starting my evening work shift as a sales associate at Coach.

The job was not very tedious at all. My tasks pretty much consisted of helping customers find their purchases and then working the register to ring them up. Just your typical, mundane retail work. The same as what I did at Michael Kors. Except, for some reason, I noticed that at Coach we received far more many returns on items than I was formerly used to.

My dull shift for the night was about to get a bit lively when a woman came in holding a white shopping bag in her hand as she entered the store. She made a beeline for the registers, practically hurling the bag over the counter when she approached. The Karen pulled a four-hundred-dollar, salmon-colored shoulder bag out, along with a lengthy receipt and pushed it in my direction.

"I'm here to return this," she coolly stated.

I put on my fakest, warmest smile, revealing my brilliant ivory teeth as I addressed her. "Hi and welcome! What seems to be the problem with the bag? Was it damaged or defective at the time of purchase?"

She shook her head adamantly. "No. Nothing like that. It was a gift for my daughter, but she wasn't thrilled about the color."

"I see..." I scanned the receipt and noticed the purchase date, comparing it to today, doing the math in my head of the time that had lapsed since. "Well, it seems this bag was purchased at our sister Coach store, but it was bought thirty-five days ago," I informed her.

"Yeah? And so what? What the hell does that have to do with anything?"

I still maintained my composure, knowing very damn well I would never let this bitch talk to me like this if I was off the clock.

"Our return policy is thirty days, mam," I let her know. "We cannot accept this return since it was purchased over thirty days ago."

"Are you fucking kidding me!?" Her voice rose into a near shout. "You're telling me you won't give me my money back because I am returning this just five days after the date of your stupid refund policy?"

I shrugged. "I'm sorry mam, but rules are rules. I don't make them. I just enforce them."

"Well, can I at least make an even exchange on it?" she requested, but in a milder manner.

I shook my head. "No. I'm sorry. Our thirty-day return policy includes exchanges."

"Well, this is absolutely ludicrous. Who is your manager!? I'd like to speak with them right away," she demanded.

Hell hath no fury like a Karen asking for a store manager, I thought to myself.

I reached for the black button on my headset to call for the current supervisor on duty. Her name was Stella.

"Stella. You have a customer that would like to speak to you."

"What is it in regard to?" she asked me over the headset.

"A return," I simply replied.

"I'm finishing up with shipment in the back. Tell her I'll be up in a minute or so."

I glanced back up at the woman, who held her R.B.F. "She'll be out in a moment."

"Hmph!" she grumbled. "Ridiculous."

I remained silent and went on about my business for the next two minutes, choosing not to say a word to the customer, until Stella arrived.

"Hi! I'm Stella!" She warmly greeted the irate woman. "What seems to be the problem?"

"This boy is insistent that I cannot return my bag," she explained, leaving out the reasoning behind it, at her blind convenience, of course.

"She purchased it exactly thirty-five days ago," I told Stella.

"Well, I'm sorry mam, but we cannot accept this item since it is past our thirty-day limit," my manager further explained to her, literally repeating what I had already told her.

"This is completely asinine! I am a loyal customer. Never in my life have I heard of such a terrible return policy at a store!" Now the woman was actually yelling. "I'll be reporting the both of you. I will leave a review on every platform there is out there if you won't..."

Stella then let out a deep sigh, scooting over so that she was now in front of the register, tapping on the screen. "We do not normally do this, but if this is your first return, I can make an exception."

"Thank you! Yes. This is my first return. See? Was that so hard? That's all I was asking." The Karen rolled her eyes, but held a smirk on her face, knowing she managed to get her way, much to my dismay.

Deep down, I was fuming on the inside. I could not believe Stella was letting this woman get away with this, only because she was a nasty fucking psycho with deplorable behavior. Stella was taking the easy way out. She just didn't want to have to waste the time to deal with the scene this woman was causing. Our district manager would probably catch wind of the bad reviews and have Stella explain to her all that happened. My manager was one who tried to avoid drama at all costs. And I did understand that, to an extent. Yet, at the same time, in her having this philosophy, she was allowing people, like this heinous woman, to walk all over her.

"Go ahead and make the return, Dean," Stella instructed. "Just punch in my manager code. You know what it is." With that, Stella stepped out from behind the counter. "Thank you. I'm sorry for your trouble and we hope to see you again soon," she cheerfully said to the woman, before traipsing to the backroom.

"And I will just need to see the credit card you purchased the item on," I said to the woman, hoping even this simple request wouldn't cause her to go all ape-shit on me.

"Yes. Here..." she said, handing off her credit card to me in a normal, decent tone, much to my relief.

I swiped it in order to make the return, printing out a second receipt for her. "You should see the balance return to your account in the next three-to-five business days or so. Can I help you with anything else?"

"No. That will be all. Thank you." She accepted the receipt and turned around, heading out of the store.

Good fucking riddance!

Since I already had the woman's information on the screen, I curiously scanned her transaction history at Coach and saw that she had made six other purse and handbag purchases over the past year, all of which were returned or exchanged.

The fucking nerve of her to lie to us and say she never returned anything here before!

But I realized I had to give up my acrimony towards the woman. I would never see her again. Plus, she was beneath me. I lived in a high-rise penthouse with a hot lawyer. She was resorting to going to Coach outlets to make exchanges and returns on purses that were just a couple of hundred dollars. That spoke volumes of how bottom of the barrel she was, compared to me.

No matter how annoyed I was with a customer, I never held on to it. Never would I return home with negative energy from the interactions I've had in my work environment. That just wasn't me and I refused to bring myself to talk about my part-time job with Frank. I knew it would be an unattractive trait in his eyes if I did that. And I worked so hard over the past year to always keep him intrigued, attracted to me, and wanting more.

I was working a closing shift tonight, just like all of my other weekly shifts. As I closed the store, I brought the salmon-colored shoulder bag into the stockroom with the other seven returned items that were made today. One would think these purses, handbags, and accessories, which were still intact and undamaged, could be resold at a discounted price or sent to an alternative vendor to be sold. But no. Under Coach's policy, I was instructed to slice and destroy these bags before taking them to the dumpster out back behind the store. It was a shame that that was what I had to do with these perfectly good products. I could easily have made a couple thousand dollars in selling all of them. What a fricking waste!

Coach Responds to Negative Viral TikTok Video
-Fashion Forward News

After a viral TikTok video surfaced, alleging Coach destroyed its returned merchandise, the company was quick to respond and modify that policy.

In the video, posted by an anonymous TikTok account, someone was seen dumpster diving in the parking lot behind a Coach store. Multiple Coach bags were found and shown on the screen. The user further comments that the bags have been deliberately "slashed" by store employees as a company "policy."

Coach immediately replied in a statement posted to Instagram, emphasizing its commitment to sustainability.

"We have now ceased destroying in-store returns of damaged and unsalable goods and are dedicated to maximizing such product reuse in our Coach (Re)Loved and other circularity programs," the brand said.

The company further commented on their philanthropy, mentioning that they have donated products "valued at over $55 million USD" and pledged to continue to implement sustainable solutions to disposing of and repurposing its goods.

Chapter 9

Jackson

Current Day...

It had been a full twenty-four hours since Dean fired me from the interview. I did just as my fiancé, Darren, had advised. *Begged for forgiveness*. I did it in an email, over the phone, and even through Dean's DMs on all of his major social media accounts, but of course, I should have known better that he was probably not the one that checked on any of them. He has hired public relations professionals that take care of all of that for him, I'm sure.

I promised myself I'd give him or someone from his team until the end of today to get in contact with me. Otherwise, I would be checking out of the hotel first thing tomorrow morning. The last thing I would want would be to continue to stay at the hotel on the company's expense for a few extra days having no interview in my back pocket. Still, there was always that little bit of information Dean gave me that I could work with to somehow create a story out of. Not to mention the testimony from his neighbors and the documents I uncovered from his ex's divorce lawyer. It wouldn't be a substantial story as it could potentially be with a full, extended interview with Dean, but I would do my best to make the most of the cards I'd been dealt.

But really, was I dealt these cards or did I over bet and go all-in on a hand I shouldn't have gone all-in on, which was why I now found myself in the predicament that I was in? Although I was sitting on pins and needles, attached to my cell phone hoping, no, *praying*, to get a phone call, text message, email, anything from one of Dean Cargill's representatives, I knew it would be unwise of me to lull all day in my hotel room just sitting by my phone, waiting for this miracle.

Plus, the weather outside was gorgeous. Well, technically, the weather was always phenomenal in Malibu. But still, it would be a sin not to be out in it and allow the sun to gaze upon me during this beautiful day. Also, I promised Darren I would try to venture to the beach at least once during this trip and who knows, this could be my only opportunity to be able to do that, with the chance that I would likely be checking out and heading back into town tomorrow.

I laid on the beach in my aviators and light blue swimming shorts, borrowing a few of the pool towels from the hotel to use as beach blankets, which would have to suffice. I allowed myself to just close my eyes and listen to nothing but the sounds of the rhythmic crashing waves, seabirds calling over the Pacific, and the gentle ocean breeze. For the slightest moment it put me in an idyllic meditative trance, one that I wished I could never come out of.

But my mind would only allow me to travel there but for a hot second, before it managed to make an immediate U-turn right back to the thoughts of my failed interview with Dean Cargill, full of *would ofs*, *could ofs*, and *should ofs*. Then, I became aware of myself glancing at my phone literally every minute, longing to see a new notification of some sort, indicating it was Dean. Yeah. This whole beach trip was not working out for me at all. It wasn't turning into the distraction it was meant to serve as. So, I gathered my belongings and trekked back to the hotel.

After taking a nice hot shower, I decided to eat dinner at the hotel restaurant, while bringing my laptop with me. Maybe it was a bit of a faux pas, but I couldn't help but want to work while downing my meal over a glass of red wine.

I needed to keep my mind busy, so I decided to try and create a scope and sequence for my news story. The one I would likely have to develop, assuming I no longer was able to get anymore sit-down interviews with Dean. I already had the major concept sketched and mapped out in my head. It was just a matter of now getting the bullet points down into a document to be saved to my computer:

> — *Create an introduction of highlighting the lavish lifestyle of Hollywood royalty and some catchy phrases to segue into how there are those who have conned their way into this life.*

> — *Discuss basic info on Dean Cargill, beginning with what everyone already knows about him: age, net worth, dashing looks and three failed marriages to his former husbands.*

> — *Now dive into what people may not be privy to: the mystery that surrounds Dean Cargill and being able to afford his lifestyle. Go into detail on his Paradise Cove Bluffs home, its cost, and mention the experience walking through the extravagant beach home.*

> — *Describe the skepticism of the Paradise Cove Bluff neighbors. Mention direct quotes from Nora Van der Sarm and her experiences living beside Dean.*

> — *Create a cloud of questions for readers that they should be asking. Jump into details on Dean's finances*

from divorce settlements based on documents from the lawyer.

— Big Reveal: Dean's actual account balances!!! Build mystery around this with how he has so much money compared to his former husband's bank accounts, when he has barely worked a day in his life besides his retail days. Doesn't make sense!!!

Just by writing the synopsis and outline of my work, I was already becoming heavily invested in the project, all too eager to start the actual story itself. The waiter at the restaurant approached the table as I vigorously typed on my keyboard.

"Can I take that finished plate off of your hands? And would you like any desserts or anymore to drink?" he asked me.

"Yes. Please take the plate," I replied without bothering to look up from my laptop screen as I continued jotting my ideas down. "And I think I'll pass on dessert for this evening, but I will take another glass of wine."

The waiter leaned over to retrieve my glass, but just as he turned to traipse away, I called back out to him. "Actually, just bring me the bottle. I think I'm going to be here for a while."

We both smiled at one another. "Very well, sir," he replied. "I'll bring it out momentarily."

"Thank you," I simply remarked, still keeping my laser focus on my computer screen. A minute or so later, I didn't even realize he had already returned with a refilled glass and the full bottle of wine sitting next to it. I took a quick sip when I saw it was on the table and I continued on my article.

I was now determined to make it back into my office with a working draft that would hopefully be enough to please my boss and Edgar Baxter. This was the only way I could salvage my career at Chatterbox News and it meant that I would have to make this story of going on the attack against Dean.

The best part about typing up this piece was that I felt no guilt about going against Dean Cargill and questioning him and his finances. All of my research thus far had pointed in the direction of Dean hiding something and being a conniving snake. Hell, I was the one that was at his house, sitting on the beach, willing to give him the benefit of the doubt and let him tell his side of the story. But he was quick to dismiss me and therefore I now no longer owed him anything.

I kept having to tell myself that this was all on him. He had every opportunity to explain himself to me, but failed to do so. If he wound up hating me after this all became published, then that's on him. He should be the one to feel remorse for choosing not to be open and honest with me in our interview.

Before I knew it, nearly two hours had passed, and the entire bottle of Cabernet was now depleted. I waited for the waiter to deliver the check to pay for the dinner and wine before I carried my laptop back up to my room. I didn't realize how much time had already flown by. The after effects of the wine were starting to hit me now. I was feeling both loose and lethargic. My mind became a fog and a sudden dreariness overcame me. The second I laid my head down against the pillow on my bed, I was out like a light.

The sun peeking its way around the curtains to obstruct my vision woke me up the following morning. I stretched and yawned heavily, prior to rising out of bed, groggy as hell. At least I only had a minor headache. I rose from the bed and entered the bathroom, running the sink water. Reaching into my bathroom accessory pouch, I grabbed the small bottle of Ibuprofen I brought with me and popped two pills in my mouth, chasing them down with water. That should be enough to do the trick.

That was solution number one for problem number one, which was reducing the hangover. Now, I just needed to get my caffeine fix if I wanted to make it through the day without dosing off at some point.

I checked the time on my phone and saw that it was already 9:30am. That gave me enough time to pack up my belongings in my suitcase and then make my way down to the breakfast café to grab a croissant and an iced chai vanilla latte with oat milk, my morning routine drink of choice, before I would have to checkout of the hotel.

As I saw the time on my locked screen, I also noticed I had quite a few notifications on my phone. Now was the moment of truth. Whatever was on this phone would help me make my final decision. If there was no contact from Dean, then I would be on my way back into the city. If I did hear from him, I would just extend my reservation for another day or two perhaps, until I could test the waters and see where he and I stood and where his head was at.

Hesitantly, I unlocked my phone and checked through my texts, missed calls, and emails and not a single one of them indicated Dean or someone from his team had tried to get hold of me.

It was settled. I rolled my luggage down to the lobby, standing in line to grab my breakfast and coffee at the café, before I returned to the main foyer of the hotel and the front counter to officially checkout.

There were two other hotel guests in front of me as I stood, waiting my turn. Pulling out my phone, I decided to scroll through some social media posts. As I opened my account, I noticed I had a DM awaiting me in my inbox. When I went to click on it, my eyes bulged with great alarm. It was a message from Dean Cargill's account. His actual, legitimate account that had 1.8 million followers.

> Hey Jackson. Sorry we ended things on a sour note yesterday. I've been thinking about how things went down and realized I probably overreacted way more than I should have. I want to make this right. If you're willing to continue with the interview, I'm more than willing to let you do it. There will be some new conditions I would prefer and I want to be completely transparent about them as we move forward in this relationship. If you are will-ing to still participate, why don't we meet out tonight? Say 11:00pm at Avec Nous in Beverly Hills? I'll already be in the area and have my assistant make a reservation. Hope to see you then.
>
> -Dean

Damn! Of all the possible times.

Honestly, a part of me last night and even this morning was re-lieved to no longer feel as much angst or pressure when it came to having to be around Dean. I had almost resolved all of my panic and worry with writing that draft at the hotel restaurant, based on the minimal information I had obtained from my research and interviews with those acquainted with Dean. That weight that I thought I had absolved myself from suddenly came crashing back down again on my shoulders.

Fuck! What was I going to do now!?

Then, I suddenly remembered what this full interview would mean for me. This would open up so many doors for more A-list celebrity interviews as well as other major media corporations reaching out to want to hire me. Who knows? This could directly lead to me being an editor-in-chief one day soon.

"Sir!?" a woman at the hotel desk called out to me. I was brought back down to reality, noticing that I was now the next person in the front of the line holding people up who were waiting behind me. "Sir, are you checking out?"

I let out a deep sigh, knowing I would have to endure a bit more drama and stress. "No. I'm actually going to extend my stay for two more days." *Just a few more days*, I kept reminding myself. Just a few more days would be all it would take to make my future hopes and dreams come true.

Chapter 10

Dean

Seven Years Ago...

I really thought Frank was the love of my life. And I'm sure he thought I was his. But that's the thing with being in a relationship with someone for nearly a year. It's all unicorns and rainbows for that blissful period you are initially together. But during that time, you're only seeing half the person for who they are. It's when the longevity of the relationship kicks in- that's when they will eventually show who they truly are. That other ugly half of them that they've concealed for as long as they could, inevitably comes to the surface. And it isn't pretty the first time you see it.

At first, I thought it was just a *bad day at work*. Frank came home grumpy as hell and just laid it into me. Everything I did was wrong. The restaurant I reserved for us wasn't what he was in the mood for that night. I wasn't giving him enough attention. Then, he resorted to making snide comments with insecurities he held onto, saying that I was likely cheating on him or probably on the hunt for someone better than him. Then the downward spiral continued. It turned into more of a *week-long funk*. I was willing to give Frank the benefit of the doubt. He was just going through something. Surely this was a short-term thing. It couldn't have been permanent. He wasn't like this. This wasn't him.

Then, the excessive drinking came. There were evenings when

Frank would drink until 2:00am on a weeknight and then pass out into a stupor. I had to wake him up from the living room couch on certain mornings because he forgot to set his alarm. I was stunned he managed to even make it into his law office okay and on time, being able to function. Some of those days, I recalled him still being drunk when he woke up. It got to be so bad, I wasn't sure what to do anymore.

Whenever I tried to bring the problem up to him, he completely deflected, telling me that I was the one overreacting and that I was worrying over absolutely nothing. But the more I brought it up over the next two months, the more hate and resentment he held towards me. Frank resorted to attacking me, saying that he could "throw me back out onto the streets where he picked me up from." That I "depended on him." So, I should be grateful to have him in my life no matter under whatever circumstances.

But that's where Frank was completely wrong. He only assumed I had no money or assets to my name. And he was sorely mistaken about that. I had saved up quite a bit of money from my side job and with much of the money he had given me over the past year and a half. Plus, I knew I could easily sell some of the extravagant and expensive items and designer clothes he had gifted me since we had been together.

Frank was a fool to think he could treat me so shitty on the belief that I was *stuck with him*. Maybe that's why he was so easily able to show his true colors to me on the whim. He was turning into a selfish, egocentric bastard. But I would never tolerate such behavior. I was too good for it. I could do *better*.

However, I did stay with Frank longer than I probably should have. I let his repetitive vile behavior persist, and I remained with him for two additional months. However, I was not the only one who saw a change in Frank. Many of our other friends noticed it too, to the point where they privately checked in with me to make sure I was doing okay. Of course, they did it in a furtive, inconspicuous way so that they wouldn't be seen as being antagonistic towards Frank, but it didn't take a rocket scientist to read between the lines they were throwing my way.

But good ole Frank became a creature of habit, which was his complete and utter downfall. During one of the late parties we hosted, Frank became so obliterated that he wound up passing out on the sofa by midnight, while a few of our guests were still here. Most of them softly trickled out one by one until we had one guest that still lingered. Steve Horschawitz was a fellow lawyer friend of Frank's who ran his own firm on the west coast.

According to Frank, he ventured out to Miami but twice a year to visit old friends. This was now my second time meeting him. Our first encounter was under calmer circumstances, which consisted of a casual sit-down at a fancy restaurant downtown with after-hour cocktails here at Frank's place. Steve proved to be a complete flirt with me and gave me so much attention that it even caused Frank to take notice and be skeptical of his actions towards me.

Now, here he and I were, the only two conscious people in Frank's penthouse. I could tell he wanted to strike up a private conversation with me, which was why he suggested we speak out on the terrace. I offered to refill our champagne glasses before I stepped outside into the brisk night air with him.

Steve was far wealthier than Frank. That I was sure of. However, he wasn't quite as good-looking and as attractive as Frank was. Something about Frank drew me in, at least in the physical sense. When it came to Steve, those feelings did not kick in for me.

"So, how is college treating you?" he nonchalantly asked me as we both leaned over on the railing, overlooking the brightly lit up city with our champagne flutes in hand.

"It's been going well. Just two more years left. I'll be graduating a semester earlier than expected with my bachelor's degree. I've been taking extra classes just to finish it sooner," I explained.

"How impressive," Steven commented. "And you're still into fashion merchandising?"

I nodded. "Yes."

"And what is your end goal, Dean? Do you want to be a fashion designer or run your own business or what?"

Truth be told, I never really gave it that much thought recently, being so content and comfortable in the lifestyle I found myself absorbed in with Frank. I've been living day to day, not really thinking about the far-out distant future. But yes, the thought of being a world-renowned luxury designer didn't sound so bad.

"Yes. I want nothing more than to have my own label. Hell, my dream would be to have my own store on Rodeo Drive," I revealed to him.

"Well then, living your life in Miami is doing nothing to make that wish come true," Steve stated, before taking a sip of his champagne. "You need to be in Los Angeles, Dean. There's far more out there in L.A. for you. I think Miami, even being as huge as it is, is still too small for you."

I held my reservations with what Steve was saying. Was this recommendation of his really something that was meant to help me, or was it something that *he* wanted? Did he want me living near him? I suddenly became very suspicious of his intentions.

"Yeah. But what about Frank? I don't think he would just upend his practice and his entire life here just to move to L.A. for me," I explained.

"What do you mean, *what about him*? Listen, Dean. I think it's time you thought long and hard about Frank. Is he really the man you want to spend the rest of your life with? If he is, then by all means, stay here. Although, I'm not sure what the merit is in staying with a raging drunk. But I think you and I know you are destined for so much greater. Frank is just holding you back from accomplishing that."

Steve was really pushing the envelope. Both of us knew he was stepping way over his boundaries by making such remarks when he was Frank's dear friend. However, Steve did have strong points here, only heightening my own thoughts in regard to leaving Frank.

"But what about college? I worked so hard to get into Miami International University of Art & Design. I have two years left there. How can I just leave it all behind? Also, where would I live? There's no way I can afford to live in a nice apartment in L.A. on a whim."

"There are resolutions to all of these things," Steve confidently stated. "Ever hear of transfer credits? Just find a college in L.A. that has a fashion merchandising program. There are plenty. And who says you even need to go to college to be a high-end designer? It takes far more than college to make it big in that industry. Connections. Networking. That's how you get yourself known in that world."

Well, that answered half of my problems, but that didn't address the other major issue. "And my living situation?"

"You can move in with me for as long as you need to until you get on your feet. I would be more than thrilled to accommodate you."

I've seen pictures of Steve Horschawitz's estate in Los Angeles. It was nearly ten-thousand square feet, with luxury Spanish-style architecture. His hacienda was truly impressive. Living there would be phenomenal. Plus, Steve throws quite the lavish parties. There have even been quite the number of celebrities I've seen him in photographs with on social media at various gatherings he has hosted over the years.

But making this life-changing choice here and now was not possible. I would need to think on it. Weigh out the pros and cons. This wasn't something I could just decide without taking the time to really dissect all of it.

"It all does sound promising. And I appreciate you looking out for me," I genuinely said.

I could suddenly feel his hand on my back, rubbing it up and down before it eventually ended on my hip, with his arm wrapped around me.

"Well, somebody has to look out for you, Dean. I know I've only met you twice, but there's something extremely special about you, and Frank is a fool if he's not treating you like a prince. You deserve nothing but the best."

"Thank you, Steve. You're too kind."

"I really mean it. I'd give you the world," Steve mentioned.

I felt like I was having a déjà vu moment. Did I not hear the very same promise from Frank when we first met? That he would *give me the world*?

Frank did give me a lot, but the world, he certainly did not. And I had to remind myself of this. He was breaking his promise to me, because the attitude and behavior he displayed now was a far cry from giving me all that I deserved.

Perhaps it was time for me to move on. Maybe I should let someone else take their turn and see if they can keep that promise to me, since Frank obviously couldn't.

I gave it another month. One last shot to see if Frank would be willing to make a change. However, no matter the ultimatums that I gave him, he took none of them seriously. He viewed them all as empty-threats, which made me come to a realization. Frank never really saw *my* self-worth. He never believed in *my* growth, *my* achievements, *my* capability in being independent. For if he did, he would have taken my warnings seriously.

It would just have to be something he would have to see to believe. It was a Wednesday evening when he returned late from work. His eyes instantly fixed on the three suitcases and other bags of luggage of mine against the wall in the main foyer. I emerged from our bedroom with more bags in tow.

"You can't be serious..." he uttered, shaking his head in disbelief. "You're not really leaving, Dean. This has gone too far now. Let's talk this through."

"No!" I nearly yelled. "I have tried talking with you, but you wouldn't hear any of it."

I proceeded to brush by him on my way out the door, to drop my bags off in the rental car I had summoned to take me to the airport. His hand grasped my arm to stop me before I could make it fully out the door. "And where will you go? Some shitty rundown apartment in the slums?"

I shook my head. I was tempted to tell him that I had already found a new job working at Burberry in L.A. Also, that I was staying with one of his close friends, Steve, in a much better place than here. Steve's estate made this penthouse look like a dump. But I could not throw Steve under the bus like that. After all, he was the one doing me a huge favor, by taking me in and treating me well. So, I went with the more mature response. "Where I go is none of your business, Frank. I'm leaving you. Any concern you have for me should be nonexistent."

I yanked my arm away from him and headed out the door, down to the lobby and out of the building to my ride that was pulled up in the front lot. I dropped my bags off in the car, telling the driver I needed to make one last trip back up to retrieve my final three suitcases before returning to Frank's penthouse for what would be the last time.

By the time I made it back up, Frank already had a glass tumbler filled with bourbon clenched tightly in his hand. Can't say I was surprised at how expeditiously he already made his drink. It's been that way for quite a while now.

"Dean... please," Frank intimately whispered, coming up to me, trying to wrap his hands around my waist. Now I was getting the emotional side from him. I had waited months for him to at least show some compassion, some remorse for the way he has treated me. But it was too little too late.

I threw his hands off of my waist and grabbed my suitcases, not daring to look him in the eyes. My decision was final, and I was more determined than ever to get the hell out of here without having to tolerate any of his sentiments. What was the point? I needed to be tough. These past few months of tolerating his bullshit have allowed me to build a steel carapace around my heart and he was the architect of it.

I strode towards the door as quickly as possible, rolling my luggage behind me. I turned my head ever so slightly to Frank one last time, allowing him to catch my side profile. "No... don't *Dean please* me. You need to please yourself, Frank. Figure your shit out. Get some help. You're a fucking grown-ass man. It's embarrassing."

It was cold as hell, but those were the parting words he needed to hear from me. Hopefully, he would take those to heart and really work to improve himself. If not for him, then for the next twink victim he would try to claim as a boyfriend who would have to endure all the shit I had gone through with him in these recent months.

Once I got into the car, the driver took off and I was on my way to the airport, on my way to a new beginning with this promising life for me in Los Angeles. As I stared out the window on the way, I held my head high, realizing I was free. It was a comforting feeling to know I had elicited so much confidence in order to muster up the courage to leave Frank and take this leap of faith in moving completely across the country. But I knew, deep down, that this was what I needed to do. Frank really was holding me back. I deserved better. I deserved to find a man who treated me right and could provide me with everything and more. A man who would still allow me to pursue my own goals and dreams, and support me in my efforts, even in my pursuits of choosing to still work in retail for my own ease of mind.

I was excited to start a new position as an assistant manager with Burberry when I arrived in L.A. It would be the perfect distraction for me, while also giving me an out so that I wouldn't have to spend every waking second in Steve's home, feeling like a complete burden and imposition to him. I even offered to pay Steve a monthly rental fee, but he refused my offer, saying that's what friends did for one another. I was appreciative of his generosity, although it was a generosity with hidden motives.

Steve would wine and dine me. He would buy me so many extravagant gifts, clothes, and accessories that it put Frank's altruism to shame. Of course, I would have to give Steve what he wanted, too. Adoration, sex, attention. But I was willing to do all of those things without any sort of complaint. At this point, I'd do anything for a better life than the one I had been living in Miami with Frank.

Millions of Dollars Burnt by Burberry
By Global News Today

In order to protect its brand, Burberry, the popular British fashion label, burned nearly $30 million worth of unsold products, including bags, accessories, and perfumes this year alone.

This number adds to the other $90 million, the total value of the other products they have been burning for the past five years.

But Burberry isn't the only fashion brand doing this. Many others continue to destroy unwanted products to prevent them from being sold cheaply or even stolen. Their defense: It maintains the exclusivity and value of their company.

Chapter 11

Jackson

Current Day…

I wasn't expecting to have to wear my fine dining attire at all during this trip, but I was once again wrong about this too. Avec Nous was a fancy French bistro type restaurant directly inside L'Ermitage, one of the most highly rated hotels not only in the greater Los Angeles area, but in the country for that matter.

It was in Downtown Beverly Hills, just off Burton Way and the place where I would be meeting Dean again for the first time since our not so pleasant experience that happened a couple days ago, where I was escorted off of his property for having offended him.

I stood just outside the restaurant in my regal blue Ralph Lauren suit and matching dress pants. Beneath my blazer was a white buttoned-down shirt with a plaid lagoon blue tie. It was just two minutes before the stroke of 11:00pm, the exact time Dean had requested I meet him by. Eating out this late in the evening was something I wasn't quite used to. By this time, I was either at a nightclub, a party with friends, or lounging on the couch beside Darren, dosing off to a show on Netflix.

It was imperative that I take an extended nap this afternoon if I wanted to be able to be on my A-game tonight without nodding off in front of Dean. Luckily, I did manage to get two hours of sleep earlier in the day, so I was more than ready to go for tonight. Plus, the adrenaline in my veins was flowing at an all-time high for as thrilled as I was that Dean Cargill was giving me a second opportunity at this interview, to make things right.

As I stepped into Avec Nous, I was astonished by how resplendent the venue was. I also couldn't believe how packed the bistro was this late at night, full of well-established patrons. Not a table went unoccupied. The place gave me all the ritzy French Riviera vibes I was expecting it to. The sans white tablecloths were pristine. The wooden floor panels were shaped in a unique, elegant pattern. The beige seats at each table were plush and more along the lines of opulent accent chairs than your traditional restaurant seating. Glossy finishes were at every turn. On the ceiling was an ornate brass lighting decoration. Three extremely large halos overlapped one another with brightly lit bulbs emerging from their outer rims.

And at the very center of the restaurant was an isolated table for two, far more secluded from the rest, with someone already there. It was Dean. I could recognize him even from a mile away. The man easily stood out in a crowd. How could you not take notice of his suave hair and charming physical build and features? Rumor has it that his chin and jawline were insured. No joke. It was disturbing at how captivating he was. Almost sickening.

As I traipsed closer to him, his head turned to spot me. His lips formed into a graceful smile as he rose from his chair, taking a step towards me with his arms spread wide. It prompted me, too, to reach out and give him a hug. In our quick embrace, my nose picked up on his soothing cologne, detecting scents of vetiver, bergamot, and cedarwood. It reeked of wealth and sexiness.

"Welcome, Jackson! I'm so glad you could make it," Dean greeted me with in a lively tone.

"Thank you for having me!" I replied with an equal enthusiasm.

He released me from his hug. "Please, have a seat. Dinner and drinks are on me tonight."

"Oh, but I couldn't..." I began to say before he held his hands up to interrupt me in protest.

"No. I insist." He was affirmative.

All I could do was smirk and nod before taking a seat across from him.

"The waiter should be coming out with a bottle of Vueve Clicquot. Is there anything else you'd like to drink besides sparkling champagne?" Dean asked.

I reached for the menu and began perusing it, unsure of what else to request. It all sounded so phenomenal and overwhelming to pick from. "What is your recommendation?"

"Personally, I like the L'Ermitage Martini," he revealed.

"And what's in that?"

"Their top-shelf vodka, which I believe is Belvedere? Also, strawberries, basil, lime, and agave nectar. It's to die for," Dean declared.

"I think you've convinced me. I'll go ahead and have that then," I decided.

No sooner than I said this, the waiter came to us with the bottle of champagne and two crystal flutes. He poured us each a glass before leaving the remainder of the bottle chilling in a metallic bucket. "And would you like any appetizers or anything else to drink?"

Dean spoke up for the two of us. "Yes. We'll each have your L'Ermitage Martini. Also, we'll start off with your Regiis Ova Ostera Caviar."

Hubba-whatta?

It sounded like Dean spoke a completely foreign language. All I heard was *caviar* in there.

"Perfect. I'll be out with that and your drinks shortly," the waiter stated, before ambling off.

Dean raised his champagne flute in the air, prompting me to hold my own out towards his, to clink them together. "Here is to new relationships," Dean said with an alluring smirk, before throwing his head back to take a sip.

I followed in suit, enjoying the bubbliness strike my tongue and throat. "Yes. I concur."

His toast did leave me pondering for a moment. *New relationships*? Perhaps this was his way of saying that he wanted to start over with us. We could begin with a brand-new, clean slate, which put me over the moon.

Soon, a lingering silence existed between us. It was awkward for a brief moment. So, I decided to lead in. "Look, Dean, I am beyond sorry for how I handled things during our interview. I should not have gone in so aggressive like that so soon."

Dean waved his hands in the air. "No. I should be the one to apologize. Had I been transparent with you from the beginning, I would have told you that there were certain topics that I did not feel comfortable discussing with you. Finances being a major one. That is my fault for not disclosing that from the get-go."

Okay. This was a really good sign. I just needed to continue to be humble, gracious, and accept his apology, while also owning my fault in the miscommunication between us.

"And I will no longer pressure you by asking questions that you aren't willing to answer. Believe me, I've learned my lesson," I explained.

"I appreciate that, Jackson."

Our sentimental moment was then put on pause as the waiter returned with our martinis and the caviar. I took a drink of the L'Ermitage Martini the moment it was handed off to me. "You weren't kidding," I said to Dean. "This is amazing. It really does pack a punch."

"I'm glad you like it," the waiter chimed in. "And are the two of you ready to order dinner?"

Dean nodded. "Yes. I'll have the Ora King Salmon."

"And for you, sir?" The waiter eyed me.

I scanned over the entrees in haste before I landed on one that sounded appealing to me. "I'll take the Bouillabaisse," I replied. It consisted of Pacific salmon, langoustine, shrimp, scallops, saffron, tomato broth, and rouille croutons.

I just hoped I pronounced the meal correctly, although I suspected that I butchered the living hell out of it, which left me completely and utterly embarrassed for my lack of sophistication in not knowing the correct pronunciation. Much to my relief, no one corrected me, though.

"Perfect. I'll put those in to the chef right away," the waiter informed us, before taking off.

Once Dean and I had our privacy again, I picked up on where we left off in the conversation. "So, what I'm proposing is, why don't I strictly be your listener? Instead of me asking any sort of questions, why don't you just divulge your story and what it is you're willing to say to me? I'll take notes and actively listen. I may ask clarifying questions about things you do tell me, but I think that's the ideal route we should take moving forward. What do you think?"

Hopefully, Dean could see that I was willing to bend over backwards to make this interview happen. Any compromise that needed to be made, I was open to accepting it. I was breaking all of my own rules as a journalist, but I wanted this damn story to happen. I *needed* it to come to fruition. I couldn't risk losing it again. The thought of not getting to do this interview with Dean was beyond dreadful. I could not picture going through what I did over the past few days.

The anxiety I had was enough to nearly put me over the edge.

"I think I like the sound of that," he responded with.

"Great. And there's no pressure. So, we can resume the interview whenever it's most convenient for you, whether it's now, tomorrow, or even later," I further added to placate him.

Dean then scanned the room, scrutinizing anyone who seemed like they were an earshot away from us before speaking once more. "I'd prefer not to have any personal conversations here in this public of a forum. It may be best that we restart the interview later tonight, or maybe tomorrow? Plus, I'd rather just enjoy dinner right now. Let's not kill the vibe," he suggested.

"That sounds good to me." Although, I really wished I had a timeline on how long this would take. That's how I functioned best, using a strict Outlook calendar where my days and meetings were mapped out to the exact hour.

Our food soon came out and after the first bite into my meal, I felt like I could devour the entire thing in just seconds. It was that damn good. But I refrained from doing so, wanting to capitulate to the etiquette that those who dined here were expected to abide by.

Dean and I proceeded with idle chit-chat as we ate our dinner. I had to admit, I was completely caught off-guard with how easy he was to talk to. The conversation between us just seemed to flow so naturally, as if we were childhood friends who met up for the first time, after years of being apart from one another. It was like we had known each other all of our lives and were catching up and reminiscing over old memories and hilarious stories together.

When we had nearly finished our drinks and the full bottle of champagne, we decided it was best to call it quits for the night.

"Oh, I completely forgot to ask," Dean changed the subject with. "Where are you staying while you interview me?"

"I'm actually in a hotel by Zuma Beach," I answered.

"Really? Well, that just won't do, will it? How about this. Why don't you stay in my casita?" Dean offered.

I nearly spit out the remains of my drink at his suggestion. I managed to take a heavy gulp to prevent that from happening. "Your place? You're not serious, are you?"

Spending the night at Dean Cargill's residence? Was I fucking dreaming? There was no way this could possibly be real. How could I, unknown journalist Jackson Cartwright, have just received an open invitation to staying the night at the famous Dean Cargill's home? Things like this were unheard of in my world.

"I am. I don't see why it's a big deal. I mean, I think it's easier for you to interview me if we're constantly around each other. Plus, I feel like it's my duty to accommodate you. So yes, I would love if you stayed at my place at no charge. My assistants will be able to cater to your every need," Dean elaborated.

Seriously? What dimension did I just fall into? This couldn't be happening. It was hard to believe. Despite me not wanting to be any sort of burden for him, I knew this was Dean's game we were playing. He made the rules. I needed to follow them if I didn't want him to pull the rug out from under me like he did the last time, rescinding the interview altogether.

I needed to just give in and avoid arguing against his wishes. "I truly appreciate that. I'll just cancel my hotel reservation, pack up my belongings and then head back to your place."

"Better yet," Dean stated. "Why don't I have my driver take us to your hotel? I can always just grab a drink at the bar and wait while you finish packing. Then we can head back to my place together."

This was not what I had bargained for, but I was beyond elated to spend as much time with Dean as possible. "That would be amazing."

Soon, Dean paid the bill, and we left Avec Nous. When we stepped out onto the street, a massive black SUV pulled up to the curb beside us. Dean and I opened the doors and sat in the backseat. I couldn't even see the driver in front of us, for there was a barricade that separated any sight of him, while also blinding him from us.

A vintage bottle of 2012 Dom Pérignon was sitting right on the floor between Dean and me. The second the vehicle was in motion, Dean popped the cork and poured us each a glass.

I could really get used to this, I thought to myself.

"You know, ironically, this was the very same bottle I drank on my first date with my first husband, Ralpho," Dean began to describe. "We met soon after I moved to Los Angeles from Miami years ago."

And just like that, Dean told me about his very early days in moving to and living in L.A. with Ralpho. He was so open and vulnerable with me. All I could do was just sip my champagne and listen to all that he had to say, mentally taking notes in my head.

Chapter 12

Dean

Six Years Ago...

It only took a few weeks and already I felt completely acclimated to the Los Angeles lifestyle. But I couldn't say I was surprised at the very least. My charm, wit, and determination guided me in making all the right decisions and having all the right conversations to make the connections that I did. Not to mention I had Steve Horschawitz to also thank for introducing me to his high-status buddies and colleagues, who then became my acquaintances and eventually friends.

Without Frank looming over me, I felt like a completely new and invigorated person. There was a newfound freedom I had discovered that I never knew I was missing all this time. It was time for me to reinvent myself and to absolve myself from anything to do with Frank and my former life in Miami.

To start off with, I completely altered my social media accounts, by deleting the old versions and completely adding new ones, uploading only my finest photographs of me wearing designer clothing and being on the most grandiose of vacations. There was a certain image I wanted to aim for, and I could tell it was already going off without a hitch.

My followers were climbing into the thousands in just the span of a week. I even garnered the attention of wealthy, affluent men who privately messaged me, wanting to take me out on dates at expensive restaurants, some even on their yachts. I was starting to make a name for myself. Who knew that Frank was the one actually holding me back from all of this?

I could easily get used to this single life. However, completely escaping from Frank proved to be a major hurdle. I received countless phone calls, text messages, and emails from him. The pscyho wouldn't leave me alone. His messages ranged from him being sad and crying, begging me to come back to him, making claims that he would stop drinking if it meant me giving him a second chance to those that were absolutely crazy with him making empty threats, calling me derogatory names like trash, slut, whore, gold-digger, etc. I realized it was in my best interest to pay him no mind, so I blocked him altogether, refusing to listen to anything else he had to say.

The drunk fool was now behind me and it was time for me to continue to move forward without him in my life.

Despite this fresh confidence I found, I still felt it was in my best interest to continue with my retail work in designer stores. Although Steven and other men were buying me expensive gifts and providing me a place to live, I could not rely on that alone. I had enrolled myself back in fashion merchandising classes and still wanted to work at my new job I just recently started at Burberry.

My hours weren't so tedious as I decided to only work part time. It opened up so many other doors for me to focus on making new friends around town and keeping Steve company, which wasn't so bad, since being close to him gave me access to all the greatest bars, clubs, restaurants, exclusive charity events and parties. So what if I let him fuck me every now and then? I was still single and believe me, the perks definitely outweighed the cost of having to offer myself up to him only once or twice a week. Despite the frequent sex we had, me living with him on his estate, and the amount of time we spent together, Steve and I weren't an item, per se. The man vowed to be a bachelor for the rest of his life. Therefore, our relationship proved to be along the lines of a *friends with benefits* type of situation, which still allowed me to be open on the market, welcoming all the DMs and offerings that prosperous gay men threw my way.

Tonight, I was finishing up a late shift at Burberry, before heading back home. Steve had already made arrangements to be hosting a party this evening. All the guests would already be there as I arrived close to 11:00pm. The second I stepped foot in the door, Steve waddled over, placing his arm around me, introducing me to some of his new friends I'd never seen before, while also reminding me of the ones I'd already met and their names, so that it wouldn't seem rude of me if I had forgotten them.

But there was a new face in the crowd tonight that I could not keep my eyes off of. I recognized him from the tabloids and from a television show or two, but couldn't quite put my finger on his name. Soon, Steve escorted me over to the man, who was on the couch, finishing a line of cocaine that was on the glass cocktail table with two other men beside him.

At this point, my attraction towards him was teetering back and forth. He was beyond sexy and definitely a D-list celebrity of some sort if I'd seen him on television, but the drug piece is what was giving me hesitation. I just hoped he only snorted cocaine socially, and he wasn't dependent on it. For now, I was willing to give him the benefit of the doubt, until I saw otherwise.

The man was in mid-laughter before his neck craned to see Steve and me hovering over him. The instant he saw me, his smile diminished, to which his face looked more awestruck than anything else.

Steve introduced us then. "Pete, Ralpho and Ken, I want you to meet Dean." Ralpho was the one in the middle who I had my gazed fixed on, but I remained polite in grinning while extending my hand to the other two men on the couch with him.

Ralpho... Ralpho Mercado.

It all then clicked. Ralpho was an actor on *The Youth and the Gallant*, a daytime soap opera. He had been on the show for at least the past three years now, to my recollection, while also making some cameo appearances on other television shows and cable network interviews.

"It's a pleasure to meet you," I indirectly said to the group.

"And you too," Ralpho replied, with his gaze still transfixed on me.

But before I could even utter another word, Steve was patting me on the back and leading me to the other guests at the party, much to my irritation.

After I made my rounds, I decided to head to my room to change for the evening. If I wanted to really capture Ralpho Mercado's attention tonight, I needed to put on an outfit that would leave his mouth watering the second he saw me again.

My walk-in closet was filled with tons of clothes I'd managed to collect over the past two years, most of which I haven't even worn yet. Tonight, I did want to wear something I have never worn before in keeping with this fresh reinventive vibe I was going with these past few weeks. An iceberg blue Dolce and Gabbana buttoned down shirt caught my eyes. I retrieved it from the hanger and grabbed a pair of ivory pants. Now, it was just the shoes I needed to decide on. Seeing the pants I now had draped around my forearm, it instantly reminded of the most recent pair of shoes I purchased at Burberry. They were mostly optic white made of leather and suede with the traditional Burberry black, red, and taupe check tartan design on the back half of the shoes.

I rushed to put them all on before proceeding into my bathroom to check myself out in the mirror, restyling and gelling my hair so that it was completely swayed back. After a few sprays of cologne, I was now ready to make my appearance once again back down at the party. As I descended the main marble stairs, I turned at the foyer and passed the narrow hallway into the grand living room, where most of the guests were. A floating black granite bar counter was caddy-cornered at the far end of the room, with a bartender behind it. I needed a drink if I wanted to keep up with everyone here who have now had multiple cocktails and even some other mind-altering substances in their system.

"And what can I get you to drink for this evening?" the young, male bartender asked me. He had long, golden blonde hair tucked into a man-bun, wearing a charcoal vest over his white dress shirt. The guy looked barely old enough to even legally drink.

"I'll have a glass of your chardonnay," I requested.

"Really? White wine at this kind of party?" A seductive voice murmured from behind me.

I immediately spun around, annoyed that someone would judge my drink choice. But much to my surprise, it was Ralpho Mercado who stood before me. Although I was initially vexed, I quickly changed my tune, realizing my main attraction was now directly standing here before me. The corner of my lips curled into a snarly grin.

"Of course. The only occasion in which white wine would be unacceptable is in some rural country saloon," I informed him. I then glanced about the room, pretending I was taking in the entire scene before me for the first time. "And the last time I checked, this venue is a far outcry from that."

My remark got a chuckle out of Ralpho. I paused to turn back around to retrieve my stemmed wine glass from the bartender, before diverting my attention back to Ralpho.

"Wow. I didn't realize Steve had any friends who were... *spunky*," he playfully commented.

I shrugged. "Let's be honest. It would be more observant and obvious for you to say that you didn't realize Steve had any friends who were *so young*."

Ralpho then held his glass tumbler up to me, to which I clinked my drink to his. "And that too!" he added. "Speaking of being so young, that begs my next question to you, Dean." Ralpho's eyes glossed up and down my entire body, sizing me up. I could have sworn I saw the tip of his tongue escape from his closed mouth to trace along his lips, but I also could have been imagining that. "How did you manage to get into the good graces of our pal, Steve?"

I took a sip of my chardonnay, giving me a moment to process his question before responding to him. I wanted to be vague as possible. The last thing I wanted was for Ralpho to think I was damaged goods and someone who was full of drama and leaching on a rich man strictly due to his wealth and situation in life, because that's not attractive in the very least. "I met him a year or so ago through a mutual friend in Miami. He actually convinced me to move out to L.A., recently."

"And you live with him now?" Ralpho arched his brow at me.

"It's just a temporary thing. Once I get settled at my new job and my college courses are situated, I'll find a place of my own," I explained. Although, truth be told, living here in Steve's massive home was a pretty damn good gig. I had no intention of leaving anytime soon, unless I was forced to due to some unforeseen circumstances.

"Is this interrogation over, detective?" I further added, before taking another drink of my wine, only this time I held a flirtatious and seductive gaze on Ralpho as I did so.

His hands waved frantically at me. "Oh no! I don't want you to think I was judging or grilling you in any way. Far from it. I'm just trying to get to know you a bit more, is all."

I smirked, signaling to him that I wasn't offended. "Well then, maybe we should continue this conversation in a more private location? So we don't have any interruptions," I suggested.

He nodded. "Sure. You know the place better than I do. Lead the way and I'll follow."

Honestly, as much as I wanted to take Ralpho to my bedroom and sexually ravage him, I knew that would be a poor decision on my part. However, it seemed that not many people were outside, so that was the next best option.

"Let's chat out back then," I recommended.

We traipsed past many of the guests at the party and opened the sliding glass doors to gain entry to Steve's oasis of a backyard. His in-ground pool was brightly lit up with a cerulean hue whose lights bounced off all surfaces of the backyard. I walked with Ralpho around the pool to a set of lounge chairs close to the far end of it. Both he and I took a seat there.

As I stared at him across from me, I could see the trickles of cobalt reflecting off of his face from the soft undulations of the lit-up pool water.

Ralpho then proceeded to reach into his back pocket, pulling out a pack of cigarettes and a lighter. "Do you smoke?" he asked.

"I mean, not really. But I'm not opposed," I said, as I reached out my palm towards him.

He offered me one of his cigarettes while he placed another in his mouth, lighting both of ours up as we took our first few heavy puffs.

"So, you're an actor?" I led into the discussion with.

"Yeah. And I absolutely love every second of it," he confidently stated.

"Really? Tell me what's intriguing about it, to you."

"There's something about playing a completely different person other than yourself. And here's the thing. It's one thing to star in a movie role where you only play a character with a quick, one-shot story, but it's another to play the role of a character in a soap opera."

"I can imagine," I said, sitting on Ralpho's every word with interest. "And you're on the set weekly, I presume, if you're on a daily show? You must be so invested in playing *Remon*."

"You hit the nail on the head," Ralpho declared. "I feel like Remon has now become a part of me. There are times when I find that I actually act and think like him, even off of the set."

I pondered about what I recalled about Ralpho's character, Remon, in *The Youth and the Gallant*. From what I could remember, he was cast in a more villainous role with secretly murdering one of the other hot men from the series, while also having sex with multiple female characters on the show, with which the women found out about it and ended up in cat fights over him.

"You're saying you kill people and also cheat on your partners?" I inquired, while holding a wily grin on my face.

It caused Ralpho to burst out in laughter. "Haha. No. Not that extreme. What I mean is, Remon's confidence and tenacity. Those are the sort of things I've learned to carry with me in the real world."

We both then chuckled together. "But enough about me," Ralpho stated. "What do you do? Steve mentioned you were just getting home from work earlier."

"Yeah. I actually work at Burberry," I informed him.

"Burberry? Are you a model or something?"

I shook my head. "Not quite. I'm a part-time assistant manager at one of their retail locations." And I wasn't the least bit embarrassed to admit this. Yes, Ralpho was a major actor and one might think that being a retail manager was a complete degradation to his profession, but I didn't think that at all. I was proud of my work-ethic just as anyone should be.

"Really? What makes you want to do that? I feel like you could get a more substantial job working with Steve or any other one of his friends here in L.A."

I shrugged. "It aligns with my career goals. I want to be a fashion designer in the future. Currently, I'm a fashion merchandising major in college. So, I think working in a fashion designer store is something to keep me busy and still in the field."

"I see..." Ralpho said, rubbing his chin. "Do you work tomorrow, or are you off?"

"I'm off, actually."

"Do you have any plans, then?" he further asked.

"A few, but they can easily be rescheduled."

"Well, why don't I get your number? Maybe we can have lunch or even dinner?"

Was this really happening? Was the sexy Ralpho Mercado asking *me* for my phone number and to dine with me?

But I couldn't hesitate or think twice on the matter and show my weakness in being shocked. I promptly retrieved my phone from my pocket, unlocked it, and handed it off for him to add his contact information.

Ralpho proceeded to do the same in passing his cell phone over to me. I inserted my phone number for him.

"Perfect," he commented as I returned his phone to him. "I'll shoot you a text tomorrow morning and we can plan something."

"That sounds good to me."

Our conversation continued. He asked about my life in Miami and I went so far as to tell him about my adolescent days in Pennsylvania before venturing off to the Miami International University of Art & Design. I explained my entire upbringing and even my low-income household and how I wanted to escape that life. Ralpho actually seemed impressed by how far I've come. But after we chatted for nearly a half-hour, I became aware of the time. It would be rude of us to remain out here alone while everyone else was likely already hanging out in Steve's lower-level game and theater room.

I then rose from the pool lounge chair, ready to head back inside to rejoin the rest of the party. But before I could begin to even walk, Ralpho stood and reached to wrap his hand, gripping the back of my neck. He pulled my face to meet his. Our lips locked.

At first I was stunned by his assertiveness in kissing me here in Steve's own backyard. But then I softly eased into Ralpho, allowing him to take the reins over me. It felt as if my bones had melted and I became light and limber. He tasted so damn good. It was hard to believe that I was now making out with *the* Ralpho Mercado, a man who likely caused millions of gay wet dreams across the nation.

Still, my legs were rendered motionless, just getting lost in the passion that existed between the two of us. Ralpho was beyond sexy and I could not believe that I was now in this position of being the main object of his affection. I'd be a fool to not continue to get to know him on a more intimate level. What was there not to love about Ralpho Mercado? The man was rich and captivating as hell. Surprisingly, he was only eight or so years older than me, which was much closer in age than some of the other men I've dated and been affectionate with, including Frank and Steve.

And that night of longingness and fervor would be a lingering memory for us. Ralpho took me out to dinner the next day. We were so consumed and enthralled with one another that we had to see each other at least three times a week. The sex was other-worldly. We were a match made in heaven. Both he and I shared these sentiments. It would be just three months later that I would move out of Steve's estate and into Ralpho's private residence at the Four Seasons in Beverly Hills, in an exorbitant condo overlooking Beverly Grove.

Just a month later, Ralpho would take me on a vacation to the Maldives. On our second-to-last night there, we would eat at the Ithaa Undersea Restaurant with panoramic views of the coral gardens and tropical fish hovering above us. It was in this magical scene where he would get on one knee and propose, to which I adamantly said *yes*. A month later, we would get married back in Beverly Hills. When we were finally at the altar saying our *I dos*, it was then that I realized that I had made it. This was the life I wanted to live. This was my happily ever after. I thought I had everything I could ever desire. What more could I possibly want?

Chapter 13

Jackson

Current Day...

It was hard to believe that one minute I was nervous about my job being on the line, having been fired from the interview with Dean and then the next minute here he was, bringing me back on the assignment while also offering me a temporary residence at his twenty-million dollar home.

But I couldn't dwell on the past. I had to move forward. And right now, I was keeping Dean waiting. He was sitting in the hotel lounge with a glass of wine in hand while I was upstairs packing up my clothes in my suitcase. The room looked like a bomb went off with how frantic I was, tossing all of my belongings on the bed, hurrying as much as possible to stuff them in my luggage. At this point, it didn't even matter how wrinkled they were. I was already on thin ice with Dean, so the last thing I wanted to do was piss him off even more. My guess was that he wasn't the most patient of a person. So, I needed to expedite this process.

However, I became slightly distracted while getting my clothes together. My mind was going into overdrive, reciting all that Dean had told me about his and Ralpho's relationship during the ride over to the hotel. I sat on every word he had given me. It was important for me to keep it as fresh as possible in my mind. Before I knew it, I had pulled out my laptop and opened up a blank document, typing out most of the story and direct quotes that Dean had provided. I couldn't afford to let any more time pass and risk me forgetting bits and pieces of the story and losing memory of his direct testimonials.

The second I found a good stopping point, pleased with what I had managed to get typed out into the document, I saved it directly to my desktop screen before shutting my computer down once again. Suddenly, I heard a loud buzzing noise coming from the nightstand table. I glanced over my shoulder to see my cell phone lit up and vibrating. I made haste to sprint over to it, hoping that it wasn't Dean trying to call me to complain about how long I was taking to get ready.

But I instantly let out a deep sigh of relief, seeing my fiancée's name flash across the screen. I picked up the phone and answered it, putting it on speaker mode, so that I had both hands free to continue to be able to pack.

"Hey there!" I enthusiastically greeted him with.

"Hi. Is everything alright?" Darren asked with worry.

"Yeah. Everything's great. Why wouldn't it be?"

"Well, I haven't heard from you all evening and it's after 1:00am. I tried texting you but never got a response."

I did feel guilty about not getting back with Darren earlier, but there was so much going on. And the last thing I wanted to do was seem rude and be on my phone in Dean's presence. "Sorry. babe. I've been super busy. A lot has changed in the last few hours," I began to explain.

"Like...?" Darren trailed off.

"For starters, Dean reached out to me. We had dinner together this evening, and he picked me back up to do the exclusive interview with him," I revealed.

"I knew it!" Darren exclaimed before laughing into the phone. "See? I told you he would come back around. All that worry for nothing."

"Yeah, yeah, yeah. But that's only half of it. Right now, he's waiting down in the hotel bar."

"What? What the hell is he doing there?" Darren inquired.

"Apparently, he wants me to stay at his place. He offered his casita up to me throughout the whole duration of our time together."

"You can't be serious!? That's insane! You have to take pictures. I bet you he has like a thousand dollar roll of toilet paper there for you to wipe your ass with. I can't even begin to imagine how nice that bed is you'll get to sleep in. Send me a picture of it so I can Google search how much the sheets likely cost. Damn. Now I really wish I was there with you."

I couldn't help but chuckle at Darren's making light of all this. It made me feel right at home. And truth be told, I was longing for him to be here with me, as well.

"I'm sure it's not that extravagant. I only got to see the main living area when I was at his home the other day, but it was nice. Nothing over the top, though."

"Well, either way, how many people get to say they had the chance to spend the night at Dean Cargill's house? You know how many gay men would kill for that opportunity?" Darren elaborated.

"True. But I'm strictly staying there for work-related reasons. This isn't some pleasure cruise," I reminded him.

"Anyway, when you do get there, I want to hear every detail about what it's like."

"Well, I won't even get to experience it if I keep Dean waiting any longer," I stated, now glancing at the clock with worry.

"Okay. Just text me later. It's a little late, so if I don't respond right away, it's because I'm dead asleep."

"Will do, babe," I agreed.

"Oh. And try to stay in your own bedroom tonight. I know how hot Dean is, but I would hope he isn't your once in a lifetime *hall-pass*, although it would be a pretty good one."

I began to snicker. The thought of even having sex with Dean never even crossed my mind, nor did I think Darren would even bring something like that up. But I was aware he was only kidding with me. "You have nothing to worry about, babe. I'll make sure I stay in my own room. Plus, I don't think I'm even Dean's type. I'm nowhere near the tax bracket that he requires the men he sleeps with to be in."

We both busted out laughing at my remark, realizing there was definitely truth to it.

"Anyway, love you. Have a good night," Darren stated.

"Love you too. Back at ya," I said, before ending the call.

I checked the time on my phone the second I hung up and quickly continued to gather my clothes in my suitcases. Once they were fully zipped up, I left the room and began rolling them down the hallway and towards the elevator, heading straight down to the main lobby.

I made a sharp left turn, in the direction of the restaurant bar in the hotel. It was completely empty except for one person. I spotted the back of a head at a table. Even from behind, Dean's hair was slick and well kempt. You could just tell he was worth a million bucks, or rather more, literally. I rolled my luggage beside the table and sat in the seat directly across from Dean.

"Sorry to keep you waiting. Took a bit longer than I had anticipated. I'm all ready now though," I informed him.

"No worries," he mentioned. "I actually didn't know how long you were going to be, so after having one glass of wine, I just ordered a full bottle of a red blend. The waiter is bringing it out now."

"Oh?" I commented. "Did you want to stay and finish it, or..."

"Yes. Why don't you split it with me? We can chat some more over a few glasses before we had back to my place."

Truth be told, I wanted nothing more than to head back to Dean's home, enter the casita and hop right in bed and go to sleep. It was the middle of the night, after all. But I couldn't let him know that. I needed to keep my pep up and follow his lead, even if it meant pulling an all-nighter. My schedule was based on his. That's all there was to it.

Soon, the waiter returned with a bottle of red wine and poured two glasses for the both of us, leaving the remainder of the bottle on the table before he ambled off.

I took a sip, savoring the full-bodied taste. "It's delicious," I complimented.

"Yeah. It's not so bad," Dean followed up with. "Anyway, so where were we in our conversation on the car ride over here?"

Yes! I screamed on the inside.

Now I became fully awake, with my inner drowsiness instantly subsiding. I was taken aback by Dean wanting to continue with his story. I assumed we could pick up where we left off tomorrow. Needless to say, it was a pleasant surprise that he was being so open with me and taking my suggestion to heart, with controlling the interview and divulging whatever it was he wished to disclose to me about his life.

"You were telling me about how you met Ralpho and what your marriage was like to him," I replied.

"Oh yes! Thank you for reminding me. So, Ralpho and I tied the knot pretty quickly, but the whole thing felt right. Being Mr. Mercado had its perks, I must admit. Our wedding did wind up becoming a big photographed event and eventually posted in some of the minor blogs. Even a few people on the streets started to recognize me as Ralpho's husband thereafter. I'm not going to lie, I did like all the newfound attention and popularity. I'm sure you can relate, Jackson." Dean paused, before shifting gears in the story to speak directly to me now. "Think about it. Whether it was in a daze or even a daydream, you had to have pictured yourself randomly walking on a sidewalk and then all of a sudden, *BAM!* Random people start coming up to you with a gleam in their eyes, speechless that they were in the presence of stardom. Then, a flock of paparazzi with flashbulbs going off in every which direction come out of the blue just to get a few snapshots of you for whatever media outlet they worked for."

I simply nodded. "Yeah. I've imagined it once or twice at some point."

It was a bold-faced lie if I ever made one.

I thought about it on a daily basis. To be rich, famous, and recognizable in a public crowd. Thoughts of my Carrie Bradshaw hopes and dreams were a daily occurrence, but there was no way I would be providing Dean with that information. It would make me look desperate. Hell, even envious that he had the life I was striving for in some capacity.

"Exactly," he responded, swirling the contents of his red wine around in his glass. "Even on social media, my followers were drastically climbing. I was even able to get that blue check on Instagram. You know the one, right? Anyway, I then realized my marriage was absolutely perfect, and I began to recognize that my life was slowly inching its way close to perfection as well. But..." Dean trailed off.

"The marriage didn't last," I filled in the pieces for him.

"Yes. Nearly a year of us being fully wed, and we were already getting a divorce," he added.

I inserted myself again to guide the discussion. "And what happened to cause that divorce? If I recall, the media had a field day with the story claiming that Ralpho uncovered something about you, but that was the extent of the story. No one knows if it had to do with your past and some even speculate that it was a looming, dark secret he found out about you during the marriage. Something scandalous. No matter how many interviews he did, he never quite mentioned the reason behind the divorce."

"Well, I am here to tell you that it is all a complete lie," Dean answered.

"Really!?" I said with shock.

"Mhmm. That's not how it happened at all. It was actually me who ended things between us."

"How so?" I asked, with intrigue.

"Well, it happened during the day, while I was working. I took off early and wanted to come home to surprise him..."

Chapter 14

Dean

Five Years Ago...

Today would be a huge surprise for Ralpho. To his knowledge, I was working from 9:00am to 4:00pm at Louis Vuitton. I started a new job there just two months ago. It seemed as if I couldn't stay put for more than a year at a major designer retail store. But what can I say? I just needed a change of pace and scene periodically. Plus, I'd rather work at Louis Vuitton than Michael Kors, Coach, and Burberry. It was more upscale, and the commission and benefits were much greater as well.

Tonight, Lana Del Rey would be performing at Exposition Park. She was one of Ralpho's favorite artists. I'd also managed to get us backstage passes to meet and chat with her over drinks. But before then, I'd planned on taking Ralpho out to dinner at a nearby Mexican restaurant. It would be a crazy, fun evening for the two of us.

However, I wanted to take a half day off of work and get home by 1:00pm to inform Ralpho of the surprise plans for tonight. It would give us enough time to shower, change clothes, and have some pre-game cocktails before we left for dinner.

I strode into the Four Seasons at Beverly Hills with a radiant smile. Tonight, would be absolutely flawless, and it was at times like these where I found myself dwelling on my past, where I lived in a small eight-hundred square foot home, ate canned meals for dinner and was barely able to afford to do anything fun for leisure. The only game I could afford was solitaire and the other basic gaming programs on the loaner laptop my school provided, which included *Hearts*, *Minesweeper* and *Freecell*. But really, who in the actual hell played *Freecell* and fully understood how the rules worked, while actually enjoying it? I'm pretty sure no one.

I couldn't believe the drastic change from just four years ago to living in rural Pennsylvania to now being a millionaire residing in Los Angeles. It was unfathomable and at the same time, I was completely grateful and appreciative of all that had been bestowed upon me and the life I now lived.

It made me love Ralpho all the more, knowing that he could love me despite us both growing up at completely opposite ends of the socioeconomic spectrum. Although I appreciated all that he was able to provide for me, I would be foolish to not recognize that I worked hard up until this point as well. I was the one that flipped the switch and made the move to Miami without a penny to my name, only to grow from there. It was I who learned the ways of the gay elitists and their lifestyle. I fit in their crowd perfectly and played by their rules. I made all the right connections, which really was what led me to this position that I was in today.

As I got off the elevator, I traipsed down the narrow corridor leading into our luxury condo. That walk to the main door felt like an eternity. It was like I was in another dimension. My entire mood suddenly changed. Now, I can't say in the moment that I knew I would enter our home only to find Ralpho having sex with another guy. But there are always those few seconds leading up to you walking in on your spouse cheating in which something just sweeps through your entire body. A sense of worry and sullenness just entirely overcomes you, even just for a brief second or so. It's as if your mind miraculously knows what's it's going to walk into. I can't explain the feeling, but those who have ever experienced infidelity and catching their partner in the act know of the very feeling I speak of.

And so, gliding into our luxury penthouse, I called out Ralpho's name, but heard no answer. I paced around the place, room to room, not finding him in our main living area, the kitchen or the office. So, as I moved towards our master bedroom, I opened the doors, only to see it with my very own eyes.

A young, blonde man was up on his knees in *my* bed, riding *my* husband's cock. His body was tan. The muscles in his back were fully contracted, revealing just how toned and athletic he was. His body arched as he bounced up and down on Ralpho's dick, heaving and panting.

"Are you fucking kidding me!?" I screamed.

Ralpho sat up in the bed to get a view of the sudden commotion, practically throwing the guy off of him. Now that I could see the man's face, he looked to be in his early twenties. He was cute, but nothing out of this world. Really? Is this what Ralpho was cheating on me with? Clearly, his expectations were far lower than I even realized.

"Dean!? Wh-What the hell!? You weren't even supposed to be home!" he yelled back, as if that was the problem. Not him cheating on me or being unfaithful. No. Apparently, I was the one in the wrong here, for coming home from work early, unannounced, without any sort of notice. Him inviting another man into our bedroom was okay though, right? So long as I was at work. Totally my fault.

Asshole!

"Really, Ralpho!? You're fucking..." I eyed the guy up and down with nothing but disgust written on my face. "This *homewrecker*! And the only thing you have to say is *why I'm home early?*" I shook by head with discontent. "Un-fucking-believable!"

I couldn't bear to picture the image of my husband fucking another man again. It needed to be erased from my mind permanently. I didn't want to even look at the two of them now. So, I turned around and headed right out the bedroom doors, running down the hall to try and escape as if a serial killer was chasing after me. I had to get out of here. Anywhere else but this place that now felt like it was a tainted, miserable home that suddenly became haunted in the span of seconds.

"Wait! Dean! It's not what you think..." Ralpho called out, catching up to me.

Really!? Was he fucking serious!? Strike two for Ralpho.

What did that even mean, *it's not what you think*? Do guys just say that, assuming it will make everything go away? Did Ralpho actually think for one second that by him saying that, I would actually listen to his point of view and believe him? Even after I just caught some trashy little flake riding him?

My stomach was churning as I realized I wouldn't be able to get out of here without addressing the issue. It seemed my body had a mind of its own. Without even thinking, I abruptly turned around to face him. My face was fuming. Embers practically emitted from my nostrils as I breathed.

"Then what the hell is it!?" I asked him in an accusatory tone. "Please, tell me what else it could possibly be, besides you cheating on me!?"

Ralpho stood, stunned, just staring at me with a saddened look. A watery glaze was cast over his eyes. I wasn't going to fall for those AS-PCA abused puppy dog eyes. Cue the Sara McLachlan song. Actually, I heard that those dogs were all fake. Producers of those commercials purposefully made those pets look disheveled and mangy to try and get more donors. So technically, the tragic-looking dogs were just trained little actors, faking it, just like Ralpho was right now, with me.

"Look. It was wrong of me. But it was only this one time. I swear!"

Ralpho pathetically fell to the ground on his knees, weeping. Behind him, I could see his dirty mistress, now fully clothed, standing at the far end of the hall, his arms folded across his chest, likely unsure of what the hell to do to get the fuck out of here.

"One time or one-hundred times. It honestly doesn't fucking matter, Ralpho. It's all the same," I tried to explain.

"But I only want you, Dean. It was a mistake. I don't even like Brad."

Ugh! That thing had a name...

"I'm serious!" Ralpho then scooted closer to me, sliding on his knees. "I don't want him. It was just my cock and hormones. Fucking dumb! I know! But please... hear me out, Dean," he pleaded.

I let out a heavy sigh and then kneeled down so that I was at eye-level with him. I stared right through his eyes, as if I was targeting his soul. "You're right, Ralpho. It *was* a mistake, and it *was* fucking dumb. And believe me, it was the biggest mistake of *your* life. The biggest fucking mistake that you'll regret for the *rest* of your life. I'm done with you. I want a divorce."

I then rose back up to my feet and spun back around, heading towards the front door.

"You can't just walk out on me, Dean. I love you. We love each other too much."

His words did not faze me one bit. I continued to ignore him as my hand gripped the door, opening it.

Apparently, because Ralpho's words were not sinking into me, he decided to take drastic measures to get my attention in this time of desperation of his.

"Where will you go? You won't divorce me. Let's be serious. You'd go back to paying rent to live with someone or in a small rinky-dink apartment. Just think this through. You're not going to walk away from all this."

And strike fucking three!

I knew Ralpho wanted a reaction out of me. He *needed* to see me cry, get further worked up because that meant I cared about our relationship and might give it a chance and forgive him. But no. I could not give him that satisfaction. Once you've lost my trust, you've lost it forever. There are no second chances.

I didn't even bother to turn back around to face Ralpho. All I could utter was, "Watch me!" before I slammed the front door shut.

I walked out of the Four Seasons with my head held high. It would only be me attending the Lana Del Rey concert tonight and I would blast so many pictures and Instagram stories of the event just to fuck with Ralpho. I knew he would be stalking me online for a while. He would no doubt see it. And no matter how many texts and phone calls he would make, there would be no response to him from me. I would only see Ralpho Mercado again when it was in the presence of our divorce lawyers, coming to a final settlement and agreement two months later. Then, I would never see or hear from him ever again.

Louis Vuitton Louisville Sluggers its Goods
By Diamond Stone Media Group

Everybody in the world knows Louis Vuitton, a popular designer merchandise brand among the elites. But what most people are unaware of is what happens to Louis Vuitton's unsold merchandise. In order to keep their exorbitant prices and maintain their exclusivity they burn their unsold products.

There are multiple reasons for why they follow this protocol. One, Louis Vuitton avoids sales at any cost. They have never been known discount any of their upscale merchandise and want to ensure that "everybody gets their products at the same price."

Another reason Louis Vuitton destroys unsold merchandise is to maintain stock control and diminish their theft prevention option. If Louis Vuitton had multiple warehouses full of their unsold items as a long-term storage site, it would be a heavy target for would-be fashion thieves.

Lastly, Louis Vuitton specifically burns bags in the United States thanks to a "duty drawback" law. Under this law, if something is imported into the United States with having already been paid, prior to it being burned or destroyed, then these duty payments can be reclaimed.

This reportedly allows Louis Vuitton to claim back any financial loss, as the duty on their products is incredibly high. Although they don't get to completely reclaim the full value lost, it does go some way towards softening the blow and is better than getting nothing at all.

Chapter 15

Jackson

Current Day...

Dean's personal driver dropped us off just out front of his Paradise Cove Bluff's beach home. As I stepped out of the vehicle, I felt like I had been transported to a completely different world. I was only used to seeing Dean's gorgeous house in the daylight. Never did I imagine that it would look even more miraculous during the nighttime.

The uplighting hit the angles of the estate in just the right places to make it glisten. The landscape and gardens around the home were also flawless. I didn't even recognize the meticulous attention to the details of the grounds as much during my first visit, but they surely stood out to me now.

Instead of entering Dean's main house, we trekked down the stone pathway beside his home, descending towards the beach. We arrived at his deck and moved down the wooden stairs, heading into the casita.

As we arrived, two men were already present there. One was behind the long onyx bar that spanned an entire wall of the main room, while the other sat on the sofa on his phone. The second the seated man saw us, he slipped his cell phone into his pocket and stood.

"Ah! Hector!" Dean stated as he leaned in to hug the guy. As they released their embrace, Dean then proceeded to introduce us. "Jackson, this is my friend and assistant, Hector. Hector, this is Jackson, the one who's interviewing me."

Hector reached his hand out to me to shake. "Nice to meet you," he said to me.

"Likewise," I replied.

"Everything is all squared away. There are three bedrooms here in the casita, Jackson. Please feel free to choose whichever one is most comfortable for you while you stay with us," he commented.

"Thank you. Really, you don't have to go out of your way for..." but before I could finish my sentiments, I was interrupted by Dean.

"You're my guest, Jackson. And so, you'll be treated just like any guest I have over."

All I could do was nod and give in, knowing it was best to not bother arguing with Dean. I knew I would not be getting my point across to him.

Hector diverted his gaze over to Dean before he strode up beside him, whispering something into his ear. I couldn't quite make it out, but I managed to overhear what Dean whispered back to him. "We can talk about that in the morning. We'll figure something out. Just make sure his lips stay sealed."

Make sure his lips stay sealed? That couldn't be good. Just who were they talking about? Now I was beyond intrigued to figure out what they were referring to, but I knew it wasn't my business to pry on the subject. It would be wise of me to ignore it altogether if I didn't want to get kicked out again.

Hector then passed by us, heading out of the casita, while Dean moved towards the onyx bar, where the man behind the bar still stood. "Care for a nightcap?" Dean asked me.

It was nearly 4:00am. I was beyond exhausted. I hadn't been up this late since I was in college. It was a complete shock that I was still standing. But I couldn't turn down an offer from Dean. What kind of guest would that make me?

"Sure. I could go for a drink before bed."

"What would you like?" Dean asked. "Julian here can whip up anything you want. Try him!"

"Hmmm," I pondered, scanning the shelves stocked with various wines and liquor bottles behind Julian. It looked as if every bottle was completely stocked and full to the brim, as if they had been unopened and untouched. I wondered if Dean ever drank much while he was down here at the casita or if he demanded the bottles be completely full at all times. I was inclined to believe the latter.

Although Julian was making Dean a mixed drink with some sort of brown liquor, I couldn't go with the same. After having had champagne and wine most of the night, I knew that it would be smart for me to just stick with that.

"I'll just have a glass of red wine," I requested.

"What kind?" Julian inquired.

"Ummm. Not quite sure. Can you surprise me?"

"Just give him a Médoc," Dean interrupted.

"A whatta?" I found myself saying, embarrassingly. The moment the words escaped my lips, I wanted to retract them.

Dean let out a chuckle. "Médoc is a region in France. Have you ever been?"

I shook my head. "No. Can't say I have."

"It's known for some of the most world-renowned Bordeauxs," he explained.

"Ohhh!" I replied, as if I had a revelation, which I did. Now *Bordeaux* was a name I recognized. "That works then. Thank you."

The young and handsome bartender poured me my glass and handed it off to me.

"I think we're good for the evening, Julian. You're dismissed," Dean coolly stated.

Quickly, Julian gathered a few supplies and then exited the casita, leaving Dean and me to ourselves.

"Please, have a seat anywhere you'd like," Dean offered as he moved to sit on one of the sofas in the main area.

I proceeded to do the same, sitting on the couch directly across from him. The moment my butt sank into the cushion, I was awestruck. This was the softest and most comfy sofa I think I've ever sat in, in my entire life. I had to lightly bounce my ass up and down on it in good measure, just to really get a good feel.

As I sat snugly, I took a sip from my wine. "Wow! This is really good!" I enthusiastically informed Dean. But let's be honest. Even if the wine tasted like it came straight from a gutter leading into a sewage drain, I probably would still have said it tasted delicious just to appease him.

"Great! I knew you'd enjoy it," he commented as he took a guzzle from his own drink.

"This place is pretty spectacular," I said to him, as I took it all in once more.

"Yeah. This was a major selling point of the house for me. Honestly, most of my small get-togethers and parties happen down here."

"Really!?"

"Mhmm," Dean nodded. "I prefer to have my main home to myself and my assistants. Maybe it's just me being picky but whatever. This casita is where I usually have all of my guests stay unless there is an overflow of people staying the night. All of my parties happen down here because of the immediate access to the beach. I can't even count the number of times friends of mine have stripped naked and sprinted from here and into the brisk water."

I couldn't help but be reminded of my interview with Dean's neighbor, Mrs. Van der Sarm earlier in the week, where she alluded to such crazy get-togethers that Dean held here. Although, Nora only told me that he had many guys in speedos running around the beach during some of his parties. She failed to mention that some of them were completely naked. But hopefully she just didn't catch those scenes on those particular evenings. I'm sure the sight of it would have been enough to put her into an early grave.

"Yeah. I mean, I wouldn't complain. It must be nice to be able to just step outside and be right on the beach whenever you wanted, after a few cocktails or just to get the scent of the fresh salty sea air," I stated.

"Well, maybe you could join us for some of my parties in the future," Dean suggested.

It took every nerve cell in my body to prevent my eyes from bulging out of my sockets. Was Dean Cargill seriously inviting me to one of his exclusive parties? This was a fucking dream!

"I would love that," I warmly said, while trying not to sound so eager and desperate.

"But the other reason I host most of my events that create a ruckus down here is for liability purposes," Dean further added.

"Liability purposes?" I repeated back with confusion.

"Yes. My lawyers advised me that having drunk men try to sprint downhill and down the stairs of my deck while drunk could end tragically. It's a lawsuit waiting to happen."

I could only imagine Dean's gay friends getting out of control and tumbling down the hill and deck with their drinks spilling and flying through the air. They would roll down like tumbleweeds, with the alcohol in their system numbing the heavy bruises, sprained ankles, and possible broken bones they would wake up with in the morning.

"Yeah. I can see how that could be a problem. It does make sense," I agreed.

Dean and I continued to chat for another few minutes as we

downed our drinks. I couldn't help but let a yawn escape from my mouth. I tried to hide it, but Dean was too quick to pick up on it.

"I think it's time we call it quits for the night. What do you say?" he recommended.

I was beyond relieved to hear him say this. I was ready to crash right here on this plushest sofa known to mankind.

"Sure. We can resume our interview tomorrow, unless your schedule demands otherwise?"

Dean sent a radiant smile my way. "Nah. My schedule is completely open. We can continue in the morning. Sleep well, Jackson."

I felt the need to repeat my graciousness once more. "You too. And thank you so much for the warm hospitality. I am beyond grateful."

"Really, it's nothing," he nonchalantly stated, wiping his hand through his sexy, wavy hair with all the suaveness in the world. As he proceeded to leave, he turned back around to me. "Oh! I almost forgot. Should you need anything in the middle of the night, don't hesitate to buzz. One of my assistants will be down right away to get whatever it is you need." He then pointed out two small intercoms, one on the wall to the left of the bar and the other on the closest wall to me in this main living area. "There's also one in all the bedrooms and their private ensuite bathrooms."

"Thanks again. I'm sure I'll be okay for the night, but I'll keep that in mind."

"Good." Dean then tapped the frame of the door with his wrist. "Anyway, get some rest. See you in the morning."

"You too. Goodnight."

And finally, Dean left the casita, leaving me all to myself. A sense of relief instantly washed over me. On one hand, I was so ready to pick the closest bedroom and just fall face first into the bed and crash. On the other, I now had the ability to allow my curiosity out of its cage and explore this place to my own content.

I did pull out my phone and open my camera, snapping pictures of everything to send to Darren. He wouldn't believe this set-up I had. He would die the minute he saw it. I then stepped into the bedrooms. Each one had a different theme. The first one looked like it came straight out of The Godfather, having pure leather furniture with dark brown oak and black features. It was made for the likes of a gangster or mob boss. Definitely not my cup of tea. The second room I peeked into had many very white marble and granite fixtures, with small gold veins running through them. It also had tons of rose gold colors scattered throughout on the bedsheets, the sofa, accent chair, and pillows in the room. I wasn't sure if this was the room I was going to claim, but it had more merit than the first option.

However, I had struck gold on the last room. It was beach-themed. The crown molding was white. The walls were a sandy color with steel blue pillows, sheets, and decorations. Just by stepping into the room, I could already feel my heartbeat slowing its rhythm, being calmed by the effect the room had on me. This was definitely the one.

I plopped right down on the bed, deciding to take one last selfie of me to text to Darren for the night.

Wish you were here. This bed is lonely without you, I typed out before sending the message to him along with the picture. I assumed Darren was sound asleep back home in our own bed, which then immediately brought on a wave of homesickness. Although staying here at Dean's home was a once in a lifetime opportunity, which I was completely grateful and ecstatic about, I still missed my own place and every little thing about it.

Resting my head against the soft pillows, I stared up at the ceiling, reflecting on all that had transpired tonight. Mostly, I thought about the story Dean shared about his initial encounter with Ralpho, the progress in their relationship and marriage, and to how their divorce occurred.

I couldn't help but feel the need to compare Dean's version of events to what the media had covered on the topic in the past. And both stories completely contradicted one another. Dean claimed it was he who called things off with Ralpho once he discovered Ralpho was cheating on him. However, all the other stories I've ever heard ran with the idea of Ralpho being the one to call it quits with Dean. But the strange thing about this was that not one news outlet ever mentioned the reason behind the breakup. The most they said was that Ralpho learned some information about Dean that gave him fair warning to want to end things between them. And that was the extent of it.

I had to weigh out both scenes in my head. Was Dean really telling me the truth? Or was all of this one convoluted lie and story he was giving me? But I had to believe him and tell his side of the story. What the hell else could I do? Yet, at the same time, telling a false story felt morally wrong to me and all that I stood for as a journalist.

If Dean was, in fact, lying about everything, would I lose all of my credibility? Would people shun me if I believed Dean's unheard-of testimony and published that information? It was definitely a conundrum for sure.

I continued to dwell on it until the dreariness fully overcame me. My eyes shut, sending me off into a deep sleep with the sound of the crashing ocean tides serving as my peaceful metronome.

A knock at my door was what finally woke me up the following morning. I stretched far and wide while letting a deep yawn escape from me.

I tossed over on to my side, not wanting to ever get out of this bed. It was so fucking warm. I curled into the fetal position, trying to remain as snug as possible. If I could just lie here forever with this permanent feeling of contentment, I think I would actually do it without any sort of reluctance.

But the second round of knocks at the door brought me back down from cloud nine to reality.

"Yes?" I called out to whoever was the source of the hammering.

"Sorry, Mr. Cartwright. It's me, Hector. Brunch is almost fully set up on the beach. Mr. Cargill requests your presence there soon," he informed.

"Okay. Let me get changed really quickly and I'll meet him out there," I said.

"Very well."

After hearing no other replies from Hector, I glanced at my phone to see that it was nearly 11:00am.

Holy shit! I didn't even realize it was that late. Then again, we didn't get the chance to get to bed until well after 4:00am. Still, I needed to get a move on. I unwillingly rose from the bed and reached for my clothes from last night. But what sort of message would wearing the same clothes from last night send? Hopefully, someone had brought my luggage in to the casita.

I opened the door to peek out of it, glad to see Hector was sitting on the sofa with his back facing me. "Ummm Hector?" I whispered to him.

He abruptly stood and turned to face me. "Yes, Mr. Cartwright?"

"You wouldn't happen to know where my belongings are, would you?"

He pointed right next to the door. I peered further out from behind the door and down to see that they were right next to me, sure enough.

"I brought them in this morning. I figured you'd want your privacy, so I didn't bother to roll them into your bedroom," he explained.

"No worries at all. I appreciate you doing that. Thank you!" I reached for my belongings and brought them into my room. Now I just needed to figure out what the hell to wear. It's not like I actually brought a specific pair of clothes for a *brunch on the beach* sort of occasion. So, I decided to ultimately go with a pair of navy swimming trunks and a plain white t-shirt. That was the best I had, given the unprecedented circumstances.

Once I was fully changed, I scanned over my bag one last time, debating on whether or not I should even consider bringing my recording device with me. The last time I showed Dean that, things didn't pan out well. But the Dean I got last night seemed to be turning a new leaf, being more open with me. Perhaps he would be willing to allow me to use it this time around. At any rate, I could at least try and see how it would go. It was worth a shot.

I went to retrieve it and stuffed it in my pocket, before coming out of the room, still noticing Hector was waiting in the main living room still. "I'll escort you out to the beach," he offered.

Although, I truly wondered about the purpose of him walking me there. The beach was just outside the casita. Unless the brunch set-up was a mile further down the beach, which I doubted since the Paradise Cove Bluff beach backyards were privately owned by residents, then I didn't see why I couldn't manage on my own.

Still, I had to acquiesce to Hector's offer. "That would be great. Thank you," I heard myself say aloud, willing to accept his kind gesture.

The two of us strode side by side out of the casita, past the deck and right into the sand. Sure enough, there was a giant ivory elongated, oval table set-up closer down towards the water. A few matching white chairs were around the table.

Hector and I proceeded to walk towards it. Even for the short walk, I didn't want there to be lingering silence the entire way. That was just completely awkward. So, I decided to make small-talk.

"How long have you been working for Dean?" I asked him.

"The past four years," Hector answered. "But I've known him for a much longer time. We've been friends since... I don't know. Nine or ten years ago?"

"Wow. So, you knew Dean back in the day, before he became this... *sensation*."

"Yeah. I was one of his very first friends he met when he came out to Miami. We sort of had a hiatus for a bit when he arrived in L.A., but eventually we reconnected and he flew me out down here to work with him. He gave me an offer I couldn't refuse. The fucker is pretty damn generous."

It was really nice to hear that Dean treated his staff well. Being in this business, sometimes I've heard horror stories about how certain celebrities treat those on their payroll. But I was thrilled to know that Dean was not one of them. At least I didn't think he was, based on the information Hector just provided me with.

"Yeah. It sounds like he's an all-around nice guy," I added.

"Anyway, here's where we part ways. Clearly, you know where you're going, right? Unless you have 20/100 vision that I am unaware of," Hector slyly remarked in a smart-ass tone.

"Yup. The only table out here," I said, stating the obvious.

"Take care. Oh, and I'll have someone come down and fix your room up for you before you return. Is there anything else I can get for you in the meantime? Any specific preferences or unusual requests?" Hector asked. "We're more than happy to accommodate *anything*."

I shook my head. "Nothing I can think of. I think I have everything

I need, but I appreciate the hospitality."

"Sounds good. Well, have a good brunch. I'm sure we'll see each other later."

"Bye," I replied back to Hector as he turned around and headed off, back in the direction of the house.

As I scanned ahead, coming closer to the table and chairs that were set up on the beach for Dean and me, I noticed how full the table was. There was an array of so many different foods and drinks, finely organized. Fruit bowls, eggs, omelets, oysters, crabcakes, scones, biscuits, sausages, muffins, a variety of casseroles and quiches, waffles, pancakes, and so much more. Then, there were the already prepped drinks - mimosas, bottles of champagne, vodka, tequila and mixers. But what really caught my eye were the Bloody Marys. The glasses were stacked with shrimp, crabmeat, olives, celery, seasonings, and a massive lobster tail coming forth from it. The entire thing looked like a culinary masterpiece, a laudable and edible form of art.

And on one end of the table sat Dean Cargill, with his back towards me as he faced the ocean. He was in a thin salmon pink shirt with pure white jeans on and barefoot from what I could see from my angle of him. I also noticed the white frames of his sunglasses on the side of his head. No doubt they were from some crazy, expensive designer. A lit cigarette also hung from his rose puckered lips.

His hair effortlessly glided with the gentle sea breeze as it blew. The man looked as if he was posing and modeling on a 24/7 basis, even though it was completely unintentional and likely oblivious to him. He was just that damn good-looking, to the point where it was becoming a bit annoying to me. I wish I could easily look like that and not have to put in as much effort to pull it off.

"Good morning," I said when I was at a close enough distance for him to hear me. I figured it was best to let him know I was behind him, so that he wouldn't be startled or freaked out, thinking someone was sneaking up on him.

"Hey. Good morning to you, too. Did you sleep well?" he checked as he threw his cigarette in the sand and smushed it to put it out.

I nodded. "Yeah. Honestly, it was one of the best nights of sleep in my life, surprisingly."

"Perfect. Well, I'm glad you feel rested." Dean then adjusted his chair, scooting it around so that he now faced the table. "Feel free to pick out whatever you want to eat."

"It's all so much! You really didn't have to go out of your way to do all of this for me."

"Nonsense! Of course, I did. You're my guest, after all," he replied.

"Well, thank you."

Both of us grabbed our plates and went to town. I decided on most of the seafood options, including the oysters, eggs Benedict with salmon, a crab and veggie frittata and, of course, one of the ostentatious Bloody Marys that felt almost like a sin to drink and ruin for how damn pretty it was.

As we devoured our meals, Dean proceeded to ask me questions about my personal life, surprisingly.

"Oh! That's great. How long have you and your fiancé been together for?" he asked as a follow up question when I told him about my love life.

"About six years now. We've been engaged for three of those six."

"Very nice. And do you two have a date selected for the wedding?" Dean inquired.

"Not quite yet. We're waiting until things are a little more stable in our lives."

As much as I was elated over Dean wanting to get to know me more, I was now wearing my journalist hat. And rule number one about journalism is to never *let in* those who you are interviewing. It's all about the story and specifically *their* story. You should never get attached to clients or those who you are covering.

"So, speaking of love life," I began to segue. "Last night, we left off with you and Ralpho divorcing. What happened next?"

I then brought out the tape recorder from my pocket and placed it at the center of the table between us. "And like I mentioned the first time I was here, I prefer to have my notes recorded, but if that's an issue for you, I don't mind..."

But Dean cut me right off before I could finish what I wanted to say. "No. Don't worry about it. It's completely fine now. You can go ahead and record the conversation."

Wow! Well, that went way more smoothly than I had anticipated. Before he could retract that statement and have a change of heart, I quickly hit the play button. A red dot lit up on the device, indicating that it was now recording.

"So, Dean, I was just asking what then happened after your divorce to Ralpho? I know there was about a nine-month gap after things were through with you and Ralpho before you met Senator Leon Merck. Then, just three months after that, you married him, making Leon your new husband. What all happened in that year of time?"

Dean had a smirk on his face as I asked all of this. "Oh, Leon! I can't help but laugh whenever I think about him."

"And why is that?"

Dean took a sip of his mimosa, while leaning back in his chair now, seeming all the more comfortable. "Because being with him felt like a complete fucking joke."

Chapter 16

Dean

Four Years Ago...

There is something to be said about being at a point in your life where you just no longer give a fuck about money. And believe me, my entire mind was once consumed with the idea of making money and having just enough of it to sustain my lifestyle. It was the one thing that gave me so much anxiety in my life.

It was the main contributing factor in me moving to Miami to pursue my college degree in fashion merchandising and being able to afford my monthly rental on my apartment.

I dated Frank and surrounded myself with men that were financially secure, because that was what I desired most in my life. Coming from my not-so-great home in Pennsylvania, I was desperate to be in a livable situation where I could afford all of the amenities I wanted, beyond my wildest hopes and dreams, while never ever having to worry about living from paycheck to paycheck.

Then, spending time with Steve and living in his home in L.A. allowed me to save and accumulate so much money in my savings. Yes, I was working at designer retail stores, but that, plus the amount of money my boyfriends and dates gave, allowed me to establish quite a substantial savings account.

On top of all of this, after I divorced Ralpho Mercado, I was the one that prevailed in our divorce settlement. Without the prenup, I was entitled to half of everything, which then officially made me a millionaire.

I'm not going to lie, I felt slightly guilty about taking half of Ralpho's assets. But because he cheated on me, it felt *so right*. The consequence was just perfect. Him having to forfeit a few million dollars felt like the punishment that served the equal amount of justice needed to forgive all that he had done to me.

Now, I was a millionaire in my early-to-mid-twenties. And let me just say, when you are a millionaire with Greek god-like looks as mine and so easily adaptable and friendly with everyone, able to make connections with the best of the best, then the world was your oyster. And every oyster you then stumbled upon always contained the finest pearl.

After my divorce with Ralpho, that was just how my life proceeded. So many rich and wealthy men requested to go on dates with me, to which I obliged. My social media pages were accumulating attention all the more, nearly growing to over one million followers under each platform. It also helped that I posted thirst trap photos of me shirtless and on lavish vacations on a daily basis after the divorce.

Now I could afford all the finer things in life, including luxury sports cars, high-class condos in Beverly Hills, secondary homes in all the major cities of the United States. My expectations were set so high that I honestly was not sure if I ever wanted to find or date a man that I wanted to spend the rest of my life with. I was finally financially independent and able to support myself to the point where I questioned the idea of spending my life next to a *significant someone*. I was skeptical of the entire establishment. Why should someone seek to be married to a single person in order to be satisfied for the rest of their lives? Why would anyone need a sole partner to make all of their dreams come true? Why couldn't you do that on your own? Hell, why couldn't you do that with three plus people that were very close in your life?

I found myself going against the grain of life and its societal conformities. At least, I thought I was that way until I met Leon Merck. It was at the Merill S. Guthrie Cancer Research Institute's annual charity gala.

My arm was strapped around my date, a renowned plastic surgeon in Los Angeles named Dr. Patrick Wetherton, as we strolled up the marble stairs, across the blue velvety carpet and into the grand ballroom. He asked me to be his plus one for the event. We had been on two romantic dates prior to this evening, and this black and white tie event would technically be the third.

An usher at the entrance of the ballroom escorted us to our assigned dinner table. The place had at least fifty round white tables that could easily fit ten people at each. Patrick and I were brought to a table in the middle of the room. Two other couples were already seated around it.

It seemed Patrick knew who at least one of them was right away, for he quickly made introductions. "Ah! Mr. and Dr. Grietling, it's a pleasure to see you as always. I want you to meet my date for the evening, Dean Cargill."

"A pleasure to meet you Mr. Cargill," Dr. Grietling greeted me with while extending his hand for me to shake.

"And you as well," I warmly replied, while also exchanging a greeting with his wife.

"Bruce here is an oncologist at the Beverly Hills Cancer Center," Patrick informed me.

"Yes. Patrick and I go way back. We both were residents at Cedars-Sinai Medical Center," Bruce Grietling added. "But it seems Patrick here decided to go the cosmetic route over the patient-care one."

Patrick let out a haughty laugh. "Well, I just followed the money, honestly. But who's to say that patient-care doesn't also fall under plastic surgery?"

The conversation went on the for the next hour or so, with some mild interruptions. Most of the discussion among the group at the table related to medicine, current research and findings, as well as comparisons among medical and Ivy League school programs. Of course, there was nothing I could bring forth to contribute to the exchange, since I had absolutely no strong medical knowledge and barely understood some of the vocabulary that was being thrown across the table during every other sentence. So, I nodded and smiled, pretending to be fully engaged with all of them, when deep down, I was doing my best to hide a yawn that was desperate to liberate itself from me.

I needed to make my temporary escape or risk embarrassing Patrick and myself with my bored yawn. Knowing that I was on the verge of nearly not being able to control it for very much longer, I rose from my seat and moved behind Patrick, leaning in to whisper in his ear. "I'm going to head to the bar to get something that's a little more potent. Would you like me to get you anything?"

Patrick craned his neck back so that his lips could nearly meet my ear. "Yes. Can you get me a bourbon, please?"

"Of course."

His lips then tilted to graze my cheeks as he landed a soft kiss on them. Patrick returned back to the table talk, which left me the opportunity to finally be able to get away from that dull babble.

I was swift in navigating between the tightly packed tables and around those who were in the narrow, confined spaces to make it to the edge of the room where the full bar counter was. There was only me and one other person at the far end of it. This man took a clear liquid drink from the bartender, which I assumed to be a tonic with liquor.

Now that he was taken care of, the bartender gave me his full and undivided attention. "Can I get you anything?"

I nodded. "Yes. I'll take one of your top-shelf bourbons and an extra dirty martini."

"Gin or vodka?"

"Vodka, and make it Grey Goose, please."

"Coming right up." He sent a warm smile my way before turning back to me to make my drink requests.

"Aren't you a little too young to be drinking bourbon and dirty martinis?" A deep, unknown voice called from behind me.

I sharply spun around to see the source of the judgmental comment. It was a man that looked to be in his late forties or early fifties by the looks of it. His skin was silky smooth, with his glowing sapphire eyes gazing at me. His snow-white hair reminded me of Anderson Cooper. He wore a light gray suit that fit snugly around his toned body.

"And shouldn't you be a little more classy and not question the drink choice of a complete stranger?" I retorted. But I wasn't finished yet. "But clearly you wanted to get my attention. Otherwise, you would have left me alone. So, tell me, what about me drew you in?"

His eyes widened with alarm at my bluntness. A sly smirk then crept up on his face. "Wow. A spitfire. What a refreshing surprise. Clearly, you're no amateur at this game."

I shrugged. "Yeah. Don't let the age fool you. I'm years ahead of most others."

"I can see that," the suave, debonair man commented. "And you are?"

"Dean Cargill."

The bartender then handed off the glass tumbler of bourbon and the martini glass to me. I retrieved them before glancing back at the man.

"Ah! I knew I recognized you from somewhere," he stated, as if he just had an epiphany.

But I knew better than to believe that. I was inclined to think he already knew who I was all along, which is why he came over to make this flirtatious introduction.

"Oh. Really?" I tried to sound as oblivious as possible, pretending to have no idea what he was referring to or how he came to find out about me. Of course, anyone who recognized me must have done so through the tabloids, social media or by word of mouth through gay circles as a result of divorcing Ralpho Mercado.

"Yes. You were with that soap opera star. Ralpho, I think his name was?" The man was performing the same act I was, trying to sound clueless, as if he were trying to come up with an answer, when he already knew it all along to begin with.

I took a long sip from my martini before addressing him again. "That I was. And what about you? Are you some sort of doctor or...?"

I paused, wanting him to fill in the blanks for me. His face now seemed startled, as if he was stunned that I hadn't the slightest inkling as to who he was. "My name is Leon Merck."

The name didn't ring a bell in the slightest. I held my puzzled expression. "Sorry. Should I know your name?"

The confidence in him did not waiver one bit. He chuckled at my naivety. "Leon Merck... the senator from Wisconsin. Do you not follow politics?"

No. To be honest, I did not. I completely steered clear of politics altogether. My life was so consumed with other things that I never really even considered dipping my foot into the political pond, even for a dabble. "Unfortunately, I do not. But a senator... that's impressive."

I had to give the man an ego boost, although I gathered his ego was likely already through the roof being a senator and all. But still, this man was probably used to compliments thrown his way on a daily basis. That was the sort of world he lived in. And I was the type of person who always made myself fit in to anyone's world. I was that successful of a chameleon.

"Thank you," he sincerely stated. "So, Mr. Cargill, what exactly brings you here to this cancer research charity gala?"

"I'm actually here on a date," I informed him, nodding in the general direction of where we were seated. "Patrick Wetherton. He's a plastic surgeon here in Los Angeles."

Leon's demeanor changed to one of slight disappointment. "Oh... that's unfortunate. Are you two together or..."

I couldn't help but blush, picking up on what the senator was putting down. "No. Not at all. We've just been on a few dates here and there. Nothing serious as of yet."

"Well, I guess I don't have to necessarily turn into a snake to steal you away from him then, do I? I can just do it with no foul play."

We both snickered at the sinister comment. "No. You wouldn't have to," I acknowledged.

"Not that I'm obligated to stay here at this gala or anything. I showed my face and made a hefty donation. I've set out what I came here to do. So, what do you say we get out of here? I know of a private jazz-piano lounge we can get into tonight, if you're interested?"

This was tempting as hell. Would there ever be an opportunity again where I could sneak off in the company of a gay U.S. Senator? Not likely. But at the same time, my morality was kicking in. It would be extremely rude of me to just leave Patrick here alone. Then again, I could always shoot him a text and lie by saying that I left abruptly because I wasn't feeling all that well. The more I thought about it, the more I was leaning towards taking Leon up on his offer.

What would it be like to have sex with a senator? To be dating him? I couldn't even imagine the connections and circles I would get into by being with him. There were so many unknowns about it, but it thrilled the living hell out of me.

So, I finally reached a decision. "Let's do it," I eagerly replied.

And just like the way I was living my life now, I walked out of the charity gala with Leon Merck by my side, never once looking back.

Chapter 17

Jackson

Current Day...

I felt more full than I ever had in my entire life, to the point where I questioned if I was bloated or not. Dean had just finished filling me in on the lapse between his divorce to Ralpho Mercado and up until the point where he had just met Leon Merck for the first time at a charity event. While he was in the middle of his story, we ate to our heart's content as well as imbibed on some of the mimosas and Bloody Marys he had one of his assistants concoct at this elaborate beach brunch he arranged for us.

Now that Dean had taken a break from reciting his life-story, I had a moment to reflect and to process on all that he just informed me. As much as I wanted to believe every word he was telling me was true, a lot of the pieces still weren't adding up. For instance, the money he had accumulated from the divorce settlement with Ralpho Mercado left many questions to be posed. Through my investigative skills, I found out that Dean barely got five-hundred thousand dollars out of the divorce when all was said and done. Ralpho Mercado was a soap opera actor, with a net-worth that was barely above two million dollars. So, how could Dean possibly afford all the things he previously mentioned to me (the luxury vacations, multiple homes across the country, designer wardrobe) with just five-hundred thousand dollars and the minimal amount of money he earned from his part-time retail positions?

Maybe I was missing something, but I couldn't just out right blurt out that I had questions about his finances. I learned my lesson the first time on that one. It wasn't my first time at the rodeo. Best not to go there with him again.

But there was also something else that was bothering me with all that Dean shared that went back to his and Ralpho Mercado's relationship. Dean had mentioned that it was he who divorced Ralpho and not the other way around. He was pretty damn clear and adamant about that being the case. Yet, this was contrary to public records, which I gathered as evidence for this story on him. And those records undeniably pointed at Ralpho being the one who served Dean with divorce papers and ultimately was the one who filed for the divorce. Why would Dean continue to lie about this to me? He had to have known all of this information was public. I was a skilled reporter. Did he think it was out of my wheelhouse to find out incriminating details on him?

The more I thought about it, the more insulted I was beginning to feel. Just who did he take me for? At any rate, I couldn't call Dean out on it just yet. I still needed to hear more from him.

For now, I was just pleased I was getting this much information out of Dean. It was more than any other journalist had ever gotten on him in the past ten years. But we weren't through just yet. I needed to see this entire thing through and that included hearing the details pertaining to his second marriage to Leon Merck.

"Why don't we take a stroll along the beach?" Dean suggested after downing another mimosa.

"Sure. I'd actually like that," I replied, which was the god's honest truth. I was stuffed and needed to walk all this food off. It was the perfect idea to avoid the sedentary stomach ache that was bound to come on if I remained anymore still.

He rose from his chair, but not before grabbing another full mimosa. I was only halfway through my drink, so I decided I would carry it with me, not really caring to grab another. But before we did walk side by side, I reached for my recording device to bring along with us, assuming we would discuss a lot more as we strolled along the wet sand, where the waves crashed into the shore.

The weather was glorious today, leaving Dean sun-kissed and even more sexy than he already was. But I kept more of my focus on the pleasantness of my surroundings and not Dean's looks and stardom.

I couldn't help but take a deep breath as Dean and I began our jaunt along the beach, inhaling the Malibu sea breeze that took advantage of my expanding lungs.

Out of the corner of my eyes, I noticed Dean retrieving a cigarette from his pockets, placing it between his lips. He reached for a lighter in his other pocket to light it up, taking a deep puff as we continued our walk.

"Do you get the chance to walk this beach often?" I asked him.

He merely shrugged. "Honestly, not really. My schedule is so jam-packed I barely have a moment to wipe my own ass. But I managed to rearrange all of my prior engagements just for us to have this interview."

I wasn't sure whether to feel honored or guilty based on his statement. Part of me felt like I was being a huge imposition if Dean had to alter his schedule on my account, but then I remembered that he was the one who requested this interview to begin with. Not me. Therefore, I was led to assume he wasn't trying to insinuate that I was the bothersome one who forced him to have to upend his entire itinerary.

"Well, I appreciate that. And yes, this beach is so amazing. If I lived here, I'd try my best to come out for a long walk as often as I could," I explained.

"If you lived here, you would be so busy being a major CEO or some sort of celebrity that you wouldn't have the time nor the energy to be able to do it that much," Dean stated, derailing my all of my pleasant thoughts on that.

But he had a point. For anyone to live in Paradise Cove Bluffs, you had to be mega-wealthy, and in order to be that well off, you had to have been some high-status celebrity or owner of some conglomerate of a company, all of which would likely leave you with a pretty tight schedule.

"Or some rich politician," I added to create the perfect segue to get back on topic to picking up where we left off with Dean's first initial encounter with the Wisconsin Senator.

"That too," he simply stated, acknowledging my comment.

"Speaking of rich politicians," I led in with. "It seemed like you and Leon Merck hit it off well when you first met."

"Yes. We did. For the first six months, things were great. But then once he went back into re-election campaign mode, it all went downhill from there," Dean said.

"That lines up with the timeline from the stories I've heard," I informed him. "But after you and him were married for four months, prior to the divorce, it was reported that Leon learned of some *unsuitable* things about you that left him filing for a divorce. But there were no further details on that. People have said it was pretty similar to the way in which the divorce went down between you and Ralpho."

Dean let out a haughty laugh. "Do you really believe that to be true, Jackson? Come on! I didn't think you were that naïve."

"Well, what happened then?" I asked with hidden skepticism.

"It was all Leon. He completely changed throughout the entire course of our relationship," Dean stated before glancing up towards the sky as if deep in thought. "Actually, now that I think about it, I wonder if he was always a lying, nasty hypocrite to begin with, but just hid it well until we were eventually married and he could no longer conceal his true self."

It was hard for me to even follow up with anything after a disgruntled comment like that, but I just needed to stick to the facts and be as unbiased and objective as possible. "I think I need you to fill in the gaps for me here," I requested. "Tell me about your relationship with Leon from beginning to end."

"Sure," Dean replied. "If you want to hear about how maniacal Leon was to the point where it became so suffocating for me, then I'll gladly tell you."

Chapter 18

Dean

Three Years Ago...

There's a difference between the perks of dating a soap opera actor from those of dating a senator. Well, there are actually many, but there was one that really stood out to me. Ralpho Mercado was able to get us into VIP sections of various nightclubs, stadiums, events, etc., but when you're in the company of Leon Merck, a Wisconsin senator, you actually get access to the most exclusive of country clubs and private lounges and bars that even a soap opera star couldn't manage to get into.

The two of us sat across from each other at a table for two in one of these restrictive lounges called the Braunleder, in Middleton, Wisconsin. The bar had a prohibitionist vibe to it. The lighting was very dim. The furniture was of the purest brown leather. The bar counters and tables were shined and glossed, showcasing the gorgeous, dark-stained cocobolo wood. We both ate a full-blood wagyu tenderloin, and dare I say it was one of the most succulent meats I've ever tasted in all my life? I had a glass of fine-aged Bordeaux, while Leon imbibed on his usual scotch on the rocks.

It had now been four months since we officially started dating one another. During our first two months together, I spent my time mostly in Los Angeles, venturing off on a plane for Wisconsin on the weekends to visit Leon. But lately, I've been spending weeks on and weeks off between both places, now that our relationship was getting more serious.

One would think I needed so much excitement and adventure in my life that I wanted my next partner to be able to supply that and keep up with me, but I actually found myself drawn to just the opposite. Leon Merck was a creature of habit. He loved fine-dining and was enthusiastic about having private small group affairs filled with talks of politics, card tournaments or even just the two of us cuddled up on the couch with a lit fireplace watching Yellowstone, White Lotus, or whatever popular new series was currently streaming that we both took an interest in. Well, they were actually television shows Leon preferred, some of which I pretended to find fascinating. He was an intellectual. I had a feeling he would be unattracted to me if I shared with him my love for The Real Housewives and trashy reality television shows. I would be content enough for now to watch those series on my own, in the comfort of my own place.

However, there was something so simple about our time spent together that I grew to cherish and appreciate. Not simple in the sense of monetarily unsubstantial and boring. That was far from the truth, because Leon, like me, valued the finer and expensive things in life. But by simple, I mean that domestic, comfortable lifestyle of spousal dinner dates and cozying up to one another on the sofa over a glass of wine by the fireplace, just enjoying each other's company and conversation.

I hoped those moments would continue in our relationship, but they soon were put on pause due to Leon's re-election campaign, which undoubtedly took far greater precedence than anything else going on in Leon's life, including me.

"I've been meaning to talk to you about your new job with Chanel," Leon said, after finishing chewing a piece of his wagyu tenderloin. Our table was isolated in a corner of the Braunleder, far enough away from anyone to be able to eavesdrop in on us.

"What about it?" I asked. Although I worked for Chanel, I was no longer in a brick and mortar store. I now worked as a brand ambassador, creative marketing director and consultant for the designer-brand company. Now that I was fairly wealthy and my social media following was growing astronomically, more designer companies offered me higher paying positions. So, why wouldn't I seize the opportunity? After all, I worked hard in the retail space to move up to this current role.

"Do you really think it's best that you work for them?" Leon questioned me.

"Of course!" I enthusiastically declared. "Opportunities like this just don't randomly happen all the time. My background is in fashion merchandising. Why wouldn't I work for such a prestigious company?"

"Well, what I'm trying to say is, do you really *need* to work for them? Surely, you know I'd support you. Why don't you work with me on the campaign trail?"

"The campaign trail? You know I don't know the first thing about politics," I tried to explain.

"I know. That's the reason why you should join me. Look, Dean... you know I have bigger and brighter aspirations beyond just being a senator. And, well, to be frank, if you're by my side, it's imperative that you also be well versed in the political arena and all that it entails," Leon suggested.

"But you know I prefer not to have to rely on anyone else," I reminded him. It was a conversation we've had quite a few times in the past few months as our relationship was blossoming even more. I would never go back to having to be under a man's financial cloud.

Gone were the days where I was obligated to commit myself to a part-ner because they pulled all the monetary strings in the relationship. I promised myself I would never go back to that lifestyle and even mentioned it to Leon on a few occasions.

"But every spouse does it, babe. Think about it. What husband or wife of a senator or higher political power doesn't fit into the role of politics? You can't just run from it. Plus, that would only hurt me and my polls if people knew of my significant other wanting nothing to do with the growth and flourishment of America."

I couldn't help but chuckle at how dramatic Leon was with his sen-timents. Surely, the country did not need me to support it to stand on its own two legs. "Yes, that may be so. However, we are not spouses."

"Oh, come on, Dean!" Leon gave an exasperated sigh. "Don't you at least think we are headed in that direction? Look. I'll be honest. You know how I feel about you. I've never felt this way about any other man in my entire life. There is just this magnetism about you. Between us. I know you feel it too."

"Of course, I do," I confirmed. "But I'm just stating the facts. We aren't yet married."

"And if we were?" Leon arched his brow at me. "Would you then change your mind?"

"I'd consider it," I left him with. Although, truth be told, I only did it to make things less awkward between us. It was best to just tell him what he wanted to hear to avoid a verbal conflict.

"That's a step in the right direction," he positively stated. "And I promise I'd make it worth your while. To show you how committed I am and appreciative of your sacrifice, I won't have you sign a pre-nup."

Well, this conversation completely escalated and went to a place where I never imagined it would. I couldn't help but let my eyes widen in shock that Leon would even consider bringing up the idea of a pre-nup at this point in our relationship, or rather a lack thereof.

"Leon, are you sure this is the right time to even be discussing this?" I asked, taking another swig and sip from my glass of red wine.

"There's never been a more perfect time, Dean. My campaign is just around the corner, and I want you to be there with me every step of the way. But I'm not just saying that's the main reason I want you to marry me. Far from it. You know how much you mean to me. I love you unconditionally. It's only a matter of time before I wind up proposing to you. Why avoid the inevitable?"

What the hell was I supposed to say to all of this? There was no way I could not acknowledge Leon's feelings for me. Therefore, I felt like I had to reward him. He deserved it, after all, for how amazing and wonderful he has been to me over these past four months.

"You're right. We're just stalling at this point," I said with a flirtatious wink. "I'd want nothing more than to be married to you, babe."

I reached across the table for his hand, and he placed his over top of mine.

"Do you mean it, then?" he asked. "You'd marry me and go on the campaign trail with me?"

"Yes!" I blurted out. "But this is not a proposal, I hope. I'd expect it to be in a more romantic setting and under different circumstances."

"But of course!" he replied. "Believe me. I know you all too well to not pop the question here, of all places."

And Leon knew better. Yet he only waited a full week before proposing to me. We took an impromptu trip to Hermitage Bay in Antigua for a quick getaway vacation, since he would be fully committed to his campaign that was on the horizon. At the resort, we spent the evening in the infinity pool, leaning over the ledge overlooking the verdant archipelago and cerulean sea with a glass of champagne in our hands. The scene was so magical that I didn't even hesitate when providing my answer. *Yes.*

We had a private wedding just a month later, and the rest was history... a *short-lived* history, that is.

I always pictured what being the husband of a political figure would look like. However, I just held onto hope that I was an exception to going with the flow of that stream. I was fucking Dean Cargill, after all. I had the confidence of a lion and the pride of a peacock. Not to mention I had my own finances sorted out and was not reliant on my husband. Therefore, why couldn't I bend the rules a bit?

It had been a full three weeks that I was on the campaign trail with Leon. And let me just say it was the driest and most dull three weeks of my entire life. Most of my time spent in bumfuck Pennsylvania was even more lively than this, and that's saying something. I desperately needed a break even if it was just for a weekend or else I was going to go insane being on the road with Leon.

Half of our time was spent driving in a black SUV traveling from place to place. It was unbearable. So, I decided to sneak away and fly to Los Angeles for a little while. Luckily, marketing executives from Chanel reached out to me and asked if I was interested in meeting them in L.A. for their own marketing campaign. Now that was a campaign I could easily get behind and not these stodgy political ones.

So, I abruptly took an Uber to the airport the minute I could get away from Leon. I left his staff members with a note letting them know where I was running off to, but that I wouldn't be too long, just two days tops.

However, the second I landed down in L.A.X., I turned my phone off airplane mode and received quite a few *nastygrams* from Leon's chief of staff, name Laura. She was a brutal bitch, to say the least. "Dean! Where are you!? You can't just fly off to Los Angeles on a whim. We are in the middle of a campaign here, for Christ's sake! Do you not fully understand the impact your absence can have on Leon's campaign... his entire career, for that matter!?"

This was completely overboard, and I was beyond pissed that she even had the audacity to speak to me in such a way. I wasn't having any of it. So, I responded back to her, being as straight-forward as possible. "I have an important business meeting that was sprung on me. Will be back in two days. There's nothing to worry about."

Within five minutes of sending that text message to Laura, I checked my phone that was vibrating in my pocket. When I pulled it out, I saw that I was receiving an incoming call from Leon.

"Hey babe!" I said, as if nothing was wrong. Although when we were back in person, I would be sure to give him and Laura a piece of my mind for how she responded to me.

"Dean... why are you in Los Angeles?" Leon sounded stern, as if he was a father ready to scold his misbehaved son.

"I told your staff that personnel at Chanel reached out to me. They called for a meeting that I couldn't turn down," I informed him.

"But we're in the middle of a campaign. You can't just disappear on me like that."

"I'm sorry, but I didn't think it was a big deal. I'll only be gone for two days." Really, it wasn't that worrisome.

"Dean, I'm trying to keep my cool right now. I really am, but you're making it impossible for me to do so. Please, just get on the first flight back home, here. I need you by my side. We have a very important dinner date tonight and other engagements to attend to tomorrow. You know the message that will send to people if you're out gallivanting around in Los Angeles during *my* upcoming election?"

"I don't think anyone cares all that much, Leon. You're not going to lose any votes just because I took a weekend business trip to L.A."

"That's beside the point, Dean."

"But isn't it? I thought that was the very point that was trying to be made here?" Now I was just completely confused. Was this really about the campaign or was this more of a control issue or power struggle Leon was having over me?

"Christ!" Leon shouted. I've never heard him this enraged since we've been together. "Just get your ass back on a plane and come back home. I shouldn't have to explain myself. Don't be so illogical."

"Illogical!?" I yelled back at him through the phone. "So, now you're resorting to insults and throwing education in my face?"

"No! I didn't mean it like that. Look, just come..." Leon tried to finish his statement, but I interceded before he could.

"Absolutely not. Not after this fucking mess of a conversation. I'm staying in L.A. whether you like it or not. I'll be back in two days. You can wait for me until then. That's final!"

I quickly ended the call before things could get even more heated between the two of us. Leon and I had moments of disagreement before, but things never blew up the way they just did. This was a first for us and would hopefully be the very last time it ever happened.

Now my mind was foggy and unfocused going into this meeting with the Chanel executives. The last thing I needed was for me to not be on my *A-game* when this conference could be a critical one for my career.

I became even more agitated at Leon for putting me through this. It was selfish of him to only be concerned with his job and not my own. The more I thought about it, the more resentful I was becoming. Whatever. I just needed to get this over with and head back to Wisconsin in a few days. Hopefully, everything would blow over by then.

Just two days later, I arrived back in Wisconsin, rolling my luggage through the front door of our home. "Babe, I'm back!" I called out, hoping to see Leon come dashing across the foyer to greet me in a warm embrace. I stood waiting for the moment to arrive, but it never came. Oh well. I assumed Leon was busy at work on his laptop or on an important phone call.

The house was too quiet for my liking. The living room and kitchen seemed untouched as I passed them. Down the hall, I could see the study door was slightly ajar, which meant that was where Leon likely was. I left my suitcase and moved into the room, only to see my husband sitting reclined in his black leather chair with his feet propped up on his desk. He held a glass of bourbon in his hand.

It left me slightly irritated that he couldn't bother to get up to greet me at the door, since it seemed he wasn't busy whatsoever. But I shunned the thought right from my mind, just glad to be home to see him again. Absence does make the heart grow fonder, even if we hadn't seen each other for but a few days.

"Hey!" I enthusiastically said to him.

His eyes glanced up at me. They were glossy and bloodshot. He was either drunk or completely over-tired. I was leaning towards the latter, considering he probably wasn't sleeping well with the campaign and all. Plus, he rarely went to bed without me by his side, which also likely added to his inability to sleep. I'll admit, I too missed him went I slept alone in Los Angeles, wishing he would cuddle and spoon me from behind, his warmth seeping from his body onto my skin.

But Leon didn't utter a single word to me. He just stared at me blankly. It was then that I realized something was wrong. This entire situation didn't feel quite right. I could instantly feel the tension in the air that lingered in this stuffy room.

Finally, Leon spoke up. "I specifically asked you to come home two days ago..."

"I'm aware. We already went through this," I reminded him, not wanting to take even more steps backward by rehashing the argument.

"Clearly, you were doing more in L.A. than just attending that work meeting," he added.

"Yes. I went out to dinner with a few friends I haven't seen in ages. So what?"

Leon then reached for his phone, scrolling through it almost maniacally, in search of something until he landed on what he was looking for. He turned the phone so that the screen faced me. I stepped forward, scanning over the contents of an article he was showing me. It was from a blog and included an image of me at dinner just last night. I had my hand wrapped around a friend's arm. Whoever snapped the photo and cropped it made it look as if the scene was a romantic and flirtatious one, although it was completely not intended that way at all. In fact, there was a group of six of us at dinner last night. I was growing accustomed to how quickly the media could alter and over-dramatize situations like this one. They did the same thing to me during my divorce with Ralpho.

"Do you think I was cheating on you? Of course, I wasn't. You should know me better than that."

"That's not the point!" Leon angrily grunted. "I could give a rat's ass if you were fucking half of West Hollywood, so long as it was under lock and key and not in the public. Do you realize what this article could do to my campaign, Dean? Do you not fucking know!?"

Leon was going overboard, to the point where he threw his glass against the wall. The brown liquid content dripped down the wall and all over the hardwood floors. The glass erupted into a million shards across the entire room. The whole scene was cringeworthy. I wanted to duck and hide in a corner, just to escape from the madness of it all.

"You're fucking crazy!" I seethed back at him before I stormed out of the room and upstairs, heading into the walk-in closet of our master bedroom. I began frantically grabbing my belongings, ready to pack them and get the hell out of here. That was the final straw. There was no way I would tolerate such behavior from anyone, even my husband. I'd worked too hard to have to put up with that sort of bullshit. I wanted no parts of it.

Just ten minutes later, as I came out of the closet to toss more of my clothes on the bed, I saw Leon leaning against the doorframe, watching me with intent.

"What are you doing?" he asked.

"What's does it look like?" I replied back to him in a smart-ass tone. "I'm leaving you."

"You're leaving me?" Leon sounded shocked and taken aback.

"Yes. I don't have time to deal with that behavior. It's beneath me."

"You can't be serious. You're threatening to divorce me all because of one stupid argument?"

"Yes, actually. As a matter of fact, I am. No one should have to tolerate violence, Leon. Clearly, you have some anger and control issues you need to sort out. And while you do, I do not want to be a part of it."

Leon then slowly ambled across the room towards me, cautious as ever, as if he were trying to tame a wild beast that could strike him at any moment if he even made the slightest movement that could be deemed as a threat.

"Babe, I'm sorry I lashed out like that. I'm just under so much stress lately. Even the slightest thing can throw off my campaign." His temperament lightened as he said this, reaching out to hold me by the wrist.

I let out a heavy sigh, feeling myself begin to relax a bit more now too by his soft touch. "Do you mean it?"

He gave me a firm nod. "Yes. I'm sorry. I'll never react that way again."

"You promise?" I further questioned, wanting a crystal-clear affirmation.

"I promise," he assuaged, now rubbing his hand up and down my arm in a soothing manner.

I wanted to believe Leon, but part of me truly wondered if he was being genuine in this moment or if he was doing his best to try to stay with me for ulterior motives. Was this just a ruse to avoid me leaving him? Because a divorce during this time would be political suicide for Leon. I tried to dissipate these thoughts away. For now, I would give him the benefit of the doubt and assume his heart was really in the right place with wanting to keep me by his side.

But just a week later, he couldn't keep it together. Another situation arose where his short-fused temper reared its ugly head once again. I had given him another chance, and he completely disregarded my feelings. A week later, I called up my lawyer, who drew up divorce papers to serve him. The media caught wind of it, and his political opponent took advantage of Leon's vulnerability and created a character assassination campaign against him. It turned out that Leon lost the election only by three percentage points in the state. I had warned him about his behavior and he only repeated it, making me look like a complete and utter idiot. Fool me once, shame on you. Fool me twice, shame on me.

Where do Unsold Chanel Purses Go?
By Fashionista Farrah

You would think that the most well-known and popular designer house would sell out all of their seasonal merchandise quickly, but for most of them that doesn't seem to be the case at all. Typically, they find themselves with a huge amount of extra stock at the end of a season. The House of Chanel is no exception. However, when their purses and handbags are left over, they already have methods in place to deal with this unfortunate overstock.

Chanel, like many other upscale designer brands, has been reported to burn leftover merchandise at the end of a season. The company claims that in an attempt to avoid the problem of counterfeiters making millions each year by finding the opportunity to produce fake designer bags off of their real ones, Chanel burns its unsold products so that no part of its brand is left to easily replicate.

Coco Chanel herself is believed to have initiated the first conflagration. In addition, Chanel is also under the mindset of disposing leftover items this way in order to preserve the luxury and exclusivity of the brand. Brands like this often believe that "it's better if only a few can afford it, as opposed to making it available to a mass audience."

Chapter 19

Jackson

Current Day...

So far, so good. I sat criss-cross applesauce on the bed back at Dean's casita, typing on my laptop. I replayed the conversation we had on my recording device, to verify I didn't make any misquotes or misinterpretations as I wrote. Dean and I finished our stroll on the beach and our brunch just an hour ago. He returned to his main home to attend to his business, which gave me most of the afternoon to get to work with further developing the story.

I had to admit, the more I hung out with Dean, the more fond I grew of him. He really wasn't this monster and spoiled gold-digger that the media painted him out to be all these years. There was something kind and genuine about him. That had to count for something, right? The only conundrum I was in was deciding on what additional research to include in my article. I couldn't just completely ignore the testimony and interviews I conducted with those who were not Dean Cargill's biggest fans. Also, there were the documents I uncovered at the law firm in regard to Dean's financial arrangements. Should I mention them in the story or not? I mean, I could easily get away with it. Once I was done here with Dean, I would likely never see him again. So, I wouldn't be fearful of having to run into him in person if I decided to pursue covering some of the scandalous details of the story.

Decisions, decisions.

But before I could even decide on this, a knock at the bedroom door interrupted my train of thought.

"Yes?" I called out to whomever it was.

"It's me, Hector, Mr. Cartwright."

"Coming!" I shouted, as I rose from the bed and walked to the door to open it up.

"Sorry for interrupting whatever it was you were doing, Mr. Cartwright, but I wanted to inform you that Mr. Cargill was just abruptly informed that he has a business meeting to attend to in New York City. He is flying out of here in the next two hours."

Well, this was not part of the plan. I wondered if I would have to go home and then return here tomorrow to finish the interview. What if Dean would be so kind as to allow me to stay here in his casita until his return? That would defeat the hours I would have to waste commuting back and forth from Malibu to the city and then back again.

"Oh, that's unfortunate," I replied to Hector. "Did he mention whether or not he wants me to leave and come back to finish the interview or...?"

Hector let out a light chuckle. "On the contrary, he actually wants you to go with him."

"Say what?" I blurted out, stunned by this revelation.

"Yes. Mr. Cargill requests your presence. We'll meet him at the airport and take the private jet over there."

My eyes bulged in shock. "Private jet!? He really wants me to join him on his private jet?"

"Mhmm. We'll fly out to New York together. While Mr. Cargill attends his meeting, we will head to the hotel and get the suite all set up for the two of you. You can relax, unpack and unwind until he finishes up."

It was as if the decision was already made and planned out with the assumption that I would say yes and join Dean on his spontaneous business trip to New York. But, of course, I knew in the pit of my gut that I would be a damned fool to turn down the chance to ride with Dean Cargill in his private jet. I've never been on one before and I'm certain all of my friends would be crazy jealous at the idea of me having this experience. If only I could somehow sneak a few selfies and photos in there to use as proof to share with them. At any rate, getting this opportunity was just one step closer to me living out my Carrie Bradshaw hopes and dreams. It felt all the more attainable and within reach.

"And how long until we leave for the airport?" I asked Hector.

"As soon as you're ready. But we'll need to leave here within the next half an hour. Will you be good to go by then?"

I nodded. "Yeah. I shouldn't need more time than that."

"Perfect. Just head up towards the main driveway when you are ready. A car will be waiting there. It will just be us two heading to the airport together. Mr. Cargill will meet us there."

"Sounds good," I replied.

"Oh! I almost forgot. We'll only be staying for one night. Furthermore, we'll likely wind up going to a gay bar or club tonight. So, dress accordingly," he added.

I scratched the back of my head in nervousness. I didn't exactly pack for that sort of occasion.

But Hector must have been good at reading people, for he instantly picked up on my facial expressions. "And if you don't have clothes, I can always get you some."

"Oh, you don't have to..."

Hector quickly held his hands up in protest to prevent me from finishing that thought aloud. "Really. It won't be a problem at all. Based on the looks of it, you and Mr. Cargill have pretty similar body-types. I can just pack additional clothes from his closet and..."

"No!" I said in nearly an outburst. "I mean, I don't want to have to wear Dean's clothes." That would be completely frigging mortifying, to say the least.

"There's no worry, Mr. Cartwright. Mr. Cargill rarely wears the same clothes more than once. His wardrobe is constantly changing. I'll make sure to pick out items for you that he has never worn before. It will be something that he doesn't even know he owns." Hector gave me a wink as he said this in an attempt to make me feel more secure.

"Are you sure it will be okay?" I asked with hesitancy although my mind was starting to be swayed.

"I'm certain. It won't be a big deal at all. I swear."

"Okay then. I'll have to take your word for it," I gave in.

"Great. Well, I will go take care of that. I'll leave you to yourself to get packed. See you soon," Hector stated, before turning around to head off.

I let out a deep sigh. My thoughts were going a million miles a minute. I cannot believe all of this was just suddenly sprung on me. I barely had time to process any of it.

I wouldn't need more than five minutes to pack, so I figured I would use this time to call Darren to fill him in on my new itinerary.

The second I called him, he picked up the phone right away. "Hey babe. How is living the dream life by the beachside going?"

I couldn't help but snicker at his comment. "It's going alright. Although I won't be by the beach tonight. I was told I'm going to New York with Dean. He had a sudden meeting pop up there that he can't back down from, apparently."

"Oh wow! When are you leaving?"

"I have to pack and be out front of his home as soon as I get off the phone with you. And I didn't even tell you the crazy part. I get to fly in the private jet with him!"

"Shit babe! Are you for real?" Darren asked in disbelief.

"Yeah. I'm not even sure I'll be able to keep my cool about it."

"Well, try your best," my boyfriend advised. "Oh, and take plenty of pictures. I want to see all of it."

"I will," I promised.

"Well, look at you moving up in the world. Just make sure it doesn't all go to your head. I wouldn't want a complete spoiled and pampered monster walking into the front door when he comes home."

I laughed. "I won't. You should know me better than that." And I hoped it was true. Despite my goals and aspirations in wanting to move up in my career and the world for that matter, I knew better than to let it all change me personally. I vowed I would never be affected by the glitz and the glamor, if I did win the lottery or somehow became miraculously rich and famous. Although, it was highly unlikely that would ever happen. For now, it would remain a pipe dream.

"I know. I'm just giving you a hard time," Darren snickered. "Anyway, I have a virtual meeting I need to hop on in a few minutes. But listen, I miss you so much. When you get home, I want us to plan our next vacation together."

"Definitely! I would love that," I told him, although I already had half of our Italy trip planned for his birthday, unbeknownst to him.

"Great. Well, then shoot me a text or call me later. Love you, babe."

"Love you too," I repeated back before the call ended.

I held a smile on my face the entire time I packed up my clothes and belongings I would need for the day-long trip, realizing how great things were going.

I was being immersed in Dean Cargill's lifestyle. I had an interview that every journalist would kill for. And most importantly, I had the most supportive and adorable boyfriend in the world. What the hell else could I possibly ask for?

In just a matter of minutes, I would be boarding Dean's private jet. Never in my life did I ever think I would say those words. Hector and I sat in the back of the car as we drove to the airport. For the most part, we remained silent. Hector was on his phone the entire time, while I pretty much did the same. However, I wanted to at least break the ice and not seem rude by being disengaged with him.

"What was he like back in the day?" I heard myself ask aloud. Hector just stared at me blankly, as if he was confused by what I was saying. So, I clarified my statement for him. "Dean, I mean. You mentioned you've been friends and you've known him for ten years, right?"

"Yeah. Honestly, Dean hasn't changed all that much since we first met. He was just as fun, lovable, and generous as he is now," Hector replied, which seemed a little vague to me.

"Really? I'm sure you have some wild and crazy stories from back in the day," I further poked.

Hector chuckled and shook his head. "Mr. Cartwright. Are you trying to find a way for me to give you some sordid details on Dean Cargill?"

"Oh, no! Of course not. If you think I have my journalist hat on now and am trying to coax you into giving me more information about Dean for my story, then I apologize. I was just making small talk is all."

"I'm only kidding. I didn't mean to get you worked up," Hector explained. "But yes, Dean is nothing like how he is portrayed by the media. Far from it. He only gets a bad rap because of his situation, as you may well be aware of. Anytime a young person marries into wealth with someone older, they instantly get judged and categorized into a certain role. Now, times that by three, because that's the number of times Dean has been married. It will be difficult for the public to view him in any other light."

"Yeah. I get what you're saying," I admitted.

"Yes. But hopefully your article will shed some light on Dean's *real* story. I'm confident it will have an impact and cause everyone to have a complete one-eighty on how they view him."

"Let's hope," I simply said, although I was unsure if that would be true. Hell, I was unsure if what I wrote would actually even be completely positive. The verdict was still out on whether or not I would mention my discovery at the lawyer's office a few days ago, in seeing the paperwork on Dean's finances or even the testimony of Dean's neighbors in The Bluffs.

"You know, contrary to what you may think or have heard, Dean actually has a very tight circle of friends," Hector said.

There were two things that were a bit surprising to me about this. First, this was the first time Hector dropped his formalities and acted as if he were actually having a candid conversation with me. He finally referred to his boss and friend as *Dean* and not *Mr. Cargill*, like he had been up until this very point. Secondly, I assumed Dean had thousands upon thousands of friends. After all, I always saw blog and social media images of him with tons of different gay men and new faces all the time. It would leave anyone to assume that he had a wide network of friends.

"I had no idea," I confessed.

"Yeah. You know, all four of Dean's assistants, including me, are his closest friends? All of us have known him for years now, long before he became the celebrity that he is today," Hector added.

"Dean didn't mention any of that to me. That's great!" I exclaimed. "And all of you don't mind being his assistants?"

"Of course not. Let me just say that we get paid far more than a majority of the other celebrity assistants out there. Not to mention that Dean pretty much saved all of us. Not that any of us were in need of saving, I mean. But all four of us had average lives and average jobs. He brought us on this journey with him and made our lives all the better for it. Plus, he doesn't treat us like the hired help. Yes, we all have our roles and responsibilities in being his assistants, but he makes us feel like *equals*, instead of beneath him."

This spoke volumes to me. From experience, I've learned that a subordinate's opinion of their boss is the one way you can tell the success of a company and the comradery of the workplace. It also told you how genuine a person was. If you studied how well a celebrity treated their staff and the paparazzi around them, you could easily weed out the rotten apples from the golden ones. And based on what Hector was telling me, I was inclined to believe that Dean Cargill was one of those rare golden apples.

I let my personal feelings on the matter be known to Hector. "That sounds extremely admirable of him. He's been nothing but kind and hospitable towards me this entire time."

"Honestly, I think Dean almost views you as one of us, Jackson, which is extremely rare, because he does not give people his trust so easily. Only us assistants and a few others are part of his inner trust circle. It has been a while since he let anyone else in. But you... it seems like you may be becoming a part of that."

I had no clue what to make of Hector's viewpoint. However, I'd be lying if I said it didn't make me feel warm and giddy on the inside. I only ever dreamed of being able to become friends with Dean Cargill or someone of his caliber. Would that be the end result of all of this? Could there be potential for Dean and I to eventually become friends when all was said and done? I guess only time would tell.

We eventually made it to the airport. The car drove through a series of secured gates and then directly onto the runway.

"We're here," Hector announced as he opened the car door and got out. I proceeded to do the same, following his lead.

"Hey Jackson!" an all too familiar voice called out. Just in front of us stood Dean with a pair of aviators on, giving the younger Tom Cruise a run for his money.

"Hey Dean," I replied back eagerly. "I appreciate you inviting me on this trip."

"Think nothing of it," he coolly stated. "It's the least I can do. Plus, I'd figured this could give us more time to chat and do the interview."

"I couldn't agree with you more," I mentioned.

"Great. Well then, let's get going," Dean declared as he turned around and headed towards the white jet that was on the runway before us.

I spun around to look towards Hector, wondering how to proceed. He must have picked up on my confusion, giving me reassurance. "Go on ahead and follow Dean. I'll see to it your belongings are brought onto the plane safely. Oh! And I forgot to mention you'll loveeee the outfit I picked out for you tonight."

Hector's warmness sent a bright radiant smile to my face, as I replied back to him. "Thanks, Hector. I really appreciate it."

"Anytime, Jackson. Anytime," he said, before heading back towards the vehicle. I decided to listen to his directions and trail behind Dean.

Holy shit! This is really happening! I thought to myself as I climbed the stairs to board the jet. I grinned from ear to ear the closer I got to entering it. I could not believe I would be on this private jet soon!

Me, Jackson Cartwright, traveling first class.

My friends wouldn't believe it, no matter how great of detail I would use to describe what I was currently experiencing.

As we entered, my head circled around the place. The floor was a completely white shade of carpet. There were leather chairs, sofas and brightly glossed mahogany tables. There was even a bar with what looked like a bartender or flight attendant behind it. I couldn't tell which, but still there was an actual person that served drinks.

"Would you mind taking your shoes off, sir?" a woman from the side of me politely asked. Based on her navy-blue blouse and skirt, I assumed she was the actual flight attendant on board. Therefore, I instantly complied, taking them off and handing them to her.

"Thank you." The woman just smiled at me and left our sight.

"Feel free to sit across from me," Dean stated, nodding to the empty spot near him.

Of course, I took that very seat he suggested.

"Please, help yourself to some champagne here." Dean tapped on a bottle of champagne in an ice bucket on our table between us that read *Dom Perignon Oenotheque Brut Millesime*. "Or if you prefer anything stronger, the bartender is right over there." He pointed behind his head towards the bar area.

I decided to make it easy without wanting anyone to have to work extra harder on my account. "I think I'll have some champagne," I told him.

Dean turned his head around to the bartender and raised his index finger in the air. Clearly, he could hear our entire conversation since he wasn't that far away. He came over and popped the bottle open and poured me a glass of champagne in the crystal flute. I thanked him as he handed me the glass and Dean his before returning back behind the bar.

I took a sip and closed my eyes, savoring the taste and allowing my shoulders and body to relax and just melt, taking all of this in.

My blissful thoughts were short-lived and interrupted as I heard the rumble of the engine and turned my head towards the window to see that we were moving across the runway and ready for take-off. I braced myself in the seat and closed my eyes, not knowing how to anticipate the lift off of the ground. My eyelids creeped open just to get a small glimpse of us moving towards a higher altitude.

Dean had a look of confusion displayed across his face. "Have you never been on an airplane before?"

I nodded and also shook my head in nervousness. "Yes. But I've never been on a private jet."

He continued to watch my reaction with amusement. "Hmmm. Cute."

Once we were high enough in the air and the turbulence lessened, I finally became more at ease and sat back up in my chair. It actually wasn't as bad as I had initially thought. I peered out the window once again to get a glimpse at the buildings beneath us that were now microscopic specs.

As soon as Dean witnessed that my anxiety was no longer apparent, he proceeded into conversation. "When we land, you will be taken directly to the hotel. I'll meet up with you there later, after I attend my meeting."

I felt like inquiring about the sort of meeting Dean would be attending to, but realized it was probably in my best interest to not pry on such matters. Instead, I just politely smiled and nodded. "Sounds like a plan."

"Great. And I shouldn't be too long. Feel free to unpack in your bedroom and then have dinner at the hotel restaurant if you'd like. Expenses are all on me," he shared. "I hope you don't mind that we'll be sharing a suite."

Sharing a suite!? I was under the assumption that we would stay in two separate rooms. Now that I was putting two and two together, it sounded like we would share a nice living space but at least we would have separate bedrooms.

"I don't mind at all," I stated with ease.

"Awesome. Once I get back, I'll probably want to get a shower and then we can change and head to the club."

Our discussion continued with him filling me in with more of the details pertaining to this short trip. When he finished giving me all of the information in regards to our schedule, we sat in silence for a brief moment, imbibing on our champagne.

"You know, Jackson, I have to admit, I am pretty surprised at how quickly things turned around for us since our first encounter. Maybe I misread the situation from the very beginning. You seem like a really great guy, someone I can *really* trust."

"Of course, Dean. You can completely trust me." I wasn't sure if this was the authentic me talking or the journalist version of me speaking. I felt like the lines were blurred and I was in the middle of the gray area between the two.

"For our next portion of the interview, do you mind not recording our conversation?" Dean requested.

Now things were getting spicy. I knew what that was code for. It meant that he would be telling me some private matters or affairs that he felt uncomfortable with sharing while being recorded. This had to be something scandalous or something shocking.

"Sure. Whatever you want," I replied, hoping to alleviate any worry he may have had. "You can trust me with anything. I swear."

"That's good to hear," he said. "Because I now feel more comfortable to talk to you about my money and financial arrangements. I know you have tons of questions about this subject already, so I might as well enlighten you."

This was finally it. I could sense that the missing puzzle pieces in my head would finally get filled and fitted into their proper positions.

Chapter 20

Dean

Two Years Ago...

The divorce with Leon Merck was final. Our lawyers agreed on a settlement per our requests and now I could move on with my life. Never again would I date a politician for as long as I lived. I was never cut out for that commitment and kind of lifestyle. Lesson learned.

But, now that I was divorced, I was sitting on a ton of money that I had no idea what to do with. It was time that I sought out financial advisors and investors who I could trust to take care of it all for me. These were the mundane things that rich people did, right? They delegated to others to complete the boring and tedious work that they didn't want to waste time doing, which included keeping track of finances.

Now, I was back in Los Angeles, living there full time, and out to lunch with Joseph Feinberg, a renowned financial advisor. We dined at La Scala, one of my favorite restaurants in Beverly Hills. The old school Hollywood vibes it once possessed still felt like it lingered in the atmosphere. There's a reason images of Natalie Wood, Warren Beatty, Judy Garland, Robert Wagner and Barbara Rush adorned the front entrance.

I had the famous La Scala Chopped Salad while Joseph was taking a bite of his Capaellini Primavera, which consisted of peas, mush-rooms, zucchini, carrots, broccoli, garlic and basil, all drenched in their house-made tomato sauce.

Once we finished our meals and caught up with one another, the waiter came to claim our cleared plates. Now that the only things between us were our wine and cocktails, it was time to get down to business.

"So, is everything in order?" I vaguely asked Joseph, not wanting to be too forthcoming, especially with the waiter walking by us.

Joseph waited until the waiter was at the opposite end of the restaurant before responding to me. "Yes. All is well. I told you, you have nothing to worry about."

"Good," I replied back to him. "Because I have an additional request."

He raised his brow at me. "Go on..."

"I want you to divvy up the millions overseas. I want at least five accounts, all of them in different countries," I explained.

"But Mr. Cargill, moving it all at once and opening these accounts, will seem very suspicious. It will surely raise red flags with the I.R.S."

I shook my head. "I didn't say it all had to be moved over at once. Do it sporadically. Every four months should do the trick. I doubt it will garner any unwanted attention."

"I'm not so sure that's a very good idea, sir. I'd recommend no more than opening two accounts a year, especially if you're going to be depositing millions into each of them," Joseph further advised.

"It has to be every four months, Joseph. My income and profits are growing at an extravagant rate. You should know this. I'd prefer not to have over five million dollars at one time in the States," I stated. "It will only lead to more people lurking and asking questions that I'm not willing to answer."

He let out a heavy sigh, annoyed as ever. "If it must be done, then so be it. I will say, this does come with great risk. Just be warned."

"I'm well aware of the risks," I informed him. "But it's an even greater risk if all of it is traceable and documented here within the United States. So, which is the lesser of two evils?"

"The offshore accounts are," he objectively commented.

"Exactly. Then it's settled. Let's take care of it right way."

"I'll start the paperwork first thing tomorrow," Joseph told me.

"Good."

"But during this time, until the accounts have been active for at least a year, I don't recommend touching any one of them," he suggested.

"No worries, there. The only time I would even think of making that large of a withdrawal is if I was investing in something major, like a huge mansion in the Hills or even an upscale beach house in Malibu," I thought aloud. "But I wouldn't think of making that great of a purchase until later down the line. Likely, years from now."

Chapter 21

Jackson

Current Day...

It was now a little after 6:00pm as we landed in New York. As soon as the jet came to an abrupt halt, it seemed like everyone was in a rush to get off. I kept up and followed behind the group.

As we descended the stairs and onto the runway, Dean shifted to face me. "Hopefully, this meeting is short and sweet as I expect it will be," he stated. "Feel free to eat dinner without me, but when I get back to the hotel, the plan is to go out on the town. What do you say?"

I simply smiled and nodded to him. "That sounds great," I eagerly replied.

"Alright. And just ask Hector if you need anything in the mean-time, within reason, that is." Dean winked playfully at me as he said this.

I couldn't help but shrug it off.

"You all set to go, Jackson?" Hector came up from behind me, asking, giving me a tap on the shoulder with the cup of his hand.

"I am. Let's hit the road."

Hector led us into our private car that would take us to whatever hotel we were staying at. As the driver took off, I stared out the window at all the mesmerizing lights lit by the skyscrapers and tall buildings that were cramped together, just as I would anticipate when navigating through the concrete jungle metropolis that was New York.

This had been at least my tenth time in New York City. Being a journalist, I'd had my fair share of stories I needed to cover here, which made me have to take work excursions back and forth from coast to coast. At least my credit card and flight points were stacking up as a result. It allowed Darren and me to get free vacations and round-trip flights with whatever destination we desired, barely having to put any of our own money down. So, that was a major perk, although it could sometimes prove to be annoying, especially when I had to come to New York for just a day or two. Then it felt like a complete waste of time. But overtime, I've learned to accept the motto of *when the job calls*. I loved my career and what I did, so that was what was most important in the end, right?

But this wasn't even comparable to any of my previous trips to New York. That was because I was here on Dean Cargill's budget and his coattails for that matter. I had a feeling I would view the experience in a whole different light compared to my normal visits.

Although I was distracted for a while as we drove through what seemed like never-ending traffic, I was finally able to relax and have some time to process all that Dean had informed me of when we were on the private jet. It was extremely alarming, to say the least. Dean must have had the utmost trust in me. Why else would he disclose that he had millions of dollars in accounts overseas? I could easily take this information and run for the hills with it. He had to have known that. But for some reason, he still felt brave enough to speak to me about his private affairs.

Knowing of his offshore accounts answered some of my questions. But there was still so much that was left unknown. How was he making these millions at such a quick rate? Was he big into the whole bitcoin thing? Did he make wise investments? Perhaps he was black-mailing his ex-husbands and was accepting hush money from them over something crazy. My mind was racing with ideas.

It only made me more curious to want to talk to Dean as soon as possible again. Who knows what other things he was hiding? No matter what, I was beyond determined to get to the bottom of it and prepared for whatever it may be.

As we drove up to the hotel, my mouth dropped once I realized where we were at. As Hector exited the vehicle, I found myself still, unable to move from my seat by how awestruck I was. The concave shape of the building was one I immediately recognized.

The Mandarin Oriental Hotel.

I couldn't believe we were staying *here,* of all places. But how quickly I already forgot that I was here with Dean Cargill, who only stayed at luxury places. So, of course, we would only stay in a place that probably cost over $5,000 a night.

"You okay, Jackson?" Hector called out, bringing me back down to planet Earth.

"Yeah. Sorry. I'm coming."

I emerged from the car and strode behind Hector into the hotel. I stood by his side as we checked in and he retrieved the keycards from one of the front hotel managers.

"We're staying in one of the top floor suites, by the way," he spoke to me as we ambled around the circular hotel lobby, that was decorated with a towering flamingo ice sculpture at the very center of it. "I hope you don't have a fear of heights or anything like that?"

I shook my head.

"Good," he responded. "Because this is Dean's favorite suite when we come to New York. They actually call it *Suite 5000* here. That's how spectacular it is, that it gets its own name."

I was beyond eager to see it. And we wasted no time in getting on the elevator and heading up to the fiftieth floor. We entered the door marked *5000.*

As soon as I stepped foot in the room, I felt like I walked into some magical place that was no longer a reality. "Are you shitting me?" I mumbled to myself under my breath.

Never in my life had I stayed or even seen such an opulent hotel suite. It was over three-thousand square feet. The entire place was surrounded by glass windows that overlooked all three highlightable locations that you would want to see from this angle in New York City. On one side, you were hovering over Central Park. At a different spot, you were able to see the Hudson River. And the greatest view of all was the bright Manhattan skyline.

How lucky was I to be able to stay in such a lavish place? After I grew tired of admiring all of the views the room had to offer, I then began to recognize the fine details of the interior of the suite.

There were shimmering silver and grey hues at every which turn. The dining room had a modern, dark rectangular table with eight velvety blue chairs surrounding it. Swarovski crystals drizzled down the backdrop on the wall next to the dining table, making it seem as though there was a torrential downpour of diamonds from the ceiling to the floor. Not only was there a main living room area with the plushest of sofas and chairs, but there was also a separate media room with a humongous flat screen television built into the wall. The entire chef's kitchen was pure white marble and there was even a bar area. My eyes were carrying me in so many different directions to admire it all at once. It was hard for me to pinpoint just one thing to focus on.

And that was only half of the major features. There was a total of three different bedrooms, each with its own swanky private bathroom. After viewing all three bedrooms, it was clear which one would be occupied by Dean. Obviously, it would be the one that was most spacious, with the largest master bathroom. That was a given. But I was surprised that Hector pointed out that I would get the next largest room, which also contained a king-sized bed just as Dean's room had. The only major difference was that my bedroom had a few, less square feet with a smaller on-suite bathroom, but it was nothing to complain about. That was for certain.

"Are you sure I can stay in this room?" I questioned.

"Yes. I will take the other one. And there is nothing you can say or do that will make me change my mind," Hector authoritatively told me, but with a hint of kindness behind his words.

"Now, why don't you head on downstairs and get something to eat? One of the attendants will bring your luggage up soon and I will unpack it all for you... unless there is something deeply personal I should be aware of that's in your suitcase that you don't want me touching?"

Oh God!

I was now grateful that I did not bring any sexual paraphernalia with me to sustain my appetite while I was absent from Darren for so long. Not that we played in the freaky department all that much, but we've had our moments of *toying* with one another. And that's not to say we haven't indulged in playing by ourselves with some sexual items here and there. Thankfully, I did not bring any of those objects or gadgets with me for this trip. That would have been completely embarrassing if Hector were to discover that.

"No. Nothing important," I commented back to him. "And thank you for offering to unpack everything."

"No problem. Now run along and get your stomach full. I have a feeling you're going to need something to fill you up, especially if you're going to the Industry Bar with Dean later. The man can party..."

I couldn't help but chuckle at Hector's playfulness. It was much better carrying a conversation with him under this sort of circumstance as opposed to the formalities he was giving me earlier this morning and previously.

"So I've heard," I truthfully replied. "But again, thank you for all of this."

"Don't thank me. Thank, Dean," Hector reminded me. "Oh. And remember to just tell the waiter or waitress to charge the bill to Suite 5000. If they raise any questions or don't believe you, just ask for the manager. They should know you're staying with us."

"Got it!" I enthusiastically said, before heading towards the front door. "I won't be long," I added before heading out of the suite and down to the hotel dining area, which was known as the *MO Lounge*.

The place was beyond upscale. It would be a rarity to ever find Darren or myself here, but I pictured Dean coming on the regular. I sat at a lonely table by the window that overlooked Central Park.

"Can I start you off with something to drink, sir?" the waitress stated, barely giving me a moment to even take my seat and scan the menu.

"Ummmm. Can I have a sparking water and..." I paused briefly to give myself a moment to spot something to the alcoholic beverage portion of the menu that piqued my interest. "Let's go with a *MO' Espresso Martini*."

Based on what Hector mentioned to me earlier, it sounded like tonight was going to be a long one at the Industry Bar with Dean. So, getting some caffeine in me wasn't completely the worst of ideas at this moment. Plus, this particular espresso martini had hazelnut, vanilla, chocolate bitters, and arrack. I just had to taste that combination.

"Coming right up," she stated, before walking over towards the bar area.

I now had the time to really browse over the menu. There were so many expensive dinner options, all of which sounded mouth-watering. It was difficult to just land on one. Not only this, but there were meals where it was recommended to add two-hundred dollars' worth of various Ossetra caviar to. It reminded me of being with Editor-in-Chief, Edgar Baxter, of Chatterbox News over a week ago at Petrossian in West Hollywood, where we had quite the assortment of caviar. But I would not dare spend that much money on my own, especially if Dean was flipping the bill. So, when the waitress came back around to hand me my drink and ask for my dinner order, I ultimately decided on the salmon croque monsieur.

As I sipped on my espresso martini, I let out a deep exhale as I watched people move through Central Park. Some were joggers, while others were taking a leisurely stroll. It was still hard for me to believe that this was where I was, sitting in a lounge in the Mandarin Oriental, sipping on a cocktail, preparing to go out to a gay nightclub in New York with *the* Dean Cargill. It only made me further realize that my life could be so much closer to this lifestyle. I could get used to it so easily. I desperately wanted to, or at least come close to it. It was time for me to sit back and relax with the finer things around me after working so hard in my career field. I wanted it so badly; I could now practically taste it.

As if on cue, my Catskills smoked salmon with parsley butter and gruyere came out. I snapped a few pictures of the meal and some selfies to send to Darren and to post on my Instagram feed before finally being able to appreciate the food. It was so delicious; I had to really dig deep to maintain my etiquette in a place like this and not scoff the whole meal down in merely a few bites, devouring the entire dinner plate. It was that damn good.

When I was nearly finished, I felt my phone buzz and saw that it was an incoming text message from Dean, telling me that he would be back at the hotel soon.

Not wanting to ever keep him waiting, I quickly tracked down the waitress and told her to charge Suite 5000 before I grabbed the check, tipped her generously (on Dean's dime, of course) before heading back up to the suite in haste.

Luckily, when I entered the suite, I just saw Hector standing by the bar area, likely preparing a cocktail for Dean.

"Ah! Perfect timing!" Hector said, when he noticed me come in. "Dean should be up any minute. Here…" He reached to hand me a clear liquid in a glass full of ice with what looked like petals of a purple orchid floating on top of it.

"It looks so refreshing!" I exclaimed.

"Try it. It's a specialty of mine."

I did as Hector recommended and tossed my head back with the drink, tasting bits of lavender, gin, tonic, among other slight hints of something else that was floral and fruity. It was really was just as refreshing as I had anticipated.

"It's delicious," I said, which raised a smile on his lips.

No sooner than I took another sip of the drink, I abruptly turned around, hearing the entrance door of the suite open. It was Dean in a black business suit with a white undershirt. Now how he managed to change into that and look so damn dapper between leaving the airport and arriving at his meeting, I'll never know. The man must have seriously been a magician or one of those quick-change acts in Las Vegas.

"I see you all have started without me," he jokingly remarked, seeing the cocktail in my hand.

My face turned red, slightly ashamed that I had been called out by him, of all people.

"I couldn't resist showing off my bartending skills to Jackson,"

Hector chimed in, saving the day by covering for me.

"He does make a pretty stiff drink, Jackson. You better keep an eye on what he gives you. You might wind up on the floor in a matter of minutes," Dean informed me.

Although, I was unsure of the context behind what he said, I hoped he meant Hector was just pouring me a strong drink and not adding other substances into its mix. I highly doubted he would do anything like that. So, I decided to take the whole thing as a joke and tame my imagination from running wild with worry and anxiety over that being a possibility.

"I'll keep note of that," I wittily responded. "But I doubt I'll have more than two drinks if we're heading to the Industry Bar in a little while."

"Oh good! So, Hector filled you in on our itinerary?" Dean asked.

I simply nodded.

"Perfect. I'm going to get changed. Let's say we take about a half an hour to get ready before we head out?"

"Sounds like a plan to me," I said.

"You'll have a blast. I never have a bad time at the Industry Bar. Well, actually, I never have a bad time no matter what bar I go to. The place could be a dumpy hole in the wall. It's not the setting that makes the best times; It's your mindset and the people you bring."

"I couldn't agree more," I concurred.

Dean traipsed across the suite and into his master bedroom, shutting the door behind him. It left Hector and me to ourselves, back in the spacious living area.

"I laid out your clothes for tonight on the chaise in your room," Hector informed me.

"Thank you. I better go ahead and change too," I replied, before making my way to my own room to get ready.

I could already feel my heart racing, ready to practically beat right out of my chest. I was that ecstatic about what tonight would bring. I've seen tons of photos over the years of Dean Cargill at bars and clubs popping champagne bottles, while dancing and having the best time with some of his friends, or rather acquaintances.

It was hard to wrap my head around the idea that I would get the chance to be one of those guys in those photographs with him. I only ever dreamed and pictured being in their shoes, spending what seemed like thousands of dollars in a single night, partying and living the life.

I glanced down at the new clothes Hector had donated to me, which seemed far more expensive than anything that was in my current wardrobe at home. Being able to see the designer shirt, pants, and shoes laid out made me continue with the thought that not only was tonight becoming all the more real, but my future, which would hopefully contain more nights like these, was as well.

Chapter 22

Jackson

Current Day...

I stared at myself in the bathroom mirror, not fully able to recognize this person dressed in a tight, pearl-colored, Givenchy shirt, with a pair of faded denim Dior jeans, that snuggly fit me, hugging my glutes and leg muscles in all the right ways. On top of all this, Hector also provided me with a pair of pure white, brushed leather sneakers with the signature, triangular Prada logo on the outside of each shoe.

I slicked my hair and even put lotions and other free products I found in the room on my face and under my eyes, before snapping a selfie of myself to send to Darren. Within seconds of me sending the message, I was receiving an incoming call from him, which I answered on speaker as I continued getting ready.

"Who are you and what have you done with my fiancé, Jackson? Do I need to call the police?" Darren instantly addressed me with.

I busted out in laughter at his over-the-top theatrics. "Haha. Well, I hope you at least like it."

"Of course! I mean, I always think you're sexy, but in that outfit... whew!"

My face immediately turned red, overshadowing the cream I applied to my face. "Apparently, there were some clothes that Dean owned that his assistant lent to me. He'd never wore them before. So, no harm done," I explained.

"Makes sense. But I'm guessing you and him are going out somewhere tonight?"

"Yeah. We're hitting up the Industry Bar. It's a popular gay nightclub here in New York."

"Oh?" Darren sounded a little taken aback. "Well, just make sure to keep your hands to yourself and make sure other people keep theirs where they belong, as well."

"You don't have to tell me twice, babe," I affirmed.

"Well, have a good time and don't get too crazy."

"I won't. I miss you..."

"I miss you too. Any update on when you think you'll be coming home?"

"As soon as I finish this story," I reminded him, although I had no definitive timeline on when that would happen. "I hope it doesn't take any more than two or three more days."

"Really?" Darren said in a surprised tone. "I was expecting longer. What makes you think that soon?"

"Just the way Dean has been acting towards me. He's opening up a lot more. I can tell he's getting more and more comfortable in my presence, to the point where he's now started sharing really private information with me."

"Like what?" he asked, sounding intrigued as hell.

"I can't say... or at least not now. I'm not sure how thin these hotel walls are."

"Well, at any rate, I'm actually going to dinner with the guys soon. I'll tell them you say *hey*."

"Thanks. I appreciate that," I genuinely stated.

"Anyway, I'll let you get back to your gig. Love you."

"I love you too," I replied.

We exchanged a few more sentiments before I ended the call.

I returned to staring at myself in the mirror, probably longer than I should have. The stakes seemed a lot higher for tonight than any other time I've spent with Dean. We would both be hanging out together in a very public venue without the need for formalities. Spending time at a gay nightclub or party was definitely Dean being in his element. Now, I just wanted to impress him more than ever in this kind of setting, hoping he would see that I could easily hang and keep up with him. The last thing I needed was to somehow bore him to death.

I felt as though I had a stronger role to play tonight than just being the journalist from Chatterbox News that was assigned to interview him. Part of me was now second-guessing myself and my feelings. Was it important for me to make a good impression on Dean this evening to get in his better graces so that he'd be forthcoming with me during more of our conversations or was my sub-conscience secretly hoping that Dean actually liked me as a potential real friend? Was I letting my desire to be a part of his world influence my decisions more so than my job with getting this cover story done? The lines between the two were starting to blur, but either way, the goals for both were still the same: impress the hell out of Dean Cargill.

I soon emerged from my bedroom towards the bar area where Hector remained since I last saw him. I wondered if he even moved from that same spot where Dean and I left him nearly thirty minutes ago.

"So, do they all fit?" Hector asked, referring to the clothes he gave me.

I held a smirk on my face, to let him know my thoughts about it. "Yeah. They couldn't fit any better, actually."

"I knew they would. And you look great in them, by the way."

"Thanks," I said, spinning around in a cute twirl for him, causing us both to giggle.

"Want another drink before the two of you hit the road?"

"The two of us?" I repeated back to him, seeming slightly confused. "You won't be joining Dean and me?"

Hector shook his head. "No. I have other matters I need to attend to, but you two will have a blast, with or without me. No worries there. Anyway, how about that drink?"

I nodded. "Sure. Hit me with whatever you'd like."

My vagueness in cocktail choice caused him to reveal an impish grin. "Careful what you wish for."

"I trust you," I replied.

As Hector went to town concocting up my drink, I watched over him carefully as he poured crushed ice into a glass, followed by pear-flavored vodka, a club and lime soda, plus some bottle with a blue liquid in it. He mixed the contents into a glass, before making a second one, which I assumed was for Dean.

Examining the drink, I was impressed by how magnificently blue the beverage was, appearing as clear and sapphirine as the South Pacific waters.

"And what do you call this?" I inquired, taking a heavy gulp from the glass.

"A Dick Sucker," Hector bluntly stated.

I nearly choked and spit out my drink all at once, not expecting him to say something so... crude.

"A whatta?" I asked, wondering if I heard him correctly.

Hector chuckled at my reaction. "It's literally called a Dick Sucker," he repeated.

"I've never even heard of that."

He merely shrugged. "You learn something new every day."

"Apparently so," I muttered just as I felt a warm hand on my back. It caught me off-guard at first, but then I instantly relaxed when I saw

Dean standing beside me.

"Wow. You clean up nicely," he said, removing his hand from my back.

"Thanks. And you, yourself, look good as always," I complimented in return to him, although I hid the annoyance I felt for how naturally hot he always was, no matter what time of day. Even if Dean spent weeks stuck in a mineshaft or cave, I bet he would come out of it somehow looking smoldering and sexy as ever.

Hector handed Dean his glass of the *Dick Sucker*, which Dean gulped down rather swiftly. I had to take several quick sips just to keep up with him. The three of us talked and joked around for the next ten minutes as we finished our drinks.

Dean checked the time on his phone before placing his now empty glass back down on the bar counter. "I think we should get going soon," he suggested.

I hurried down my drink before placing my glass beside his. "I'm ready whenever you are."

"Alright. Let's hit the road then," Dean remarked.

Soon, we left the suite and made our way down to the main lobby. As we exited the hotel, I saw a limousine sitting right at the main entrance. The chauffeur had the door held open, addressing us. "Welcome, Mr. Cargill and Mr. Cartwright."

Well, this was certainly a surprise. I was anticipating a black SUV, just like the few I had driven in with Dean since my stay with him, but I gladly welcomed this upgrade.

"Thank you," Dean politely replied back to the driver, before climbing into the limo. I trailed right behind him, choosing to sit directly across from him. The interior was bright with neon lighting. The colors seamlessly shifted from one to the next, every five seconds. There were crystal-glass decanters of various shapes and sizes, with tons of liquor bottles crammed together on a stand beside us.

"One for the road?" Dean asked with a wily smirk on his face.

"Why not?" I said, before he made us a drink.

We clinked them together before taking a sip. I could already feel a buzz coming on from how quickly the drinks were coming. I wondered how I could possibly make it through the night with a sound mind, but I would make a conscious effort to do so.

In between finishing the drink, Dean pressured me into taking two shots of tequila, which I could not refuse. Eventually, we came to a stop and once the door opened, I felt relieved to get some fresh air, hoping sobriety would somehow strike me in the face, but it didn't.

Dean put his arm around me and we made our way past the bouncer and right into the bar. The place was dimly lit, with mostly hues of pink and red. We walked towards a seated area that was blocked by a scarlet, velvety rope attached to multiple gold stanchions. One of the nightclub workers stood by the rope and unclipped it to let Dean and I in to what I assumed was a reserved section just for the two of us. I sat on one of the leather sofas that was present, while Dean sat in an identical one directly across from me. A table with buckets filled with three different champagne bottles and flutes separated us.

Dean wasted no time in popping one of the bottles, allowing the pressure of the foam to overflow onto the floor and table before he could pour it into our glasses. Luckily, I spotted bottles of water at the end of the table, which I immediately grabbed and chugged, before taking a sip of the champagne Dean had poured me.

"Thanks for coming out with me tonight!" he practically shouted, so that his voice could be heard over the loudspeaker that played a popular remix to a current top pop song.

"Thanks for having me!" I enthusiastically declared back at him.

"Wanna dance?" he asked me.

Already!? We just sat down, for crying out loud.

However, I couldn't let my true thoughts be known to him. So, I stood up and just smiled down at him. "Sure. Let's go."

Dean was quick to rise from his seat and grab me by the hand, leading me through the crowd and past the bar, towards the dance floor just as the DJ started playing a club remix to Beyoncé's CUFF IT.

The floor was jampacked. You could barely lift your elbow without hitting the person next to you. Dean and I stood face-to-face and were practically forced up on each other as we began to sway and dance, getting lost in the song, throwing our hands and glasses of champagne in the air.

> *We're gonna fuck up the night, black lights*
> *Spaceships fly (spaceships fly)*
> *Yeah, unapologetic, when we fuck up the night*
> *Fuck up the night*
> *We getting fucked up tonight*
> *We're gonna fuck up the night*

As we danced through two more songs, a tap by a stranger on Dean's shoulder eventually ruined our transcend to the dance club clouds.

"Hey! Are you Dean Cargill!?" a cute guy loudly asked, so that we could hear him over the music.

Dean nodded with a bright ivory smile. "Yeah."

"Oh, my god! I knew it!" The handsome stranger turned around to tell one of his friends, before glancing back at us. "I just have to say, I am a huge fan! I absolutely loved you in *Classic Nick*. You were amazing!"

Classic Nick was a gay rom-com that came out about a year ago. It was Dean's big and one-and-only break into acting thus far. He starred as Nick, a charming, gay jock who had commitment issues. It was Nick's high school friend, Spencer, who was a nerdy geek that wound up falling for Nick, although Nick always found a way to ruin things between the two throughout the movie because of his evasive nature in being tied down. Eventually, they wound up falling for each other. The End.

The movie was actually directed by Roger Friedman. He and Dean met on the set of the film, which is where they fell in love and got married. Roger thereby became Dean's third and final husband... for now, that is.

"Awww. That's really sweet. Thank you," Dean said to this fan of his, before turning to face me. "We were actually about to sit back down, right Jackson?"

All I could do was nod.

"Take care!" Dean replied to the guy, before dragging me back to our private seating arrangement in the Industry Bar on the leather couches. This time, though, we sat side by side on the same sofa.

"I take it that you always get ambushed when you're at a gay bar?" I questioned.

Dean was already pouring us more drinks, as he replied. "Give or take, but a majority of the time, yes."

"Do you ever get tired of it?"

"Not really," he said, handing me off a glass of more champs. "I'm constantly reflecting on where I came from, to where I am now, you know? I have to remind myself of that and be grateful for this opportunity. That's why I'm always appreciative of the paparazzi and followers. I revel in the attention they give me."

I could tell Dean was being honest with me. After all, even I was aware of how nice Dean treated his staff and fans in public. So, what he was telling me now in this moment was aligning with what I've heard before. As for whether or not Dean was being truthful about everything else he was telling me up until this point in time... the verdict was still out on that.

"Well, that's really admirable of you," I lauded. "Most other celebrities can't stand the constant microscope they are under."

Dean snickered at my comment. "Well, I'm not most other celebrities, now am I?"

"No, I guess you're not."

I could tell Dean was slightly drunk already. Truth be told, I was as well, although I was still completely coherent with my thoughts and all that I was saying and thinking. I had to press on now that *Classic Nick* was just brought up by the guy on the dance floor. It was the perfect transition to get Dean to talk to me about his most recent ex-husband, Roger Friedman.

"You know, I think *Classic Nick* was a great movie, too. And I'm not just saying that because I'm here in front of you now. I've actually seen it three times already."

"Really?" Dean sounded shocked by what I revealed.

"Yeah. I mean, you and Jack Dayton had great chemistry in it. It was just an overall feel-good movie."

"Thanks, Jackson. That does mean a lot coming from you."

"Anytime. But of course, the real chemistry was happening behind the cameras, right?"

"Something like that," Dean replied before taking another sip of his champagne.

He was extremely vague in his response, but I needed to press him further on the subject. Now was the perfect time to get him to talk about his ex, honestly. Hopefully, the liquid courage that was flowing through his veins was enough to get some deep confessions out of him.

"I thought you and Roger were an amazing match, by the way, at least from the pictures I've seen of you two online and in various magazines. You always looked so happy together. Anyone who viewed a photo of the both of you could feel the connection that existed between you and him."

This comment managed to elicit a warm smile from Dean. "Yeah. Roger was the real deal. Everything about him was perfect. We loved each other so much, it was nearly sickening."

It was odd to hear Dean speak about one of his ex-husbands in such a positive way. On the former occasions where he discussed Ralpho Mercado and Leon Merck, he spoke about them with such animosity and disdain, but now, this was not the case at all.

Based on the glimmer in Dean's eyes, he seemed almost nostalgic with regret when referring to Roger. It was something I wasn't quite expecting, but nevertheless, it was a pleasant surprise to see Dean so wistful.

"So then, what happened between the two of you?" I inquired. "If things were as perfect as you say, there should have never even been a divorce, right?"

From past news, I gathered the gist of why Roger and Dean wound up divorced, which was due to *irreconcilable differences*, as the media so broadly put it. Not much was said on the matter, and both parties were always so private about their separation. But now, I would finally get to hear one of their sides of the story as to what happened. I sat on pins and needles, studying Dean closely, hanging on every word he was about to hopefully tell me.

"That's how my love life has always been, Jackson. You should know that by now. I think things are perfect one minute, and then they just blow up in my face when I least expect it. Maybe it's just me being delusional when I'm in a relationship, or perhaps I'm just ignoring all the downhill warning signs? But my marriage to Roger was no different from the rest."

Chapter 23

Dean

One Year Ago...

Being back in Los Angeles permanently had felt like a huge weight had been lifted from my shoulders. This was the place where I belonged. There was something about being in the frequent cold weather of Wisconsin, while having to deal with those aristocratic politician types day in and day out, that put a complete damper on my spirit and motivation. As I read my lines aloud, I would sneak a glance over at Roger out of the corner of my eyes. He was studying me intently, except there was a twinkle in his eyes as he did so. I could have sworn he was staring at me longingly, and I completely welcomed it.

I now had so much more free time on my hands. Recently, I signed a contract to work as a creative director for Cartier, but that enough left an unsatisfied feeling in my mind, body and soul. There was so much more I wanted to do, and it wasn't until recently that the idea of being an actor became an interest.

There were so many locations in Los Angeles that offered acting classes. It was pretty easy for me to find a prestigious school that would enroll me, with my promised additional monetary donations and all that I could afford to provide them with.

And I chose to believe that my acting coaches and instructors were true in their statements, saying that I had promising talent and could easily turn my acting skills into a successful career. I was that good.

They didn't just tell everyone that, right? At least, I was hoping they didn't.

At any rate, once I felt comfortable enough and really thought I was ready for some big roles, I sought out an agent that could try and land me some of these gigs I only dreamed of. Horace Winchester was a renowned agent who launched so many starting careers of some of the biggest names in Hollywood today. The man stood at a confident five-foot-five, and apparently the word *confident* was quite the understatement based on the stories I've heard about him. He was half Italian and half Irish, with a raspy voice resembling Danny DeVito, although it was even raspier, given the years of cigar and cigarette smoking he had under his belt.

Luckily, one of my celebrity friends was a client of his, so they were able to get me an interview with Horace. Before we even finished our initial meeting, he was already offering me a glass of scotch and extending his small Tyrannosaurus Rex arms across his oak table to give me a handshake, along with a contract that one of his secretaries was striking up and printing out.

"I promise you Dean, with your looks, talent and that audition and casting video you just showed me, I can guarantee I will find you a huge role in just a matter of weeks!" Horace exclaimed with great conviction.

We clinked our glasses together once I sent an electronic copy of the contract over to my lawyers to read the terms and conditions before they gave me the okay to sign away. Horace Winchester was officially my acting agent, and I was more than thrilled at the possibilities that would be coming out of this partnership between the two of us.

And I wouldn't have to wait very long until I got a break. Horace called me just two weeks later with a promising lead on a role under a newly famous director named Roger Friedman. He was the equivalent of a Ryan Murphy, recently taking a step into the movie directing pond, from the television and sitcom world, which he was famous for. Apparently, three Emmy Awards and two Golden Globe Awards in television weren't enough for him. He wanted to take his shot at the Oscars in the Hollywood film industry, which was why he was suddenly jumping ship into directing movies now.

"You are being offered the role, Dean!" Horace shouted over the phone to me. "They aren't interested in casting calls or any further auditions. Just say *yes,* and the part is yours."

"It sounds like an amazing opportunity. Tell me about the role," I requested.

"It's going to be a gay romantic-comedy called *Classic Nick.* You, Dean, will be playing the lead role of Nick. What could be better than that!?"

I was over the moon, but wanted so many more details. I had to have them.

"What sort of character is this Nick?" I further asked Horace.

"From what I gather, he is a high school jock who sort of has a tumultuous relationship with his counterpart, a gay nerd named Spencer. The two establish a relationship well into their college years, only Nick has commitment issues and finds a way to pull away from Spencer, the closer he gets to him. Hence the title of the film, *Classic Nick.*"

"So, it sounds like I'm a villain at first? Some might even compare me to a bully?" I asked to clarify for more understanding.

"Not to that extent. You're not a bully, per se. You just don't see eye to eye with the other main character. It's an enemies to lovers type of thing."

"Got it. I feel like portraying a bully would not be the sort of thing to help my image," I honestly told him.

"Of course. I would never seek out a part that would cast you in that sort of role. But I'm telling you, working with Roger Friedman in a starring role is something you do not want to turn down, Dean. So, what do you say?"

"I'll take it!" I eagerly blurted out. "When do I start?"

"Let me sort out the salary and financial arrangements, and then I'll send you a formalized contract in the next couple of days. Also, expect a phone call from Roger Friedman in the very near future. He'll want to be the one to officially offer you the role."

"I just can't..." I dramatically spoke to Jack Dayton, a famous, young gay actor, who was playing the role of Spencer, the geek who would inevitably fall for Nick. The two of us stood behind the bleachers of a high school football stadium, lit up at night. I then ran off the set, as if my emotions were running amok and weighing heavily on me.

Jack let out a deep sigh and muttered under his breath. "Classic Nick, running away when anything gets too tough to handle. Will things ever change?"

"AND CUT!" Roger Friedman yelled over the entire set. "That's a wrap on the scene. Let's take a break before we switch gears. After lunch, we'll head into the locker room and pick up on the scene of Nick talking with his football friends, having an internal struggle when he hears some of the guys make fun of Spencer."

"Oh, and Dean, can I have a chat with you for a moment?" Roger asked me. Although it sounded like a request, it was more of a demand. He was the head honcho in charge here, after all, as the director.

Before I could head over to him, Jack Dayton approached me,

wrapping his arms around my waist. "That was a great scene, Dean. And we did it all in one take."

"We sure did," I replied back. The proximity between him and me off-set left me feeling a bit awkward, but that's how Jack was, ever the eternal flirt.

"Maybe you and I could hang out tonight? Just me and you. You know... to sort of build the chemistry between us off camera? It will only enhance our characters' relationship with each other on camera."

"I'll have to check my schedule, but let me get back to you on that," I briskly stated, still completely distracted by Roger's summon.

I walked over to the director as the crowd around him scattered to leave us two alone. "I hope I didn't mess anything up. Did I?" I checked with him, seeming a little unsure of myself.

Roger shook his head. "No. Not at all. What makes you think that?"

I shrugged. "Just nerves..."

He smiled at me endearingly. "You're doing great so far. There's nothing for you to be nervous about. Trust me."

"Thank you. I mean, I know I'm new to acting and what not, and I still have a lot to learn," I humbly stated.

"Well, you're learning pretty fast and I'm extremely impressed. But anyway, that's not the reason I want to talk."

"Then what is it you called me over for?" I asked, cutting right to the chase.

"It's about Jack..."

"What about him?"

"I hope he's not making you feel uncomfortable or anything. He can be known to be a bit... *aggressive*, when it comes to some of his fellow actors."

To be honest, Jack Dayton was more so annoying and overly flirtatious to the point where it already crossed that line of professionalism.

But I don't think *aggressive* was the appropriate term I would use to describe his behavior.

"No. He's completely harmless," I assured Roger, not wanting to create any sort of on-set tension or drama.

"Okay. Good. If he ever does cause any issues, don't hesitate to let me know. I'm not sure what other directors and producers Jack is used to working under, but I don't tolerate anything like that on my watch."

Roger's protective nature was admirable. I found it to be a fairly attractive quality in a man who could be that way. It elicited a bright, warm smile from me.

"I appreciate the concern. I will be sure to do that if I ever do feel uncomfortable," I let him know, before proceeding to make my way to where our next scene was to be shot at.

I barely made it five steps before Roger called back out to me. "Dean, wait. There's something else I wanted to ask."

I stopped in my stride and turned my head to give him a view of my side profile. "Yeah?"

"Would you want to have dinner with me tonight? Perhaps I could give you a few tips on acting and things of that nature over a couple of cocktails?"

Was this even real right now? Was *the* Roger Friedman asking me out on a date? Well, technically, he simply referred to it as a dinner, but I wasn't born yesterday. I could easily read between the lines.

I was well aware of Roger Friedman being gay. However, he kept his social and personal life low-key, not really sharing much with his fellow co-workers, and all of the public for that matter.

I'd be a fool to refuse an opportunity to have a private sit down with Roger. So, whatever plans I had for this evening, I would have to have them rescheduled, because there would be absolutely no way that I would make Roger Friedman wait on me. Actually, I wondered if he ever waited on anyone, period.

"That would be great," I said in return to his dinner date request.

"I can pick you up at your place around seven this evening?" he offered.

"Sure. I'll text you my address later."

"Perfect. Well then, I guess we should head over to the gym locker rooms?" Roger held a coy smirk on his face as he wittily asked this.

I couldn't help but bust out in laughter. "I suppose so. Although, I feel like you are way more excited about it than you probably should be," I flirtatiously said to him, with a wink.

"Well, only because I know of the scene that is about to take place there, and it's bound to be a spectacular one."

"Then, let's really make it a *spectacular* one," I repeated back to him.

The two of us then headed over to film the gym locker room scene. I had to change into nothing but underwear and drape a white towel around my waist to make it look like I was completely naked underneath. Once my make-up artist touched me up, while also wetting my hair and slicking it, to make it seem as though I just got done with an intense football practice, I was ready for the scene to take.

For this scene, there were other actors also stripped down to just underwear with towels wrapped around them. They were playing as Nick's football teammates and were having *locker room talk*, poking fun at Spencer. It was the scene where Nick would first stand up to them, in Spencer's honor, allowing the audience to see that Nick does have a heart beneath the jock and assumedly cold exterior they would assume he had.

As I read my lines aloud, I would sneak a glance over at Roger out of the corner of my eyes. He was studying me intently, except there was a glint in his eyes as he did so. I could have sworn he was staring at me longingly, and I completely welcomed it.

$500 Million in Cartier Watches Destroyed in Just Two Years

By World Fashion on a Dime LTD.

Richemont, a Swiss-based watchmaking company destroyed nearly $500 million of its designer timepieces over the last two years. The reason being, to avoid their unsold watches being sold at discounted prices.

The company decided to take drastic measures after stocks of its designer watches began popping up in display cabinets in Asian markets amid a crackdown on corruption in China. Cartier was worried that thousands of unsold items would wind up being discounted in the so-called "grey market" of unauthorized and illegal resellers, which would thereby depreciate the value and exclusivity of the company.

Chapter 24

Jackson

Current Day...

The club experience was surprisingly shorter than I had imagined it would be. Dean barely gave me any detail about his and Roger's love life before he suddenly became distracted and immediately wanted to leave the Industry Bar.

"I'm sort of getting a bit bored. Want to go back to the suite and veg out?" he suggested to me over the loud, raving music.

"Sure. I wouldn't mind that at all," I replied, before taking another heavy gulp from my bottle of water.

"Then, let's hit the road," Dean added, before taking one final long drink of his champagne before rising from his seat.

I followed him out of the club and onto the streets. Even the damp New York night atmosphere was a brisk welcome for me compared to the stuffiness in the nightclub. It felt like I had escaped from some underwater cavern and finally made to the surface for fresh air.

Dean seemed to be in a rush as he speed-walked right into our limousine that was a few cars down, parked along the curb near the club. I hopped in behind him and, without a moment's notice, the driver instantly took off.

"Whew! What a night," Dean said, to diffuse the initial silence in the limo. "Sorry if I cut that short. It's just been a long day with the flight, the meeting and now being at the club and all. I want nothing more than to just get into comfy clothes and recline on the sofa with a nightcap."

I was more than elated about this. Honestly, I wouldn't have minded if that was our entire plan for the night from the very beginning. I would have rather just bypassed the trip to the gay nightclub altogether.

"That sounds pretty amazing, right about now," I truthfully admitted to him.

"Perfect. Glad to see we're on the same page then."

We eventually made it back to the hotel in much quicker time than when we left to go to the Industry Bar. Most of the traffic seemed to slightly die down compared to earlier. As soon as Dean and I entered *Suite 5000*, Hector greeted us in the main foyer. "Welcome back. I see your night was cut a bit short. Everything okay?"

Dean let out a deep yawn. "Yeah. We just wanted to head back here early and get settled in with a nightcap before bed."

"Gotcha," Hector acknowledged as Dean trailed off into his bedroom, shutting the door behind him.

Hector then turned his focus back to me. "There's a silk robe hanging in your closet if you want to undress into something more comfortable. It sounds like you and Dean are going to have another drink or so before you head off to bed?"

I nodded. "That was the impression I was under."

"Okay. Well, go ahead and get changed. I'll prep a drink for you both in the meantime."

"Thanks, Hector."

I then headed off into my bedroom and opened my closet door, instantly spotting the gray silky robe with the white lining that Hector had referenced.

Quickly, I rushed to throw off my clothes, just tossing them on the bed, before placing the robe over my body. I decided to at least keep on my boxer-briefs, imagining the horror of sitting in an awkward position on the sofa or even the tied strap of the robe coming undone to give Dean and Hector a peepshow.

As soon as the robe wrapped around my body, I simpered with delight at the silky soft touch it left all over my skin. I wondered just how much this robe actually cost and if it was a robe Hector had brought with him or if it was supplied by the hotel. Nevertheless, I'm sure it was expensive either way.

I soon emerged from the bedroom, relieved that Dean was not already reclining on the sofa in the main living area waiting on me. However, I did see another bottle of champagne, this time Cristal, sitting in an ice bucket with two crystal flutes beside it.

"I'm going to sleep for the night," Hector announced, coming from out of the kitchen area with a charcuterie tray in his hands that he had prepared for us. He laid it down on an open spot on the table. "Have a restful night, Jackson. See you in the morning."

"You too," I said, as Hector went into his own bedroom.

I plopped down on the couch and let out a heavy sigh of relief, just as Dean was coming out of his room, wearing the same exact robe that I had on. He flopped down on the spot right next to me. It took him no time at all to pop the cork of the Cristal and fill our glasses up, handing one of the bubbly drinks off to me. We clinked our glasses together before taking an initial sip.

"Believe it or not, I prefer these types of settings more so than the bar scene," he opened up with.

"That does kind of surprise me," I admitted. "And why do you like this better?"

"I feel more relaxed and my authentic self in a one-on-one or small group setting. When I can actually be intimate in a private room and not have to put on a show as the celebrity Dean Cargill people view me as, then I'm more at ease. You know?"

"I mean, that makes sense. Although, I've just seen so many photos and story coverages about you being at tons of wild parties and club events over the years, I pictured that being your happy place."

"I can see where you would think that," Dean stated. "Anyway, another reason I wanted to come back here is because of where we were headed with the conversation about Roger."

"Oh?" I was confused. I just assumed Dean wanted to abruptly shut down the interview altogether for the night. I had no idea he was actually planning on talking about Roger Friedman more with me.

"Yeah. There's obviously more to the story. And I'd rather talk more openly with you about it here, rather than in a public venue where there are eyes and ears all over," Dean explained.

"Sure. I can completely understand that. Again, this is your interview, Dean. It's all under your terms. Whatever I can do to make you the most comfortable, I will gladly do it."

"Really?" Dean asked, to gain more reassurance.

"Of course."

"Then, do you mind not using your recording device on this conversation I now want to have with you?"

I left the recorder in the bedroom, assuming we were done with the interview for the remainder of the evening. So, that wasn't an issue to comply with. However, I was suddenly becoming more and more antsy wondering what could be so secretive and private that made Dean now want the recording the device off the table. I sensed he was about to tell me something mind-blowing.

I could just feel it!

"Not at all. We don't need the recording device," I stated.

"Oh, and one more thing..." Dean added.

"What's that?"

He got up from his seat and headed towards Hector's bedroom, knocking on the door. Hector soon opened it. "Hey, I need to you to pull the paperwork..." I heard Dean say before then carrying the conversation into a complete whisper.

What paperwork was he talking about? Why did he need it now, of all times? I thought to myself.

It took two minutes for Dean to finally come back over to sit beside me on the luxury sofa. Hector also followed behind Dean, then taking a seat in the accent chair across from us. Hector had what looked like a packet full of papers with a pen in his hand.

"Are you sure you want to do this, Dean? There's no going back," Hector asked him in a warning tone.

"Positive," Dean said.

"What's this about?" I was now more confused than ever.

"Dean wants to share private information with you, Jackson," Hector explained. "However, there's a caveat to this. We need to be absolutely one-hundred percent sure that we can trust you with what Dean is about to disclose."

I then glanced in Dean's direction. His facial expression was blank, giving me no read on him.

"Of course, you can trust me," I answered, knowing this was the response they needed to hear in order for me to be able to pry any more scandalous or imperative information out of Dean.

"Well, to be sure of that, we would like for you to sign an N.D.A.," Hector continued. "What Dean wants to share with you is damaging if word got out about it. It could ruin his entire livelihood to the point where he would likely face time behind bars if the public knew..."

Behind bars!? What the hell was going on? What did you do Dean?

"But what about the story I'm writing? How can I even write it if

I'm forced to sign this?"

"Everything we discussed up until this point is fine for you to use," Dean replied, while pulling out a cigarette and lighting it up between his rosy, luscious lips. "Even what I mention about my divorce with Roger. All of that is fair game. However, there will be an aspect of the story that you'll need to keep private."

My mind was now going in a million places at once, not able to fully comprehend and keep up with any of this. "And if I don't sign..." I said aloud.

"Then we have to squash the entire interview," Dean chimed in again. "But I have faith in you, Jackson. I know you'll sign it. I believe in you."

Dean believed in me? The words had an immediate effect on me. I felt proud. Having Dean Cargill believe in me sent a rewarding rush through my veins. It made me feel important, like an actual *somebody* who mattered. And that's what I wanted to get out of this all along, wasn't it?

I let myself have an internal debate for all but a minute before I finally let out a heavy sigh and took the pen out of Hector's hand. I gave a sideward glance back at Dean. "And I believe in you too," I mentioned, before returning my attention back over to Hector and the papers he was now laying down on the table before me. "Where do I sign?"

"Right here," Hector stated as I initialed and signed my full name in certain parts of the agreement. Once I was done, I handed the pen back over to him.

"Anything else?" I checked.

Hector shook his head *no*. "That about covers it. And let me just remind you, Jackson, violating this N.D.A., means that..."

But I interceded, cutting Hector off before he could even finish his thought.

"I'm well aware of the consequences. You have nothing to worry about."

"Very well," Hector stated before turning towards Dean. "I'll scan and forward these to the lawyers now. You're free to tell him whatever to your heart's content."

"Thank you, Hector," Dean replied, before Hector returned back into his room for the remainder of the night.

Once Dean and I were once again by ourselves, in private, I piped up. "Dean? What's going on? What is all of this about?"

"Like I said before. I trust you, Jackson. I trust you enough to tell you my biggest secret of all. I hope you realize this."

"I do," I sincerely said. "Your secret is safe with me, Dean. Whatever it is, I'll keep it between us. I promise."

Dean studied me carefully, as if he was trying to gauge my facial expressions to see if he presumed I was lying or not. Eventually, he let his guard down and finally continued. "Well, let's get right to it then."

Chapter 25

Dean

Half A Year Ago...

Third time's always a charm, right? At least, I assumed it was. And I was pretty certain I was accurate with this one. Roger was unbelievable. As a movie producer, there were layers to him that I was learning about with every new encounter we had with each other.

For instance, he was a family man who really took care of his mother and sister. He visited them often and supported them both emotionally and financially. Roger was also philanthropic, to say the least. He didn't just donate his money to charities and foundations, but his time as well. He could spend hours helping at homeless shelters, supporting animals, and speaking at major fundraising and charity events.

Then, there was the way he treated me. There was this adoration Roger had for me that Leon and Ralpho never once had. It was as if he would be willing to give the world to me. He loved me that much. And that was the other thing about him. He loved me for *me*. He always said that if I was stripped of my money, celebrity status, etc., that he would still feel a connection to want to be with me. Our personalities just clicked, and we enjoyed each other's company so much that it didn't really matter the condition of the setting we were in. And that's what I loved most about Roger Friedman.

It didn't take very long for him to decide to propose. It happened just five months into us dating. I accepted without hesitation and then we were wed quickly, just two months later. Now, we were on our honeymoon.

We laid in bed one evening in our overwater bungalow at Soneva Jani in the Maldives, just listening to the soft sound of crashing waves as we glanced up at the gorgeous mosaic of stars in the night sky. We hovered over the crystal-clear lagoon that was beneath us in our luxurious hut. The roof was retractable so that we could open it up in the evening to embrace nature all the more.

My guilt was slowly rising in me, like a pool of unsettled bile in my stomach, giving me the urge to want to vomit at any given moment. This was how it was with the other men in my life when I would have to eventually confess my deep, dark secret to them. Of course, I was practically forced into coming out with it to Ralpho and Leon. When the topic of finances came up with them, there was no rhyme or reason as to how I was making far more money than the both of them. When we were married, of course, they snooped through my accounts now that we were in a domestic partnership. And so, I came clean with them the minute they grew suspicious of me.

But with Roger, there was no reason for him to have to ask any questions in regard to my financial status. After all, as far as he knew, I made out just fine in the divorce settlement with Leon. And now, with my endorsement deals and social media posts with product place-ments, I was rationally able to afford everything I had for that alone. Plus, there was now my acting salary, which was a bonus on top of all this.

I could easily keep everything hidden from Roger. But what if there was a chance, years down the road, where he would find out about it? How badly would it hurt him to learn that I had been dishonest with him from that very first moment we met on the set of *Classic Nick*?

If given the opportunity, I could have easily concealed everything from Leon and Ralpho for as long as I could, which I actually did. But with Roger, things were far different, and the thought of this betrayal lingering on my shoulders just kept eating and tearing away at me.

How would he react to all this? What if he just up and left me the moment I revealed everything? But I loved Roger and no matter what, I had to come clean, for his sake.

"Babe. There's been something we need to discuss," I said, with my head tucked into the side of his chest, just beneath his armpit as his arm wrapped under to hold me while we laid tucked into one another in the bed, staring up at the stars in the sky.

"Sure. What is it?" Roger asked, so endearingly.

Now, I couldn't help but have to rise out of the comfort of being next to him. I came out of bed and began pacing around.

"I don't know how to say it, Roger. I really don't." The tears in my eyes formed. I suddenly felt a tightness in my chest that was pulling at me. It felt like some sort of panic or anxiety attack.

Roger jolted up out of the bed with a deeply worried expression written on his face. His hands gripped my shoulders tightly. "Dean. What's wrong? You know you can tell me anything."

I tilted my head to the side, just staring at the ground as my tears fell. It was too painful to have to look him directly in the eyes, knowing the hurt I was about to cause him.

"I'm so scared, Roger. If I tell you, you'll never view me the same way again," I defeatedly stated.

"You can't really believe that, Dean. Whatever it is, we'll work through it together. I promise. Nothing you say to me will ever make me love you any less."

"You say that now, but you don't even know what I'm about to tell you and the devastation it could cause to our relationship, our marriage, for that matter. What if I told you that I could go to jail for something I did, or rather I'm *now doing*? Would you then feel the same way?"

"Of course, Dean. Now come on. Just be open and honest with me. I don't want there to be anything that you feel the need to have to hide from me. There should be no lies or secrets between us."

As Roger's tight grip lessened on my shoulders, I moved to the edge of the bed and took a seat, bracing myself for all that I was ready to confess to him.

"I have over one-hundred and fifty million dollars in offshore accounts," I began with.

Roger's eyes bulged with alarm at the mention of the amount. "One-hundred and fifty million!? But how is that even possible?"

"I run a business, Roger. What started out as a small illegal trade hobby turned into a black market empire," I started to explain. "It all began nine years ago, when I first moved to Miami and began working at a Michael Kors store. When I worked late shifts, we were instructed to take unsold, offseason merchandise and undamaged returns to our stockroom to be shipped out of the store. These were products that were in perfectly good condition. It was thousands of dollars in a single week's worth of bags, purses, wallets, accessories, clothes, etc., that were being sent to an incinerator all to be burned. Can you believe that's millions upon millions of dollars being wasted, all so that a company can keep its exclusivity all for its luxury status?"

I took a moment to catch my breath. Roger just remained silent, listening to my every word.

"And Michael Kors isn't the only designer company to do this. Almost all of them do it, whether it be Burberry, Coach, Gucci, Chanel, Cartier, you name it. I was on the ground floor, able to see all of this happening with my own eyes. Then, the idea came into my head. If I could somehow take these unsold products with me, cut down the prices and sell them secretly, I could easily make a killing in profits. And that's exactly what I started doing. It was small scale at first. I created private social media groups and accepted online payments from customers who wanted these crazy price markdowns on these authentic items. I even shipped the bags and products out myself."

I let out a deep sigh, remembering the struggle I had of going to college full-time, working retail part-time, while also maintaining this lucrative side hustle I had going for me. I woke up early mornings to get my shipments out before classes. I tirelessly worked late into the night, managing only to get a couple hours of sleep. But the money came in so quickly. I couldn't believe that I was already making thousands of dollars per week, before I was even old enough to legally drink.

"I knew what I was doing was against the law. But then, I thought about what these designer brands were doing, in causing harm to the environment with their burnings and then there's the landfill issue on top of it. I'm not saying I'm a climate change savior or anything like that, but in an indirect way, I am helping to protect the environment. Also, I rationalized that I'm not actually *stealing* anything, at least on a level of technicality. These products were worth zero dollars to the company at the time I was retrieving them."

Roger rubbed his hands over his eyes, still in shock at all that I was telling him. "But how did you get to over a hundred million dollars? That's absolutely insane."

"Well, I was able to make connections with retail workers on the inside at multiple store locations across the country and not just with Michael Kors, but with Burberry, Coach, Cartier and even Chanel, just to name a few. Let's just say I pay these workers under the table for them getting me their unsold merchandise that would otherwise be sent back to their warehouses. Eventually, my business was growing so fast that I had to hire assistants to help me out. But I couldn't just ask anyone to help run it. It had to be people that were loyal to me and that I could trust with my entire life. So, I reached out to some of my best friends in Miami, including Hector, who you've met. All of them are part of the growing business and helping run my regional warehouses I have in Miami, L.A., and New York. The operation was growing at a scale that was too much for me to keep up with on my own. I had to hire workers and set up these warehouses to get all the shipments in, only to be sent out to my customers in a timely fashion. Eventually, I was able to get some of the top-tier luxury goods and even have high-end celebrity clients seek me out for some of the merchandise. You wouldn't believe some of the names on my client list, even if I told you."

"I still can't believe it, Dean," Roger simply stated.

"I know. It's hard to believe. But it's the truth. I hired skilled financial advisors who have helped me out along the way. It came to a point where I had to open up offshore accounts in other countries to deposit all the money in. The I.R.S. would become extremely suspicious and I would surely be red flagged if they caught wind of this quick accumulation in accounts that were on American soil. Right now, I'm doing my best to slightly scale the business back a bit. I feel like I'm at a good place where things have finally plateaued and I can feel safe about this entire operation not getting out to the feds."

"So, this is what you've been keeping from me all this time?" Roger asked with disappointment in his tone.

"I didn't mean to. I really didn't have a choice. I couldn't risk getting you involved and then things were going so well for us in the beginning. I didn't want to spoil anything we had going."

Roger arched his brow at me. "And you don't think that telling me all of this now is spoiling our honeymoon?"

I couldn't help but chuckle at his comment. It was odd for me to laugh at a time like this, when my relationship and marriage were possibly in jeopardy with all that I revealed. I wondered if I was just being delirious or if maybe it was a sense of relief that was now overcoming me. Getting all of this off my chest and out in the open allowed the guilt I held onto all this time to finally subside. So, there was that alleviation, at least.

"I just couldn't hold it in any longer. Being here with you all alone and just this entire scene of being in paradise was eating at me. I just felt now was the time to come clean with you," I tried to explain. "I understand if you decide you want a divorce or..."

The second I mentioned the possibility of divorce, Roger reached out and scooped me in his arms. The side of my face pressed against his torso as gravity continued to work on the remaining tears in my eyes. They trickled down the skin on Roger's abdomen.

"A divorce?" he repeated back to me. "Do you honestly think I want a divorce from you after hearing all this? Of course not. Look, we'll get through this Dean. I love you no matter what. That's not going to change. We can fix this. Just promise me that you won't lie to me about anything else. Okay?"

"I promise," I managed to utter in between sobs.

Roger then pulled away from me. I glanced up at him to see a grin on his face. It looked as though he was trying to contain himself from laughing, which was extremely bizarre, especially at a time like this.

"What's so funny?" I sternly asked him.

"Nothing. I'm just stunned now, thinking it all over. So, you were like, what, eighteen years old when you started selling all of these designer products?"

I nodded.

"It's kind of impressive, actually," Roger clarified. "At that age you started a successful black market business and now have profited over one-hundred and fifty million dollars off of it, all for yourself. How many people can actually say that about themselves?"

Impressive. Well, that was one word some could use to describe it. But then others would use words like *illegal, thief, heist, disgusting, vile, deceitful.*

"How can you be so calm about this? You don't feel betrayed or even scared one bit?" I asked.

"I mean, I'm a little scared. Scared that there's always a chance my husband could be caught and go to prison for life. Maybe I also feel a little betrayed, but I understand why you had to keep it a secret from me. But we can get through this together, Dean. I married you because I love you. Whatever trouble you're in, I'm in too. We can make this work."

I gave Roger a long and tight hug. "What did I ever do to deserve you?"

"It's hard to say," he joked.

And Roger did keep his word for as long as he could. I thought we would make it out on top with all of the reassurance he was giving me. But just two months later, after our honeymoon, we inevitably went through a separation period, leading to my third divorce.

Chapter 26

Jackson

Current Day...

And there it was. The bombshell had been fully dropped on me. It exploded my mind, leaving it in pieces all over the place. I needed time to process all of this before I could begin to think about putting it all back together.

The news was far worse than I had imagined. Dean Cargill was a criminal. He made millions and millions of dollars in selling designer bags and accessories illegally. He was lying to the world, and he had been lying to me as well throughout this entire interview process.

So many questions were swarming around in my head. It was all so much to digest.

Why did Roger Friedman divorce him after what sounded like Roger wanting to support Dean in keeping his black market business concealed?

How has Dean not been caught in the past ten years?

Why was he telling me his deepest secret, knowing very well I could tell others?

What was my role in all of this?

I continued to brood over that last question.

Dean was able to see the panic and disturbed look on my face. I rose from the seat beside him and paced about the suite in my gray silk robe.

"It's a lot to process. I'm fully aware," he calmly said to me.

I threw my hands in the air, losing all cool. "You've put me in a really tough spot that I never wanted to be a put in. Now, I'm an accomplice to hundreds of millions of dollars being stolen from companies around the world. If I keep this a secret, I could potentially risk going to prison, too. My entire career is now on the line here, Dean! Do you not understand that?"

He let out a sigh, as if he were annoyed by my sudden outburst. "I do understand how you're feeling. But you are absolved of any crime. You signed the N.D.A."

"That doesn't mean shit, though! It's still a crime, Dean. I'm pretty sure that trumps any N.D.A clause. Christ!" I placed my hands to my temples, feeling the onset of a migraine.

"No one will ever know that you are aware of my affairs, Jackson. It's impossible for anyone to find out, unless you make it known to them. Mine and Hector's lips are sealed. Your name will never be mentioned, even if, by the slim chance, that I ever am implicated and caught. I've covered my tracks carefully over the last decade. I don't intend on being sloppy now."

"I still don't understand any of it. Why have you told me all of this? Why involve me? It makes no sense," I tried to rationalize aloud. "What is your end goal here? You've tricked me into interviewing you, gave me an account of your full life story and then tell me about how you made all your money, knowing very well I will not be able to write about any of it."

"You can still write the cover story on me. There's nothing holding you back from doing that. You just won't mention a thing about my *side hustle*. Is that so hard to understand?"

I shook my head. "I'm a journalist, Dean. Telling the truth is my only morality clause in my career. It's what I'm expected to do. It's really all I can do. Yet, you want me to write a false narrative on you? One that I know has cracks, holes and missing pieces? How can I create an article that's supposed to be my best work when I'm holding back all of this information that I'm now aware of?"

"Because it's the story that will launch your little, pathetic career," Dean replied in almost a demonic way I've never heard him speak to me before. "I've given you a once in a lifetime opportunity here, Jackson. How can you not take this bait? This story on me will catapult you. Do you have any idea of how many doors this will open for you? Is this not what you wanted all along?"

"And how the hell do you know what I want?" I rebuked.

"Oh, come on, Jackson! How naïve do you think I am? I run one of the world's most successful illegal operations and you honestly believe I wouldn't get a full background check on you before selecting you to be the one to interview me?"

My mouth dropped. I was stunned and rendered still. "You actually had someone run a background check on me?"

Dean nonchalantly took a sip of his champagne in a relaxed pose before responding. "Of course. Put yourself in my shoes. Wouldn't you have done the same?"

"If I was in your shoes, I wouldn't be scamming everyone..." I rebuffed.

"That's besides the point. Anyway, I've learned a lot about you far before I finally decided to pick you for this task. It was the article you wrote a month ago about Roger and me that caught my attention. You were the only journalist who actually wrote on the matter from an objective point of view. Everyone else was quick to form their own opinions and cast blame on me for the divorce between the two of us. But, for some reason, you did not. That piqued my interest in having someone that I believed that I could actually trust. Then, from the background check and some social media stalking, I was able to put a label on you."

"And what label would that be?"

"That you're the same as me," he replied.

"We are definitely not the same." I quickly corrected him. "I would never do something criminal."

"Maybe not. But what I mean is you are looking for a higher place in this world, as I once was. I've seen your posts and photos. You admire all the finer things in life. I read somewhere how your goal was to be the next Carrie Bradshaw, no? You dream of a rich and lavish lifestyle, one full of fancy cocktail events, parties on yachts, extravagant and luxury houses, right?"

"Yes. But I want to get there by doing all the right things. I don't want to have to lie, cheat and steal to move up in the world," I clarified to him.

"Omitting information is not the same as lying, Jackson. All you have to do is tell *my version* of the story and you'll be in the clear. Is that really so difficult?" he asked.

This was all too much. It was hard for me to even think right now. I took a seat in the accent chair across from Dean, trying to regain my composure. "I honestly don't know anymore."

"How can you not know!?" Dean was now becoming more of the aggressor. "I thought you were stronger than this, Jackson. I painted you as being someone like me. Someone who would seize opportunities that were presented to them. Someone who knows what they want and isn't afraid to take risks to get them. You're supposed to be grabbing the bull by the horns, yet you sound like a damn wimp right now. Buck the fuck up! I'm the one throwing you a lifeline here. Don't be a fucking fool to turn it away."

I kept my gaze fixed on the ground. I couldn't look Dean in the eyes;

not at this moment. Could I actually go through with this? I was still unsure of myself.

But if I was going to write a full story on Dean, I would be needing the full truth from him in its entirety. And right now, I was led to believe that everything he ever told me about his life was a complete fabrication.

"What about everything you told me about your ex-husbands?" I then brought up. "Was all of that a lie, too?"

"Bits and pieces," he confessed. "What I told you is exactly the version I want you to tell the world."

"And speaking of your exes, do they know about all of this? Was this the big scandal that put them over the edge to divorce you once they learned of it?"

Dean nodded. "Yes. Ralpho and Leon know about my side endeavors."

"But how is that possible? How have they not reported you to the authorities?"

"Easy answer. *Embarrassment*. Do you think they would really want to tell the world they were married to someone who stole millions of dollars from various designer companies? It would destroy their careers. Skeptics would assume that they were involved in everything I was doing. And if others didn't believe they were involved, they would at least question their knowing of all that I've done. Everyone would think they just turned a blind eye to the entire thing, and that is damaging to them, too. They would likely have to go to court with me and face years of litigation if they spilled anything about it. This would destroy them just as badly as it would destroy me. Plus, I paid them handsomely to keep their mouths shut. After all, I could afford to do it," Dean said with a sly grin.

"You really are something else..." was all I found myself saying to him.

"I've been underestimated my whole life, Jackson. I'm sure you can relate. Aren't you tired of being underestimated? Don't you want people to view you as a player, a major competitor in leagues that are far bigger than the one you are currently in? Be honest with me."

All I could do was nod.

"Exactly. And let me just say, I still do trust you, Jackson. I know this is all a lot to digest right away, but I have faith in you. Don't you feel at least a bit honored or even giddy that now you're in on one of my biggest secrets? Think about that. I literally allowed you to hold some of my cards, to hold my life in your hands. You have to realize that. I know you'll do the right thing by me here."

There was no denying that this was true. I was finally starting to view this from a different angle; One that wasn't strictly based on morals and good faith. Now, there was that aspect of loyalty and *quid pro quo* to consider. I would be doing Dean a huge favor and he would be doing me one. Would I really want to burn this bridge?

"So, what's next for you when this is done?" I further inquired. "There's still something you haven't told me. What's the purpose of me writing this article? What's in it for you?"

"Great question. You see, I need someone to write a story who is actually in my corner. It will cause a cascade effect for other news outlets to follow in suit. Painting me in a positive light and showing I have good character will lower the target on my back. Think about it. People tend to go after celebrities a lot more who are horrible people. More investigations are conducted to bring the wicked A-listers down far more to than those who are saintly. I'm well aware of what the public's current view of me is, and it's important to spin that around."

"But that's going to be a tough sell. Even you have to admit that this might be a far reach, even beyond my capabilities as a writer."

Dean smirked, as if he liked this challenge. I wondered if this sort of thing did get him off. "It won't be that hard. If there's one thing everyone loves, it's an underdog. They respect a great comeback story. And let me just say, I have created the perfect plot twist for this comeback story."

"Oh yeah? And what is that?" I asked, wondering what else he could possibly have up his sleeve.

Dean then pulled out his phone and began calling someone. "Hey babe, it's safe to come out now... Yeah... We're here in the living room."

Babe!? Who was he talking to? What the hell was going on?

Before I could even react to ask Dean who that was on the phone, I heard his bedroom door open. I turned my head, catching a figure emerging from it. My eyes must have been deceiving me. I rubbed them again just to make sure I was seeing who I thought it was. I realized I really wasn't dreaming.

The man came forward and planted a kiss on Dean's cheek before taking a seat next to him.

"Roger!? Roger Friedman?" I stated with disbelief. "It can't be. Have you been here this entire time? Wh-Why are you even here right now?"

"You don't get it yet, do you, Jackson?" Dean asked.

Nope. Not a clue.

My silence sparked Dean to continue. "The divorce between Roger and I was a sham. Well, let me clarify that. The divorce actually did happen, but we never stopped loving each other."

"That's ridiculous..." I heard myself thinking out loud.

"But is it?" Roger then spoke up. "A public divorce would definitely not look good for Dean. However, it was a sacrifice that he needed to make. Because with another divorce on Dean's plate, it would provide more evidence for his substantial budgets and actual net-worth. People would naturally assume Dean acquired millions of dollars from his divorce to me. It would allow the suspicions against him to taper off. Less chance for someone nosy and with power to look into Dean."

"I... I can't believe you're involved in this too," I commented.

"We're *all* in this together," Dean swiftly clarified. "Roger and I have already done all the planning and legwork on this, Jackson. We've loaded the bases. Now it's time for you to bring us home."

What was I supposed to say at this moment? I felt extremely uncomfortable and unwilling to provide them with an answer on the spot like this.

"I need time to think, Dean. Can I take at least a day to two to mull it all over? It doesn't feel right for me to give you an honest answer, now."

"A day!?" Roger exclaimed. "You really need a whole day to..."

But Dean held up his hand in protest, to interrupt Roger. "A day will be fine. I'll give you your space for a bit. Hector will book you a separate flight home first thing tomorrow, so that you don't think we're hovering over you. Why don't just you and I meet up the following morning? Stop by my place in the Bluffs and we can decide where to go from here. Will that work?"

"Yes. I think I'll have a final decision by then," I promised.

"Good. Well, I don't know about you, but I think it's time to call it a night," Dean recommended. "Oh. And don't forget about our N.D.A. I would think twice before trying to get someone else's opinion to help guide you. That would be in direct violation..."

"No. I won't do that. There's nothing to worry about."

"Glad to hear that," Dean replied, before tapping Roger on the shoulder, signaling that it was time for them to head off into the bedroom.

"Goodnight, Jackson," he and Roger said to me back-to-back.

"Goodnight to you two, as well," I replied, before high-tailing it to my bedroom, immediately locking the door behind me.

I would undoubtedly be up for the remainder of the night, trying to think all of this through. Who the hell could even bother with sleep at a time like this?

Chapter 27

Dean

One Month Ago…

The divorce with Roger was beyond believable. At least, based on the news and media coverage of the entire series of events following the divorce announcement, it seemed to be that way. Just as we had suspected, I came out as the villain when all was said and done. But we knew this was bound to happen. I've become so used to it now. Even with my two other divorces, terms like *gold digger*, *whore*, *slut*, *user*, *leech* and other words with similar connotations were continuously thrown around. That was the price I was willing to pay if I wanted to continue to fly under the radar and not give anyone a reason to snoop around my financial situation.

Roger and I had to be inconspicuous if we wanted this whole scheme to remain convincing. We did our best to try and only see each other but once every week or two. One of us would try to remain incognito when visiting the other. Those nights that we spent the evening together were beyond romantic and lasted into the early morning, with us having wild and passionate sex for hours on end. Absence makes the heart grow fonder and the dick grow yonder.

We figured that we would have to keep this charade up for months, until our divorce was completely settled, which we were expeditiously trying to make happen. Thereafter, we wanted things to cool down with the paparazzi before we would make it seem like we made a mistake, rekindled, and then wound up back together. But that wouldn't be for another couple of months at least.

Tonight, I remained alone in my beach house in Paradise Cove Bluffs. I asked my assistants to give me some privacy for the remainder of the night. So, they were down at my casita, working and tending to my business affairs.

I sat on my beige sofa by the warm fireplace, swirling a glass of red wine in my hand, while gazing out the window at the dark horizon. The only lights I could make out were from the specs of stars in the night sky and the faint bubbles from the rolling waves striking the sand. This was how I meditated—good wine, a crackling fireplace, and observing the darkened sea.

My trance was cut short when I noticed the screen of my cell phone blinking. Roger's name appeared, prompting me to answer it right away. "Hey babe," I greeted him with.

"Hey. How is your night going?"

"As good as it's going to get, I suppose. Just trying to unwind, sitting here on the couch, thinking about things..." I stated with absolute vagueness.

"What kind of things are you thinking about?"

"Just all of the stories and articles I've come across these past few weeks. People trying to insert themselves into our lives and write about us as if they were present during our entire relationship," I confessed.

"You shouldn't worry about that stuff, Dean. What did I say about reading into negative comments? Don't ever give them feedback and the satisfaction they want. Best to just ignore it altogether."

"I know, I know. Sometimes, I just can't help it. But I managed to come across a story that wasn't so bad."

"Oh really? That's a shocker," Roger said in surprise.

"Yeah. Some columnist from *Chatterbox News*. Jackson *something*,

I think his name was," I tried to recall.

"What did the story say?"

"It was objective. The divorce was mentioned so matter-of-factly. Actually, there were some positive remarks in the article, including the mention of my starring role in *Classic Nick* and how great I treat the paparazzi. It talks about you in complimentary ways as well. Nothing negative whatsoever."

"Give that guy an award!" Roger announced.

"Really. But too bad *Chatterbox News* isn't some world or nationally renowned media outlet. If only this story cast a wider net... the wonder it could do for my character," I thought aloud.

"Actually, that's not a bad idea, babe. Maybe you should consider reaching out to this guy. Think about it. He's already partially on your side and obviously knows all of the malice that's been thrown your way, yet he's choosing to ignore it and spin everything positively in his story about you."

"And let's face it, giving him a chance to actually interview and get quotes directly from me will get enough attention in itself. It's probably unlike any interview he has done and will ever do at this *Chatterbox News* place," I added. "I can see the merit in all this."

"Any stories that give you accolades and good attention are what we need right now. The fewer critics you have, then the fewer skeptics you have. The last thing we need is for someone with a vendetta to try and get nosy and search for a way to tear you down."

"Hmmm. Well, I'll have to do more research on him to see if he's a good fit."

"Yeah. Look into it more. Let me know what you find out," Roger said.

"Sure. I have nothing better to do tonight." I then let out a heavy sigh of annoyance. "Ugh! Two days can't come fast enough until you arrive. I miss you."

"I miss you too, babe. Keep the bed warm. I love you."

"I love you too," I replied, before ending the call.

I browsed online and discovered the name of the journalist—Jackson Cartwright. It wasn't too hard to track him down on social media. By the third picture I saw of him, I could immediately sense that he was gay. But the next picture of what looked like a boyfriend kissing him sealed the deal. Jackson's social media accounts were *neat*. His photos were carefully orchestrated and put together to include scenic vacations, nice dinners, and him dressed up at certain events with groups of friends. The only thing messy was the many *Sex and the City* references in his captions and multiple memes of Sarah Jessica Parker.

Was he that obsessed with Carrie Bradshaw?

It reeked of a man who desperately wanted to be in a permanent, rich lifestyle. This was exactly the sort of guy I could easily befriend. All it would take was for him to get a taste of my world as the bait and I could then easily reel him in. I would let him interview me to give him the publicity he likely always had wanted. I would tell my version of the truth and be the one to create the narrative that would go into his article and story about me. It sounded like the perfect plan.

It was nearly decided. Now, I just needed to make a few extra calls, hire a private investigator to do a thorough background check on Jackson, just to verify that I knew who I was dealing with. Then, I would have one of my assistants reach out to someone high up at *Chatterbox News* and specifically request an interview with this Jackson Cartwright.

I would just have to play my part right and ride this out. It would all be worth it in the end.

Chapter 28

Jackson

Current Day...

Be careful what you wish for.

It was one of those pieces of advice I often gave others throughout my entire life. It came with the territory of running gossip columns and stories on major celebrities, while discovering some of their great scandals and downfalls from their pedestals.

Now, I found myself on the receiving end of this very same guidance I had been giving to everyone else over the years. I had fought tooth and nail to discover Dean's financial situation and what he had been hiding from the rest of the world. Now that I had uncovered his deepest, darkest secret... or rather he just blatantly told me it, I wished he never mentioned it at all.

This was a can of worms that was just too large for me. A multi-million dollar heist was what this whole thing had actually turned out to be. Who knew that Dean Cargill had the balls to even run a business like this? Hell, how did he even have the intellect and skills to pull something of this caliber off for the past ten or so years without even remotely getting caught yet? Part of me was disgusted by the whole ordeal, while the other completely admired Dean's grit and tenacity in attaining such a feat at such a young age. I guess I was a feeling a combination of these sentiments. *Astounded* would be the more appropriate term to use. I was astounded and left speechless by the entire affair.

Needless to say, I could not sleep at all in the hotel last night, when Dean revealed all that he had been keeping from me. My adrenaline was spiked and there was no use bringing it down. How could Dean do this? Better yet, I was even more surprised that Roger Friedman was involved in all of this as well and was supporting Dean through thick and thin.

And worst of all, was what this meant for me. What if Dean does get caught and I'm somehow implicated in this? I could wind up with a criminal record when all was said and done. Dean believed that I was safe because of the N.D.A. he made me sign. But let's be real. Just how protected was I from the agreement? There was still a risk, no matter what the outcome.

Also, I shouldn't forget that I was now under legal obligation to not be able to expose Dean because of the N.D.A. Me violating it would allow Dean to completely ruin me. I was between the ultimate rock and a hard place and I could not help but blame myself for my part in making this happen, for being so obsessed with wanting to figure Dean Cargill out. *Be careful what you wish for*, I repeated in my head over and over again, punishing myself for landing me in this predicament.

Luckily, Dean was respectful about allowing me to have a full day to figure things out. I needed the downtime to really think all of this through. The following morning, I had Hector book me a flight back to Los Angeles, first thing. I made haste in packing up my belongings to stealthily make it out of the suite without being noticed by Dean or Roger. I called for my own Uber to the airport, not wanting to have to bother disturbing any of them for a ride or relying on Dean's hospitality any longer.

Once I landed in L.A.X., I knew heading straight home to Darren was out of the question. As Dean reminded me before he went to bed last night, I couldn't tell a soul about his black market designer merchandise business. Going home to Darren would only leave me vulnerable and tempted to tell him of all that I had heard. And I couldn't be selfish and put Darren in the same risky place that I was currently in. Therefore, I had to leave him in the dark in order to avoid having him involved in any part of this.

So, I decided to head straight back to Malibu and stay in the same hotel that I had previously been at, before Dean offered me to spend the time in the casita of his beach home. It would be convenient to also commute from there to Dean's house in the morning to give him my final verdict on whether or not I wanted to go through with his proposition, which was writing a fabricated story based on what Dean wanted me to say in the article.

As soon as I checked in, I changed out of my clothes and into my swimming trunks and sunglasses, deciding to head straight to Zuma Beach to give me some fresh air and time to relax and think everything over.

I sat on a towel, plopped in the sand, just staring out into the sea. The beach was surrounded by high, mountainous cliffs. They formed a gulf-like shape, as if they were preparing to wrap around and consume you whole. That's exactly how I felt in this very moment, inundated, like the world was closing in on me. It was all so much pressure. Something I'd never been prepared for.

But what would be the best course of action? Should I take the moral high-ground and just confess everything to the authorities? It would end poorly for Dean and I would likely be scarred in my career and for the rest of my life, for that matter.

Another potential option I didn't even consider that I was now recognizing was that I had the ability to just walk away from all of this. It would be the best move if I wanted to wipe my hands clean of any wrongdoing. But then again, there was always that small fraction of a chance that in the future, if Dean were caught red-handed, who is to say that my name would not be brought up in the conversation? I could be charged in the conspiracy since I had knowledge of these illegal matters all along. Keeping this concealed for a long period of time could open up the chance for multiple charges to be pressed against me, if people did, indeed, find out I knew all about Dean's side hustle.

I felt weak, used and abused by Dean Cargill and his crew. I was Dean's puppet in all of this, just some toy that he came across that could help him further his own gain and avoid any problems in the future. Not to mention, I was also Edgar Baxter and *Chatterbox News'* pawn in this process. They needed me to put them higher on the journalism map with this exclusive interview with Dean.

Walking away from all of this would only put me in the same situation I was in before all of this went down. I would be a weak and unheard-of reporter with *Chatterbox News*. Did I really want to go back to my tiny cubicle and be stuck there for probably the next few decades until I would retire?

I had to keep reminding myself of my end goals. What did I want to accomplish from all of this? My initial intent was to actually use Dean to hurl my career in journalism. It would be the greatest stepping stone I could utilize to get me one step closer to being the next Carrie Bradshaw.

Dean was employing me for his own benefit, so why shouldn't I return the favor and take advantage of being let in on his undercover operation? If I was going to go down this route, then I needed to plan it all out carefully, because just like Dean was doing now, I would have to outmaneuver everyone around me if I wanted to make this work and move further ahead in the world.

Surprisingly, I slept easily last night. I spent part of the night down at the hotel bar, trying my best to relax over a glass of wine or two. By the time I made it back to my room, I crashed into the bed and fell asleep in less than ten minutes. Maybe it was because I had finally come to a resolution after I left Zuma Beach this afternoon.

The more I thought about the decision I was going to make, the more confident I felt about my choice. I would remain steadfast and nothing more was going to deter me from letting Dean know what I had decided upon. The assurance I held onto for the remainder of the day was what ultimately allowed me to drift off into such an easy slumber.

By the morning, I felt as fresh as a daisy, waking up to take a nice scalding shower, before getting changed and checked out of the hotel, preparing to head to Dean's home in Paradise Cove Bluffs.

I had to remain headstrong. I did not want to seem fragile and powerless in front of him, just as I was last night. *Grab the bull by the horns*, I muttered to myself the moment I saw Dean's magnificent home out of the Uber car window, just as he recently said.

But nerves instantly got the best of me. I could feel a slight queasiness in the pit of my stomach coming on. As I stepped out of the vehicle, I tried my best to stay focused and maintain an optimistic approach. *Easier said than done*. The sinking feeling still wasn't subsiding, so I would just have to bite the bullet and try to ignore it altogether.

I made it down the driveway and before I could even walk up the stairs of the porch to knock on Dean's door, Hector was already waiting for me.

"He's down on the beach," Hector simply said, using a hitchhiker thumb to point in the direction of it.

"Oh? Is that where we are meeting at?"

Hector nodded. "Yeah. That won't be an issue, will it?"

I shook my head. "Nope. Just lead the way."

We walked down the side path of the home and down the deck to the pier. We passed the casita and Hector halted before he stepped foot in the sand. "There are chairs and a table out there. Same spot where you had brunch at yesterday. Is there anything else you need?"

"No. Nothing else. Thanks, Hector."

And with that Hector headed back in the direction of the main beach house, leaving me alone to take my shoes and socks off, before striding across the sand to meet Dean who was out by the water, sitting on a white foldable chair.

I couldn't help but think back to this same moment just days ago, when I first came to this house to meet him, back when the question was still out on how Dean could afford to live here in Paradise Cove Bluffs. But since then, the riddle had been solved. It was hard to believe that it was just a mere couple of days since then. It felt like I had been on this adventure for weeks, even months now. However, I couldn't help but also reminisce on all the stories Dean told me, all the potential lies that he led me to believe about his life story and his ex-husbands. Doubt started to seep in. Could I believe anything he would tell me again, from here on out? I guess it didn't matter if I trusted him or not, because I would just be reciting his version of the truth, based on whatever it was he wanted me to include in my story.

"Hey," I called out when I was an earshot distance from Dean, not wanting to startle him by sneaking up from behind.

"Hi," he reciprocated once he removed a cigarette from his lips, but barely tilted his head to look at me. His eyes were hidden behind his brown aviators. "Here. Have a seat," Dean further added, dipping his head towards the other empty white chair that was just a few feet away from him.

"Thank you..." I uttered, before sitting beside him.

"So, I take it you've made a decision?" Dean asked, cutting right to the chase.

"I think so," I said, with a hint of eagerness in my voice.

But before I could give him my full answer, he was already interrupting me. "Before you say anything, I wanted to ante up the stakes for you. I've had time to think over the past day too, and I wanted to provide you with an additional opportunity in my offer."

"Oh?" I replied in a surprised tone.

"Besides the article, I want to offer you the chance to write a memoir or some sort of novel about me. Honestly, I don't think a simple article is going to be enough to cover my full story. I mean, it's a start, but we could get so much more out there by going down the publishing route. What do you think?"

Not just an article, but a full book!?

Damn. Was Dean serious right now? Well, he had to have been. Otherwise, he wouldn't have presented the idea to me.

"You want me to be your writer... a published author?" I repeated back to him.

"Yes. And I'll sort out all the contracts and agreements. I'm sure we can easily get a literary agent and land you in one of the top publishing houses. All you have to do is just worry about the writing. With as much of a mystery as I am, everyone will want to get their hands on this when it's made."

The wheels in my head were spinning so fast that the nuts and bolts on the cogs were coming undone. Before I could even think, my mouth was already moving. "Yes! Yes, I'll do it! Holy shit!"

There was no possible way I could contain myself and keep cool. All I could think about was the fame I would garner in the writing world. There would be so many more doors that would be opened for me with a book deal. This was it. This really was my big break. It was all going to happen, and I was certain it would, because of all the knowledge I now had on Dean. There would be no way he would go back on this with risking me turning on him.

Dean displayed a wide grin at my reaction. "You know, Jackson, I think this is the start of a wonderful long and *loyal* friendship between us." He heavily emphasized the word *loyal*, for obvious reasons.

I stood up from my chair in front of Dean, digging my feet deep into the sand. I extended my hand out to him, wanting to officially seal the deal. "Let's shake on it then. To an amazing partnership..."

He just stared at me like I had multiple heads growing from my neck, not reaching his hand out to meet mine. Instead, he covered his mouth with it, trying to hide the laughter that he was now giving. He could barely contain himself.

I raised my brow at him, a bit annoyed that he was laughing at my expense. "What's so funny?"

"Oh Jackson! If you really want to write my memoir, you're going to have to learn a lot more about me," he stated.

I wasn't sure what that had to do with skipping on the handshake and snickering at me. "Like what?"

"For starters, I don't do handshakes when I make a deal." Dean then turned to the side table and reached for two glasses of champagne, handing one off to me. "I only drink and cheers to them."

I couldn't help but now laugh with him. *But of course...*

We clinked our champagne glasses together before he made a toast to close this agreement. "*Now*, here's to a successful partnership."

"So, we really are doing this?" I asked again just to confirm that this wasn't a hoax.

"Yes. This is really happening, Jackson. Quit second-guessing everything all the time. Trust me. I'm going to make you so rich, my little *Carrie Bradshaw*."

Chapter 29

Jackson

Two Years Later...

I sat in a white swing made of sturdy plywood on my new front porch, sipping on a freshly made coffee. It had become a daily tradition for Darren and I to sit out here every morning from 6:45-7:15am to have an earlier morning chat while getting our daily ritual caffeine fix, and watching the sunrise, here in Malibu.

Just a few months ago, we decided to purchase a new beach home along Trancas Beach, just west of Paradise Cove Bluffs and Zuma Beach. The place was no immaculate, twenty-million dollar house with a casita, but it perfectly fit mine and Darren's needs. Of course, the home did cost us just north of four-million dollars, but a *certain friend* of mine insisted on making the purchase for us. Dean called it a Christmas bonus that he wanted to reward me with, while I jokingly referred to it as *hush money* from him. We both laughed over it at drinks at the bar as we sorted through our financial agreement and the paperwork needed to make the purchase. Dean, surprisingly, was with Darren and me every step of the way with the realtors and the home walk-throughs before we closed on settlement.

Our relationship has only grown in the past two years. Dean and Roger wound up back together recently, which was a shock to the world, but not to me, of course. I was even able to introduce Darren to Dean and Roger. The four of us clicked and made a regular thing of vacationing together and going out a lot, doing normal, double date, couple things. However, Darren was still kept in the dark on Dean's illegal fashion designer merchandise business. It was all in his best interest, although I still felt guilty about withholding this information from him, when we were a couple that practically told each other everything. No secrets were ever kept, except for this one now.

Darren naturally assumed Dean and I hit it off two years ago and developed an authentic connection. To his point, Dean and I did form a great bond together, but it was with the foundation of me gaining knowledge about his black market operation. That was the catalyst in us creating our professional partnership, which eventually led us to becoming much better friends. And now, Darren and I lived just miles away from Dean's Paradise Cove Bluffs home, often visiting Dean when he invited us to one of his lavish parties which sometimes could get out of hand late into the hours.

Our weekends were now always booked with dinner dates, events, mini-vacations, etc., but we still worked on weekdays, enjoying each other's company on gorgeous mornings such as this, on the porch, feeling the gentle sea breeze waft its salty aroma right by us.

"What's on the agenda for you today?" Darren's question completely distracted me from watching the golden sunrise over the sapphire waters.

"Trying to tie up this story I need to get in before tomorrow's deadline," I replied.

"Well, I'll try to not bother you then for most of the day."

I couldn't help but grin before placing a soft kiss firmly on his lips, not worrying about our morning coffee breaths. "I like when you bother me from my work. I always need the break."

Two years ago, I finally wrote the piece for *Chatterbox News* on Dean Cargill. Just as everyone had anticipated, the story blew up and went viral. Other media outlets also posted the column, giving me and *Chatterbox News* full credit and negotiated royalties for reposting and publishing the article. I made a killing profit from the story and so did *Chatterbox News*. The Editor-in-Chief, Edgar Baxter, was beyond pleased and grateful for all of my hard work on it. But, just months after the story went live, I decided to end my employment with Chatterbox. A new opportunity presented itself where I could run my own gossip column called *The Sandal Scandals*. Half of my company's coverage was based on local news stories here in Malibu, and the other half discussed scandals and the latest ongoings of major celebrities on a broader scale. I already had seven other journalists working for me, all of us writing our stories, virtually, from the comfort of our own homes. I learned from the mistakes of *Chatterbox News* and refused to purchase a small office space and have everyone crammed into cubicles like a group of sardines. Plus, promoting jobs that worked remotely allowed me to cast a greater net to hire highly qualified employees from anywhere in the country. So, it was a win on all fronts with me making that executive decision.

In the end, it also helped mine and Darren's relationship. He too worked virtually. Most of time, I have heard horror stories of couples working from home together, constantly seeing each other day in and day out and getting into arguments and it causing a flatline in their relationship and sex-life, but Darren and me were not one of those statistics in those stories. We gave each other appropriate space during the day, when needed, but otherwise, we really enjoyed the more time we now had to spend by each other's side.

So, *The Sandal Scandals* continued to grow and flourish. It was performing so well that even Dean wanted to make a huge investment in the company, which he did. It was only going to expand from here on out.

"Oh, I forgot to ask. Do you have everything in order for next week?" I checked with Darren.

"Yeah. Flights and all the hotels at each stop are taken care of. One of Dean's assistants said they will flip the transportation bill," he informed me.

"Perfect. I'm a bit nervous, to be honest. This being my first time doing this sort of thing."

"Oh, you have nothing to worry about, babe. You're a journalist, for crying out loud. If anyone is skilled in public speaking, it's definitely you."

"If you say so," I conceded.

Next week would be the official start date of my book tour. As promised, Dean Cargill allowed me to write a full biographical novel on his life. We wound up going with *The Real Classic Nick*, for the title of the work. It took me about nine months to write the full book. Then, it went into its editing phase, among the other tedious tasks in publishing, before it was officially released just one month ago.

Because of Dean Cargill's name, the publicity behind the book skyrocketed and was featured in so many online articles, in major bookstores, as well as mentioned on morning local and national news networks. Those who already read advanced copies of the book were raving about it. Already, I had celebrity agents reaching out to me, requesting I write a biographical novel for their clients.

I instantly agreed to two of the offers, in particular, for celebrities I was extremely fond of. After all, I had made a huge six-figure deal on *The Real Classic Nick*, and continued to collect royalties on each sale. From a financial lens, I wanted the same kind of deal and would likely get it if I were to write about other A and B-list celebrities.

So, next week would start the book tour of *The Real Classic Nick*, on the east coast. Darren even agreed to fly out and join me throughout the span of the entire tour, so long as he could stay in the hotels during the day and work at his job through their Wi-Fi. Such was a major perk of teleworking.

"Oh yeah, I almost forgot," Darren added. "Dean wants us to stay with him at his new place when we travel to New York."

I rolled my eyes. "That man will find any way to keep us on his charity case list," I joked.

Darren just shrugged. "Hey, I'm not complaining about it, and neither should you."

"Haha," I laughed. "I guess you're right about that."

So, life had completely changed for me, for the better. Already, I was the CEO of my own company close to the age of thirty and I had managed to publish a New York Times best-seller. This, by far, surpassed all of my expectations. Never in my wildest dreams did I imagine that all of these lifetime goals of mine would come to fruition so soon for me. And it was all thanks to that devious and deceitful (yet suave as hell) Dean Cargill. Because of all that he had done for me and was continuing to do, there was one thing that was certain: No matter the articles we wrote about in *The Sandal Scandals*, and no matter all the juicy, scandalous and outright trashy stories we covered, not giving any celebrity a break, Dean Cargill would be the only exception to that rule. For him, I would never discredit his character.

Chapter 30

Dean

Two Years Later...

This had to have been one of the top five most gorgeous beaches I had ever been to in my entire life. Roger and I were reclining in lounge chairs on the white sands of Grace Bay Beach in Turks and Caicos. If there was ever a way that I imagined myself walking into heaven or to some afterlife, it would be striding across these sands and through these crystal cyan waters. That's exactly how I would forever picture myself dying, with my soul leaving my body, heading towards the next adventure that would await me.

I reached for my drink, which was some sort of chilled blue rum runner. I couldn't recall the name of it. All I knew was that it had rum and blue curacao in it. Nevertheless, it was the perfect beach cocktail that I sipped on, while Roger stuck to some piña colada mixed drink that looked as equally delectable. He turned his head after glancing up from his tablet, peering out of his caramel Maui Jim aviators at me. "You should see some of these reviews of *The Real Classic Nick*. They're incredible! Not to mention it's only making more people rent and buy the actual movie. I have to admit, I was a little skeptical of Jackson at first, but he really does possess quite the writing skills."

I couldn't help but display a wide grin on my face, from ear to ear, pulling off my Louis Vuitton sunglasses to get a better view of Roger as I spoke. "I could smell it from a mile away. Ever since I read that article he wrote about our divorce, I knew he was the perfect person to help me with all this, and I couldn't have been more right about it."

"I guess I do have to admit that you do have an eye for talent," Roger acquiesced.

"But even beyond that, I'm so glad we met him and Darren. I know all of it was under false pretenses at first, but now, I really do value the friendship we all have with one another."

"Yeah. I actually find the two of them quite charming," he added.

"Mhmm. But I do appreciate all that he has given me. Jackson has gained all my trust and the fact that he has indirectly worked to help protect my safety and well-being... that means so much to me, beyond anything else," I confessed.

"But you do have to consider that it was an equal trade-off. You were the reason that Jackson is where he is at right now. He even mentioned it at dinner just a few weeks ago. If it wasn't for you, he'd be stuck at that horrible media company he was working for, sitting in an office, doing the same monotonous and mundane writing he had grown accustomed to."

"Either way, I still appreciate him, just as he appreciates me. It's why our relationship is all the more, stronger."

Roger just stared at me longingly. Even this, I could recognize behind the shades that concealed his eyes. "I know how huge your ego is, and it hurts me to say it every damn time, but do you know how damn sexy you are? Christ!"

He was too cute. I busted out in laughter. "And I appreciate every time you tell me that, no matter how much you have to fight your inner conscience to do so." I leaned over to give him a peck on the lips. "And you are beyond sexy too, babe," I added to reciprocate him with.

We then sat back and continued to enjoy the drinks and the views of this paradise. It was after a few minutes of silence that Roger then felt the need to break the ice once more.

"What do you think about us getting married again?" he inquired.

"Married? Like when?"

"What about here? Maybe today or tomorrow?" he elaborated.

"Are you serious!? You want to have an impromptu wedding here, on the beach all of a sudden?"

"I don't see why not? We love each other. We always have since filming *Classic Nick*. And we've never stopped. The whole divorce was staged, but under law, it's important for us to still get remarried."

"I get that and I'd want nothing more than to marry you as soon as possible. But..." I trailed off, wanting Roger to pick up on my thoughts, to which he tried to oblige me with.

"But... you want a spectacular and elaborate wedding with tons of people, right?"

"Haha. Exactly!" I gave him a wink. "This time, I want an even bigger wedding with more paparazzi and all. It will only make the public admire us more and promote my ratings. Don't you think?"

Roger laughed. "You're not some political candidate who NBC analyzes to see if their likability rating has increased or decreased by certain percentage points for their upcoming election."

"Yeah, but you know what I mean."

"Yes. I get it. Then, I will wait a little while. I'll make sure my proposal to you is just as flawless as our second wedding will be," he guaranteed.

"Promise?" I asked.

"Promise."

The word *likability* was actually something I realized that I prioritized more so now than I ever had before when it came to the public's opinion of me. Ever since the tables had turned with a majority of people no longer viewing me as a gold-digging whore, much to Jackson

Cartwright's credit, I valued the compliments of strangers and their laudable comments towards me. I had a whole new faith in humanity now that I had significantly less hate mail and troll bots making online homophobic comments about me.

It was funny to actually now look back on all of those very same people who made terrible remarks about me and my three failed marriages, with them assuming I was some sort of sugar baby and a social-climber. Little did they know that I was far more wealthy and richer than all of my husbands at the time of me marrying them because of the business I had grown. So, the joke was really on them.

And they were also wrong about Roger all along, too. Most critics guessed that Roger and I would be divorced within a year of us being married. From a literal sense, they were right, but deep down when it came to the truth and our actual love for one another, they were completely and utterly wrong. Roger was the man I wanted to be with for the rest of my life. I loved him unconditionally, and he felt the same with me. People have used the expression *third time's a charm* a lot in pop-culture and I have to say, there was some real merit to it.

"You know, babe. I did have some new creative ideas with *the business*. Wait until you hear about my thoughts on how we can expand it even more," I said.

Roger let out a heavy sigh. "Are you ever satisfied, Dean?"

"Of course! How can you even ask that? I'm always satisfied. But just because I'm satisfied doesn't mean I can't set new, higher goals for myself."

And really, that has always been the thing with money, fame, wealth, power, and the thrill of taking big risks—you may have accumulated so much of it, but it still was never enough. You always were left wanting more. Personal growth was a never-ending cycle.

Acknowledgements

This book followed my obsession with the Anna Delvey story and I loved that I had the opportunity to make this with the idea of Anna Delvey in mind. Something about this novel just clicked and there were times when I literally wrote 5,000 words in just the span of two hours. It's how invested I felt about this story.

Thank you, Matt and Ed, for being my rocks during this writing experience. You've helped me so much along the way.

Have to give a big shout out to my friend Cate and my amazing Instagram family and friends. Your support and affirmations mean the world to me!

Thank you to Spectrum Books and its family. It's a pleasure to work with each and every single one of you. I look forward to working with you all on future projects as well.

And thank you to my mother Gina, brother Jimmy, and the rest of my family and friends for your love and support.

Most importantly, thank you to the LGBTQIA+ community. I will continue to support my community and give us more fun reads in the near future!

About the Author

B.J. Irons works in the field of education as a college professor and educational leader. Many of his personal experiences as a gay man have contributed to his books. Being a part of the LGBTQIA+ community himself, B.J. hopes to continue to bring more colorful and fun fictional works to his LGBTQIA+ readers.

Other Titles by B.J. Irons

The Greek Mythology Series
Meduso: Book 1
Arrogance: Book 2
Orpheus: Book 3
Hermes: Book 4
Hephaestus: Book 5
(Coming soon)

The Bosses of Bane Series
The Onyx Demon: Book 1
(Coming Soon)

Stand-Alones
The Cul-de-Sac
Rippling Waters
Sinfluenced
The Gift That Keeps on Taking
The Fire Island Ice Queen
Second-Guess

Excellent LGBTQ+ fiction by unique, wonderful authors.
Thrillers
Mystery
Romance
Young Adult
& More

Join our mailing list here for news, offers and free books!

Visit our website for more Spectrum Books
www.spectrum-books.com

Or find us on Instagram
@spectrumbookpublisher